SIFP

W9-BSZ-121

# MARY
# AFTER
# ALL

\* \* \*

**A Novel**

# MARY
# AFTER
# ALL
\* \* \*
## A Novel

## BILL
## GORDON

THE DIAL PRESS

MARY AFTER ALL: A NOVEL
A Dial Press Book / January 2005

Published by The Dial Press
A Division of Random House, Inc.
New York, New York

This is a work of fiction. Names, characters, places, and incidents either are the product of the author's imagination or are used fictitiously. Any resemblance to actual persons, living or dead, events, or locales is entirely coincidental.

All rights reserved
Copyright © 2005 by Bill Gordon

Book design by Helene Berinsky

No part of this book may be reproduced or transmitted in any form or by any means, electronic or mechanical, including photocopying, recording, or by any information storage and retrieval system, without the written permission of the publisher, except where permitted by law.

The Dial Press is a registered trademark of Random House, Inc., and the colophon is a trademark of Random House, Inc.

Library of Congress Cataloging-in-Publication Data

Gordon, Bill, 1964–
Mary after all: a novel / Bill Gordon.
p. cm.
ISBN 0-385-33642-X
I. Title.
PS3607.O593M37 2004
813'.6—dc22    2004049418

Manufactured in the United States of America
Published simultaneously in Canada

BVG   10   9   8   7   6   5   4   3   2   1

For Tami and Willie

# MARY
# AFTER
# ALL

* * *

### A Novel

# Chapter 1

## TONY

Tony the Horse was a hit man, and he wore a size 13 ring. His bride, Frances, was a plain woman—very shy, Italian, just off the boat. When she ordered their wedding rings, the man at the jewelry store said, "Please, lady, what kind of a man are you marrying?" Frances wouldn't go back. When the rings were ready, my mother had to pick them up.

Tony was very gentle, really, very soft-spoken; he started me on my stamp collection. "Every girl should have a collection," he'd say. "Something worth money later on." He was only my father's second cousin, but Frances was barren; Tony thought of me as his own kid. He used to stop by our house two, three times a week, and he'd bring stamps from England, Brazil, Portugal, Switzerland—all over the world. Stamps with princes' faces and houses tucked away into hillsides—not little dirt hills with weeds and billboards and railroad tracks, but mountains—green mountains with mansions, sometimes castles, tucked right into their sides. He used to tell me that he'd take me there—to those houses, to any place I wanted—when I was old enough. He never spoke above a whisper; still, his throat was often sore and he always carried a box of Vicks cough drops.

Tony threw his girlfriend out a window once—but this was years before I met him, years before I was born—and he used to curse, holler, throw things: a big temper; you never knew what he would do. But these were just stories I heard, things my aunt Delia brought up when she fought with my mother: "How could you spend time with that man? Let him near your daughter? He threw his girlfriend right out the window."

"Did you know her?" my mother would say. "Did you know her; did I know her? Worry about your own goddamned house."

A man once stabbed Tony with an ice pick—at least that's what Aunt Delia told me. "Twelve times, right in the chest," she said (my parents tried to keep this from me), "so Tony threw him out the window too. That's what sent him to prison!"

But I knew none of this when I met him. And I never even met him until I was seven.

He just showed up at our doorstep one night. The bell rang while we were about to eat dinner, and my father ran down the stairs (we lived on the second floor), came back up with a stranger.

"Look, Lena," he said to my mother. "Look who it is."

To me, Tony looked like a professor. He wore round wire-framed glasses and a brown suit that matched his hat. And I must have just seen a movie about a professor—my mother was always taking me to the Loew's Theatre on Journal Square—because that's the first thing I thought when I saw him: *a professor.*

He was a tall man, much taller than my father (my father was handsome, but stout), and when I think about it now, he was probably only six feet—but that was rare back then.

He was wide, too. We had a skinny hallway—the whole house was narrow—but from where I sat, Tony filled it from side to side.

Tony stayed for dinner that night and he and I became friends. Fast friends. He told me about his stamp collection, a little hobby he'd picked up while he was "away." (I was just learning to address and mail an envelope at school.) After that, he'd show up twice a week with a white cloth bag. It looked like a mailbag, the kind you see stuffed under a mailbox—canvas, I think. He would pull out a black leather book. It had blank pages with plastic covers and boxes drawn on them. On the top of each page was the name of a country, so you could match up the right stamps with the right places.

The first time Tony brought his stamps over, it was springtime. My father and his band played a lot of weddings, so he wasn't there when Tony arrived. My father walked in while we were still sorting through the stamps, though—almost three hours had passed. He said a quick "hello" and then he whispered something to my mother. He walked off into their bedroom—it was right off the kitchen, like mine (every room led to the kitchen—every one but the living room)—and he kept himself busy. About a half hour later, though, when I went into the bathroom, he pulled his cousin aside.

"Listen," he said (I overheard all of this; I stayed by the bathroom door), "you know you can visit any time you want."

"Thanks, Dom, that means a lot to me."

"You can eat, keep company, play with my daughter—she seems to like you."

"I like her, too," Tony said.

"So long as you stay on the straight and narrow."

"You're the only real family I have," Tony answered. "You think I'd make trouble for you?"

"I don't want you to make trouble for anybody," my father said. "Especially not in this neighborhood." Then, as an afterthought: "I don't even cut card games anymore."

This was the first I heard about card games.

"Not even that, Dom?"

"She's getting big, Tony—she's in the second grade. That's not how I want her to see me."

"I see," Tony answered.

"And I mean what I'm saying!"

"That's fine."

"I mean *straight*," my father told him.

Tony came over twice a week—sometimes more, like I said—and he always had new stamps. God knows where he got them—I don't remember that part. I remember that I'd run to meet him and we'd dump out the envelopes (the postmark sections; the rest were cut off) on the kitchen floor, sift through for the rare stamps, the interesting places—Australia, India—hold them over my mother's tea kettle—sometimes she'd help us—and steam them off.

And people in the neighborhood started talking, saying, "Tony the Horse is back," watching him while we sat on the porch, while we took a walk to the corner for some lemon ice (we only did this once, really, then my mother put a stop to it). So my mother made us stay inside when he visited, even if it was hot.

"I don't want a spectacle," she said.

"What are they talking about?" I asked her.

But she wouldn't say.

And it wasn't long before I got tired of this—the stares from neighbors, the comments from Aunt Delia in the hallway . . . my mother avoiding my questions. I could see that my mother liked him. Sometimes I thought she liked him better than my father. Between the band and the days my father worked on the trucks, he was hardly home, anyway. She wore her hair in two big swirls that met in the middle back then, and she made sure to set it with two rollers the size of beer cans on the nights before Tony came. She even fixed Tony up with Frances—a friend of her cousin in New York. She didn't just get the ring; she helped plan the whole wedding (for all I know, she picked a plain girl on purpose).

And Tony was coming all the way from New York to see us— my mother and me. He lived on Cherry Street in Manhattan, so it wasn't such a quick trip. That seemed very nice.

But still, people talked. People seemed afraid of him. I was looking out my front window once as he walked down Mallory Avenue, and two old men crossed the street just because they saw him coming.

So one day I decided to ask my mother flat-out: "Did my uncle Tony go to jail?"

She never lied, my mother—not directly—so she sat me down in the living room on her new green chair with the blue leaves. "Mary, don't tell your father . . . but, yes, your uncle made a terrible mistake. He made it, he paid his debt to society, and now that's all done."

"What kind of mistake?" I asked her.

"You asked a question and I answered it. Now, that's all I'm saying—you're too young."

"Is what Aunt Delia says true?"

"What did your aunt Delia tell you?"

"She says Uncle Tony's dangerous."

"That Delia better watch I don't get my hands on her," she said.

"Is my uncle Tony dangerous?" I asked her.

"No, Mary," she told me. "He's not dangerous to you."


In the third grade I had trouble with my math teacher, Mr. Bauer. I was never very good with numbers—I'm still not—and this Mr. Bauer was making things worse. We were learning the multiplication tables and if I asked him a question he'd pretend he didn't hear me. But then he'd call on me. He wouldn't answer my questions, but he'd pick me out for his own. And then, when I'd answer wrong, he would laugh. Right out loud. And the other kids would laugh with him. He was even threatening to fail me, leave me back.

It had been a whole year, now, since I'd met Tony, and besides that one night when he showed up drunk, sloppy, knocking things over (my mother had to feed him two pots of coffee), he'd kept his promise to my father.

I mentioned this to Uncle Tony—Mr. Bauer, I mean—one day while we were going over some new stamps. He was putting a cough drop in his mouth when I told him—licking his lips, then wiping them; folding the top of the box: he was very deliberate about these things—and at first he wasn't very impressed. He said that maybe Mr. Bauer was just old and had some trouble with his ears. Then he continued sucking, clicking, trying to slide a new stamp between the page and the plastic covering. I remember it was from Cuba—he'd just come back—and it had a picture of a Cuban lady on it: she was dancing and her hair was pulled, tight, into a bun. I remember thinking that she looked almost like Frances—by then they were engaged—but the lady wore red shoes.

I said it was possible that Mr. Bauer had a hearing problem, but I didn't think so, because if I asked a third question or a fourth, he would yell.

Uncle Tony stopped clicking. He slid the cough drop to the side of his mouth so he could speak, and it made a bulge in his cheek. Then both his hands went still.

"He yelled?" Tony asked me. I thought he might finally yell himself—that I might finally get to hear it, but instead his voice dropped even lower. He stared right at me; he concentrated hard.

"Yes," I told him.

"What did he yell?"

"Nothing," I said. "It was just a sound. An *aaaagh* or an *ooooh*."

Tony asked me if I thought "Bauer" was a German name. Tony didn't like German men—German women either. Something about his brother, the war—I wasn't supposed to ask about that either, and I didn't.

"Maybe," I said. "It might be German. Probably . . . I think."

"You've told me about this Mr. Bauer before, haven't you?"

I hadn't, but I nodded anyway.

"I see," Tony said. "And then what happened?"

"He threw a piece of chalk." And this was true—he did

throw it; he threw it at the boy next to me, but it was the same day and it almost hit me.

"He threw it at you?" Tony asked me, and somehow I knew he wouldn't wait for an answer, which he didn't. He lifted his hand, his left hand, the one that was resting between the stamps and the plastic, and he reached up to wipe his forehead. It was beginning to sweat. His hand must have been sweating too, because some of the stamps stuck to it. As he moved his hand, three or four stamps lingered, then floated down onto the table, the floor. One of them kept sticking and made its way up to Tony's forehead—it was the new one from Cuba: fresh glue. It stuck to his forehead for a second, then it floated down with the rest of them. But Tony was staring straight at me.

"The chalk flew over my head," I told him.

"How far over?"

"Just a little."

"How much is a little?"

"A little," I said, and I lifted my hand over my head—two inches, maybe—so he could see for himself.

Tony told me that I should pick up the stamps and put them in my book. He looked at his watch and said it was only four o'clock. He said he was going to have a little talk with this German man named Bauer, and see whether he had a hearing problem and whether that hearing problem could be fixed—and I said, well, that sounded like a very good idea, because I was tired of having to yell my questions in class, and Mr. Bauer didn't seem very happy either. Tony picked up his brown hat—never black, always brown with a red or green silk ribbon around it—and started heading for the door.

We'd been sitting in the kitchen, as usual. My mother was

there, too, but she was on the other side of the room, near the stove. She was making *koulyatch*—a long braided bread with fennel seeds—so she was rolling the dough, stretching it out, seeding, braiding . . . ignoring us.

"What did you say?" she asked me, when she saw Tony get up. Then, as he tried to walk past her, she said, "What?" this time to him. "Tell me what happened. You were sitting nice; now that look."

"Nothing," I said. Tony was past her now, his hand on the doorknob.

"What?" she said again. This time she was yelling—not at anyone, just yelling: at the ceiling, the window, the cabinets—"What?"

"I just told him about Mr. Bauer."

My mother wiped her hands on the dish towel and ran to catch up with Tony. She had a frantic look on her face, like the stove just caught fire. She grabbed him by his shoulder and told me to go to my room. I tried to gather up my stamps, and she said, "Just get going." So I did—but I stayed listening by my door. I heard a chair squeak—loudly—and I knew it was him; she'd made him sit down. Then another squeak—not the metal this time, just a fast stick-and-slide across the vinyl. She was sitting too. I heard some mumbling back and forth, and then her voice, clear like a shot: "Stop it," she said, and she slammed her hand on the table.

"Stop what, Lena?"

"Just a piece of chalk, Tony," she said. "A little girl and a piece of chalk."

"Lena?" he said. "Did I say it wasn't?"

"Don't play dumb, Tony. Don't make me call my husband."

I heard the bottom of a chair scrape the floor; someone was getting up. I couldn't tell who. I was hoping it was Tony. I held my book close, tried to keep quiet, not breathe. Then I heard a match strike, the click of the stove. It was her; she was making coffee. Uncle Tony would drink it. Mr. Bauer was safe . . . for now.

This is not a story about my uncle Tony. You can look him up, though, if you want. He's in the history books: Tony the Horse, Murder, Inc.—not some wannabe gangster like the rest of them. He stopped coming around by the time I was eleven— something about a black man ("negroes," we called them) in a train station, a concussion (Tony didn't like "negroes" either). . . . My father had to bail him out, and after that, he said, "Enough, Tony, you're back to your old ways."

I just wanted you to know that this was how I started out— and I know a lot of little girls have someone (a father, brother— mother, even) who says that they'll kill for her—but in my case it happened to be true. He was a professional; he'd done it before; and if necessary—I knew this for those few years—he would do it for me.

And there'd come a time—yes—when Tony wouldn't be there for me. When my father was gone, my mother was gone—when I felt like there was no one and I had to stand up for myself. But that's not how I started; I never could have seen that then.

## Chapter 2

## SINGING

I was born in 1945, late March, in the Margaret Hague Maternity Hospital, up on Clifton Place. Maybe you've heard of it—fifteen floors, a penthouse even: the biggest maternity hospital in Jersey City. The biggest in the country when it was built, back in the thirties. (I gave birth there myself, eighteen years later.) It was built by Boss Hague—"I am the law" Frank: mayor for thirty-six years; a hand in every pocket, ties to Washington. My grandpa Joe, my father's father, was a street sweeper. Once a year he'd have to visit the Boss, pay his respects. Literally. A Christmas bonus—but the other way around. Twenty-five dollars—which was a lot back then. A hundred if you were a cop. A hundred dollars a year to keep your job. If a building went up or a street got laid down, Boss Hague had a piece of it; he controlled every union; he "signed off" on every law. If you crossed him . . . well, no one did. For his mother, though, he built a hospital: in her honor, in her name. A mama's boy—typical Irish: Jimmy Cagney on the rooftop, machine gun in his hand: "I did it for you, Ma." I don't like Irish men. It's true they can be handsome: the light eyes, dark hair—and they do get things done. It's even true that I married one. But on the whole, I find them nervous, long-winded, cold.

My other grandfather—my mother's father—was named Louis. He ran a speakeasy downtown. But that was long before I was born. What *I* remember was the gambling and the cards—by then it was a "saloon"—the red and black chips; all those men in black hats blowing cigar smoke, making bets, asking me to say my name.

"Ma-rrrr-ia," I'd say, and I'd let the *rrr*s roll. At school and at home, I was Mary, and we only spoke English (my mother didn't want me to be "backward"). The men would talk about San Paolo, St. Constantine, and all the little towns near Calabria. They'd tell me what a good Italian accent I had, that if they closed their eyes when I talked, I made them think they were there.

"But you're not *Italian*," Charlie would butt in. Charlie Cupacoffee. He was the waiter, but hardly anybody ate—when they did, they went up to the bar, for privacy. At the tables, it was coffee. Little cups and a lot of refills. So it was "Hey, Charlie—cup-a-coffee." "Charlie, Charlie, CUPACOFFEE." And the name stuck. People think it was because he drank so much coffee, because he always had a cup in his hand—which he did, sure, later on—but I knew him back then, when he was only fourteen, and already that was what you called him. And it's a shame to say, but he was already sticking his nose where it didn't belong, already asking for trouble.

"You're *not* Italian," Charlie would say, as though I was talking to him, as though anybody was talking to him. "And neither am I. We only *lived* in Italy," he'd tell me—he'd tell everybody. "We're Albaniase."

"Who?" his father would yell—his name was Charlie, too—
"Who the hell only lived there? You're from here." And he'd stab
the table with his finger.

"You," Charlie would say. "People like you. People like
Grandpa Louie."

"Shut up," my grandfather would holler—from the bar, the
sink, wherever he was. And he wouldn't even look up. "Pour
the coffee," he'd say. "Pour the coffee, Charlie. And don't call me
your grandpa. I'm not your grandfather—enough is enough."

Sometimes, they'd ask me to sing—these men. I couldn't
really sing. My father was a musician, so I knew that. (I knew
this from the time I was five; from the time he came into the
bathroom and told me. I was in the bath, singing, and he walked
in—no knock—just walked in and told me, point-blank: "You
have no ear.") And I knew what real singers sounded like: I'd
heard the radio; I'd been to the clubs in Newark a few times. I
didn't care, though; it didn't matter. My grandpa Louie was a
whole different side of the family. To him, I sang beautifully. I'd
sing sad songs—the ones my mother listened to when she was
alone: when my father was out playing; when all her friends had
gone home and the kitchen was empty, and she'd listen while
I sang along. Songs by Billie Holiday and Big Maybelle, and
Bessie Smith before them: women my mother told me about—
black women with drug problems and hard lives. I'd sing their
songs about floods and walking through fires and men who'd
left—and I was only six, seven, eight years old, but the men liked
hearing these songs from me, just like my mother did. And I
liked singing them. I'd stand on top of a chair—a folding chair,
but I never fell—and I'd let my eyes stray down to the floor for
the low notes. The men would clap at the end—between every

song, and again at the end. Some would wipe their eyes with the paper napkin Charlie would put down next to their coffee cups, next to their beer glasses—or they'd pull their handkerchiefs from their pockets—their breast pockets, top left. They were old men, most of them, and up close they smelled like garlic and old smoke. But from my chair, looking down, I could only *see* them; not even their faces—the mushy lips (they all had false teeth) and wrinkles and dark circles—but their clothes. I'd look straight at their ties—they all wore ties, striped, and ironed by their wives. None of them worked in an office. Like I said, they were old. Most of them didn't work at all, just booked numbers, made bets—wannabes; the kind Uncle Tony wouldn't even talk to—or they collected pensions from the pencil factory, the ironworks, the Colgate factory. But still, they dressed.

I'd sing the song about smoke rings, and dreaming—the only one my father taught me himself (my mother's favorite—she made him teach me for her birthday)—and at the end, when I'd sing the line about the smoke rings, about how they'd rise through the air, Charlie—if he wasn't too busy—would grab a cigar from one of the men. He'd try to blow some for me, help me act out the song. Just for this, he expected me to split all my tips—and sometimes I did. But not often.

Grandpa Louie made his own wine for the saloon. He did it in the real basement—the one underneath the saloon, the one with the dirt floors. The men (always men; another rule from Boss Hague: if a lady wanted a drink, she had to stay home, go to Bayonne—go to New York) drank this wine from short, thick, rock glasses. There were two giant wood barrels down there in the basement—vats—where he kept the wine (it was always red), and I somehow got the idea that there were wolves in those vats. It must have been from a story Aunt Beta told me—she worked days at the pencil factory and read wild books on her lunch breaks, paperbacks that she stole from Woolworth's (I thought nobody else knew this then)—so she was always telling me about circus men and snakes or monkeys or wolves. Aunt Beta lived upstairs with Grandma and my aunt Dot, who used to baby-sit me between my visits with Grandpa Louie and the time my father picked me up (my mother worked part-time). Dot was always going out, so she was always getting ready. She had beautiful clothes: hand-dyed silk dresses with two, some- times three different layers; high-heeled shoes with ankle straps and fake buckles—shiny, complicated buckles that had hidden snaps underneath; and big hats with netting and pins. She had a fur jacket, too—a brown, waist-length fur jacket that she called a "chubby"—and I asked her one night (I must have been very young, five or six) if she'd made it.

"Made it?" she said, and she rolled her eyes upward, took a sip of Scotch (she hid her drinking from my grandmother).

"Then did Grandpa make it?" I asked.

"My father?" she said. "My father buy me a fur?" And with that, she put her hand on her throat, near her necklace—very dramatic—and rolled her eyes again. She was still getting ready to go out, still putting on her makeup. She was talking straight into the mirror, looking at me through the corner of her eye, in the reflection.

"*Make* it," I said. "I asked, did he make it?"

"Make it?" she repeated.

"Yes," I said. I picked up the sleeve of the chubby, just a little, so she could see it. "Did Grandpa make this from the wolves in the wine barrels?"

Aunt Dot turned around and walked over to the bed. Then she leaned over and pulled me toward her. "I think you're crazy," she said. "I've always wondered, you know. My sister is crazy. [She meant my mother.] I've always wondered, and now I know. You should watch what you say," she told me, and she pulled the fur away, out of my hands. "Other people won't be like me. They'll make fun."

Aunt Dot was a whore. She slept with Mafia men—real Mafia men—and they were all married. Usually they were men from New York; men my uncle Tony introduced her to; but a few were from Jersey as well. One of them had a wife who found out. She chased Aunt Dot down First Street with a loaf of bread in her hand (stale bread; she'd put the bread aside, maybe for days) and she beat Dot all the way down the block. And I know a lot of people might have stories about an Aunt Dot or an Aunt So-and-So who was a whore and who somebody—somebody's wife—beat with a loaf of bread (a lot of people downtown, anyway) but usually it ends with the Aunt So-and-So crying— crying and mending her ways. But my aunt Dot didn't cry. She knew what she was; she only ran because the woman, the wife, was bigger than she was. She slept with that man for ten, fifteen more years. And later on, even after that, when Aunt Dot quit her secretary job, when she started making loans from her living room, it was that woman's husband who put up the backing.

\* \* \*

But this chapter is about singing. It's about singing, and I want to finish it up.

There was no piano when I sang. Not even a guitar or an accordion—I didn't want one. Just my voice and the sound of cards shuffling—the plastic chips falling, clicking high-pitched against one another, almost keeping time. As I got older, I learned to talk the songs, mostly. Sometimes I'd pick out one man in the crowd and look into his eyes for the big notes. I'd get more quiet instead of loud. Then I'd pause, let him react, let the others watch him, and I'd take a breath, continue. And this one day—it's always this same day—jumps out: I'm twelve and I've just sung "That Old Devil Called Love." Charlie is almost eighteen. He doesn't pour coffee anymore. He sits at the table—always the same table, the one to the left, near the bar—farthest away from me—where his father used to sit. (His father, Charlie Sr., is dead by now, and his mother is still who knows where? She ran off when he was a baby. So Charlie stays in the basement most nights with my grandpa Louie.) Sometimes my grandmother comes downstairs—the saloon is still in the basement—and she pours the coffee if Charlie's too busy and I'm singing (I help now too). But then she runs right back upstairs. Charlie likes to look at me. I notice that my voice sounds better when he's watching. I go home and tell my mother. She says, "No. Please, Mary, not him." By now she's already sick. It's a bad day—it's been an even worse week. She grabs her stomach like I've kicked her, made her sicker. "Not him," she says, "not with that family." She tells me that I'm too young for this, that she won't let me go back. "This is not the life I want for you." I go a few times more anyway—I take the bus and sneak back—but she's already talked to my grandfather; he won't let me in.

It's ironic that Charlie died in a coffee heist. This wasn't until the seventies, after I was married, had children, lost touch—by then he was just someone you heard about occasionally. I'd run into him at Al's Diner on Communipaw Avenue, or the Colony Diner on Route 440—always with the newspaper, the coffee cup, his sad black hat—always talking a mile a minute, running back and forth to the pay phone. I introduced him to my two boys—once—when they were still little, and they loved the name; kept saying it over and over in the car on the way home— "Cupacoffee, Cupacoffee, Charlie Cupacoffee"—until, finally, my head started spinning. I had to pull over to the side of the road.

Now, this was a bad time for me: pinching pennies; taking Valium; my husband working late, always working late—no interest when he got home. I used to run into the girls I went to high school with at the ShopRite: Judy Scerbo, Stella Schilizzo, Carol Salerno. (I'm using their maiden names—we did that with each other.) They were all on the Valium too. We joked about it later—years later. About the crashing with the shopping carts, the dropping food in the aisles. I joined the Woman's Club after that, did volunteer work. Then I went to work at the bank—we all went to work—and it got better. All except for Helena; she didn't go to work. People made fun of her. She went to night school—Jersey City State College. "Big, fat Helena," people said (it was Judy, mostly), "she'll be a big, fat librarian." She became a teacher, then a principal, then a freeholder—wound up the first female mayor of Jersey City: Helena Malvesi. She even lost weight.

But I'm jumping too far ahead.

I used to drive around for hours—sometimes with my boys and sometimes just by myself. I'd think about him sometimes—Charlie—about how he wanted to go back to Italy, about how he wanted—even started—to write the family tree. He told me once, when we were still kids, that we were fourth cousins. And maybe we were, but nobody listened to Charlie anyway. He came to school with me once too. It was before Mr. Bauer. Kindergarten, I think. At #33 school, there were too many kids, so they broke us down into two groups—morning and afternoon. On family day, they made both groups come in at the same time. My mother was sick—just a cold—and all my aunts were busy, so she asked my grandpa Louie to take me. But he didn't want to go alone—he never liked to go anywhere alone—so he brought Charlie. When we got there, the girl from the morning class was in my desk and there was no place for me to sit. I told my grandfather that I needed a seat, and he told Charlie. Charlie walked right up to the girl and turned her chair upside down. She fell onto the floor, crying like a baby—and everybody looked, so my grandfather yelled at Charlie. He told Charlie that he'd gone overboard, that he was always going overboard, and he hit him with my pencil case right in front of the class. Charlie had to say that he was sorry to the little girl, who wound up sitting back down, and I still had no seat. Later, when I was in the seventh grade, Charlie used to meet me after school and walk me home. Again, it was Grandpa Louie who sent him. I never talked to Charlie while we walked—I knew I wasn't supposed to. Not in public. I was too young; his family was "no good" (he had no family, really, and people looked down on him for that). Charlie had dark skin and it was blotchy—he was half

Sicilian, which he never talked about, and that happens sometimes with Sicilians—and so people, some people, thought he
was dirty. It wasn't true; he used to scrub his face for hours; used
to try to rub off the blotches, and it may have worked, because
there were a few years—maybe between twenty-one and twenty-
five—when Charlie's face looked smooth, when he almost looked
handsome.

I never cheated on my husband; never, not once. And if I
had, it would not have been with Charlie, not after what he became. But I used to think about him—at night, when I was out
driving and my boys were in the back of the car and my husband
wasn't home. I'd think about a lot of things: about why Charlie
never went to school and nobody ever asked why; and why,
still—even though he never went to school, not even when he
was eleven or twelve—he was always talking about the Ottoman
Empire and some emperor who none of my teachers even knew
of named Skenderbeg, who'd left Albania or died, and so people
had to leave Albania, had to settle in Italy, and those were our
ancestors; and I'd look at my boys' faces in the rearview mirror
and wonder what they might look like if . . . if who knows? . . .
if they weren't half Irish.

But that was what happened: Charlie Cupacoffee died in a
coffee heist. He and his partners stole a truck filled with coffee.
They held it for ransom—ten thousand dollars. It wasn't so un-
usual to steal a coffee truck back then—any truck, really; a lot of
trucks got sidetracked in Hudson County. It was even in the
*Jersey Journal.* Charlie was the one left watching the truck; but
when his partners came back, they didn't want to cut the money
ten ways. And rumor has it that they weren't his partners; that he
barely knew them; that he just found out about the deal and

pushed his way in. But be that as it may, he opened the garage door and there they were—nine men with guns. The police found Charlie wrapped in a shower curtain, stuffed inside the trunk of a car. The car was in a parking lot—the one behind the Cadillac Hotel, near the Newark/Elizabeth border.

Chapter 3

## THE BUSINESS

I was a cesarean baby. My mother had very small hips, they had to open her up to get me—had to pick me out. She got an infection from it, but she'd had a miscarriage before me, so this was nothing in comparison—she never complained. And I don't know what that means about beginnings—being a cesarean—about struggle and personality. But I know what it means for the face. It means that there's no crushing, no waiting for the nose to puff back up, for the head to round off—and none of that spotty, angry newborn skin. I was a beautiful baby. Beautiful. And I stayed that way. I could leave this out, not mention it: but then this would be someone else's story—and why would I tell it?

To tell the truth, I don't photograph so well. Never did. My skin looks like anybody else's in a photo, but it's not. It's smoother, darker, more even. I've heard Barbara Stanwyck, the movie actress, had the same problem, though her skin was fair. And my eyes look brown, almost ordinary, in a photo—but they're not brown; they're black, perfectly black. You don't see black eyes so often.

My mother was beautiful, too—before she got so big. And then she lost the weight—all of it. But that was from sickness. I look at pictures of my mother, now, and I see three different women—she always said two, but I see three—the pretty one, who looked like me; the fat one; and the last one—that crooked old lady with the thinning hair. She couldn't walk by herself—not at the end—she couldn't even stand up straight; and she refused to use a cane. I used to lean her up against me—this started when I was a teenager—hip to hip, and put my arm around her shoulders. And that was how we walked: to the bathroom, the car, the corner deli. And it worked. It worked just fine. But after a while it was hard to tell—hard for me, maybe for her too—which one of us was limping. That's the problem: you can live too long in the world of the dead and dying, and you can forget; you can forget that you're not one of them.

And for me, it was even more confusing because I grew up in the business. My uncle Birdie started his funeral home in our basement. If you know anything about Jersey City at all, then you know that Birdie is a millionaire. Marelli's Funeral Home—the place Birdie grew into—is just down the street from Our Lady of Victories church. Birdie gets a steady flow of business. He always did. The whole parish goes to Birdie's sooner or later. But in the beginning, when he first started out, he'd paint the faces and dress the bodies in our basement. He did *everything* down there. And I can still remember the sound of the embalming fluid: a click of the switch, the swoosh in and out, the squeaking—why always squeaking?—in the drain. It's hard to believe, now, that he did the embalming down there—us living upstairs—but I guess he had the right plumbing, permits, ventilation. And I doubt I ever really heard a swoosh—there were two floors between us—but that's how the mind works, sometimes . . . you imagine things, fill them in. I was only six when he moved out, sold his floor (we kept the other one) to Uncle Archie and Aunt Delia. (I probably never saw a dead body sit up, either—maybe my mother saw it, told me—and so I never asked Uncle Birdie if the man had been resurrected, and he probably never told me that the man had just had a muscle spasm. But I remember that too.)

My parents, whenever they made up, would go out dancing—late at night, after my bedtime. And they fought a lot, so they made up a lot. They never hired a baby-sitter, because Birdie was always working downstairs. I used to sneak down there, after they'd left, and watch him. One night—I remember this like it was yesterday—there was a little girl. She had on a white dress—her Communion dress, I decided. Birdie was painting her lips with a brush—he always did it that way, but this brush was smaller than the others, and Birdie was crying. I felt sorry for my uncle, who never went out dancing, and I walked in to talk to him. He picked me up and held me in his arms. I asked him why he was crying. He told me that the girl looked just like me and it had scared him; made him think about the little girl's parents, about her aunts and uncles and cousins; and he usually never thought that way.

I asked if I could look inside the box, see her face, and he said I could "just this once," and he leaned me forward. I thought her nose looked big—so wide for a little girl—and I was mad that he'd said she looked like me. But I noticed that her lips, even with the pink coloring, looked just like mine: they were full (maybe even fuller than mine) and the top one puckered up, way up, toward the nose, like she'd died in the middle of a kiss. He said that I could touch her if I wanted to, and I did—but I never expected her hand to be so hard—and it *was* hard—and I started to cry too. And then Birdie had to carry me back up the stairs.

Birdie got cheap once he made his money. My father borrowed a suit from him once, and it looked better on my father, so Birdie said my father could keep it. It was a nice suit, gray pin-striped and double breasted, but not new. A month later Birdie asked my father if he could borrow fifty bucks. When my father asked for it back, Birdie said, "What, after I gave you that suit?" That was his way; he made you pay for everything. In the funeral business, there's a hundred-percent markup on everything: caskets, clothes, car rentals . . . everything, even organists. A lot of people don't know this. Still, when a relative—say, Uncle Archie—passed away, Uncle Birdie would give twenty, thirty percent off—tops. And then he'd smile, like he was doing you a big favor.

## Chapter 4

## MY MOTHER

There's a picture I have. My mother cut it out from the *Jersey Journal*. It's of a block party—a street fair. An Albaniase feast—not like the block parties my kids knew, with the rock music and the cotton candy. My father is playing the Albanian bagpipes, the *Kadamunza*. His cheeks are puffed up, his mouth is pressed tight up to the horn, and his arms are wrapped around the skins. The bags on the *Kadamunza* are big, like the sound they make—they roar, they don't peep or whine like the Irish bagpipes—and they take a lot of wind to get going, a big set of lungs and good breath control. My father had both. You can see the concentration, the tightness in his eyebrows, the tension in his fingers.

But his eyes are on my mother (I wish she could have noticed this). And there are other people, other eyes, all on her too. She's dancing. Her skirt—not a skirt she'd normally wear but long, from another century, another place—is flying high. Her left hand is on her hip and her right leg is lifted, bent. She's spinning—

you can tell by the slight blur in the photo, the sweep of her hair—a spinning teacup. She looks like she could fly.

My father playing . . . my mother dancing, upstaging him. I'm in the photo too. Just a baby, one year old. I'm in my aunt Delia's arms on a folding chair in the middle of the street—there were folding chairs and tables that lined each side of Mallory Avenue—and we're watching, too. Me and Aunt Delia, who I never liked or got close to, in the background. I'm tiny, I'm young, but you can tell that I'm watching, not just staring into space. Or maybe I am. But it's a specific space. The space in the center of the street with my mother in it.

She hadn't danced in a year, she told me later, when I was eight or nine. She was sitting on her bed, my father was out. . . . My mother had a dressing table with a stand-up three-way mirror, and I used to sit in front of it, play dress up. (These were good years—I want you to see her this way.) I'd borrow her makeup, paint my cheeks red, tie a fake-silk kerchief around my head (turbans were in style). Or a scarf. She'd help me. . . . You could see yourself from all angles in that mirror, and I'd tuck my hair in, turn my head back and forth, make sure I looked perfect. My mother would sit behind me, reach forward from the tip of her bed to help me. . . .

She was playing with the balls on the fringe of her chenille bedcover that day—the day we had this conversation—flipping through a photo album with her other, free hand. She still had perfect hands.

"That was the first time," she said. "The first time after the hospital, the infection—after you," and she grabbed my face, squeezed it, so I'd know she wasn't angry. "My comeback!" she called it—she laughed—"and the photographer showed up. I'd danced every year before that, ten years maybe. I still had my figure—I got it back fast, most of it—and that was the one time he showed up for."

My mother, she looks at no one in the photo. Her head is turned to the left, and her eyes are looking straight up. You can see the pull in her neck, the definition in her jawline, her arms outstretched—a beautiful woman about to fly away.

## Chapter 5

## GRANDMA ANGELINA

She grew up so poor, my mother—ten kids in that one crooked house on First Street, my grandma Angelina at the stove all day long.

My grandma Angelina lived upstairs from the saloon, like I said, and she never came down. Hardly ever, anyway. And Grandpa Louie rarely went up—not even at suppertime. My aunt Beta, my mother's oldest sister, brought down the food—at least by the time I went there—and Grandpa Louie slept most nights in a single bed behind a curtain at the back of the club.

My grandmother hated the saloon; she hated the men— "bums," she called them.

"Stay up here with Grandma," she'd say. "Play nice with Aunt Beta. [Beta was like a kid herself.] Whatta you want with all those old men?" she'd tell me. "Stay up here, Maria; it's not right."

But who the hell wanted to roll dough and hang laundry? I'd always sneak back down. She'd have to come down looking for me—she hated this, too; she never wanted to set foot down there if she didn't have to—and after a while, she gave up. "Just don't tell your mother," she'd say when I came back upstairs, and she'd point her finger, stare, make me promise not to tell. She knew my mother wouldn't mind—not back then—she only wanted my mother to mind. She wanted my mother to be like her—and then she didn't. It's always like that with Italian mothers: they want you to step out, be different—but then they don't want to be embarrassed.

I want you to know about my grandma Angelina, too— about her marriage, about what she came from and how she lost it—because people think that all us Italians did so well once we came here, and no matter how poor we were, it was better than what we left. But that wasn't always the case. My grandma Angelina didn't find any bed of roses over here. A rotten marriage is a rotten marriage and sometimes you're better off staying at home.

She didn't come from poverty, my grandmother. She came from a good family back in Italy. Her father was a tax collector who owned an olive grove too. She had nice clothes, even a hairdresser.

Grandpa Louie tricked her into coming to America; he said he had money waiting on the other side. He used to walk past her house every day on the way to—who knows?—not school, for sure, or work; he never liked to work. Grandma was pretty when she was young. She had a picture—only one picture from home—and she kept it tacked to her bedroom wall: she had a round face and a tiny nose (a nose like mine, with the little up-turn at the end). And she had light skin for an Italian, even light for an Albaniase. And she was smiling in the picture. Perfect teeth. Movie-star teeth. I get my teeth from her, too, like my mother did. Her hair was in a bun, but it didn't make her look frumpy; just ladylike.

Grandma's parents didn't like Grandpa Louie; they thought he was no good—and he wasn't, really, no matter how much I loved him. But my grandma was a rich girl—so sheltered. Grandpa told her that he loved her; he convinced her that things would be all right, that she should go with him to America, that he had family waiting: family with money, enough money for the two of them—for their children once they had them. Grandma told me that she snuck away. She waited until her mother was at the olive grove one day and she ran. Grandpa Louie had gone first to make it look good, and she followed. He'd left the ticket with one of his friends. The friend was no good either; he kept trying to kiss her. She had to sail alone. She told me about how the boat rocked. It rocked so hard she couldn't sleep—and she was a sheltered girl, like I said, naïve; when she did fall asleep, someone stole an earring right out of her ear. It was a gold earring—her mother had given it to her two weeks before she left.

She wore the other earring for the rest of her life. Very fine gold: a circle with a rose hand-carved through the center. Two weeks before my grandmother died, she lost the other one—"I don't like this," she told my aunt Dot.

And two weeks later—two weeks after she lost the second earring—she was dead.

## Chapter 6

## NEEDING TO MOVE

I used to write to Joan Crawford—to a lot of the movie stars—when I was a girl. . . . Lana Turner, Bette Davis, Rita Moreno (she was new then, just starting out, but I liked her—the Latin Spitfire, they called her—she had dark skin like mine). I was twelve, thirteen, fourteen years old. . . . And they'd send me 8 by 10 photos with their signatures—it's too bad I never saved any of them, because they'd be worth something today. I was good at copying their looks, too. Not just drawing the eyebrows or shaping my lips; I could make the expressions.

I'd wait for my mother to go to sleep—all those pills I had to give her, even then, one after another—and I'd slip into the bathroom. I used to stuff tissues in my school blouse and smile in front of the mirror, frown, make my eyes water, look horrified.

Then she'd yell for me—"I need my codeine"—and I'd have to wipe my face, pull out the tissues, go running.

My mother had a very rare illness—scleroderma. It's like an

arthritis, but inside; it eats away at you, hardens your arteries, your stomach lining, your skin. . . .

She got it when I was twelve.

Dr. Janislovski said it was a slow disease, but that's not how it happened. . . . She quit the curtain store right away. She took to the bed. Just a few months after the news. . . .

*Mary, get me some water for this pill.* She could barely do a thing for herself. *Mary, go get dinner started, I'm tired.*

She wasn't *so* sick then—not yet, not as sick as she got— but my father had a girlfriend. A Polish woman named Judy (I know that now—I didn't at the time). My mother was *playing* sick for him, but he was never home. It was for him that she was playing—yes—but she would act it out on me.

And she pushed my aunts away—not just Dot and Beta but the married ones, the ones in Rahway and Elizabeth that we used to visit . . . the ones who used to visit *us,* have dinner. She pushed the aunts from my father's side away too.

"I've got Mary," she'd say when they called her. "Don't worry. I'm fine."

And who knows how sick she really was then? I'm not a doctor. But I knew my mother. I knew her inside and out, and I could tell there was something about her that was pretending— I'm talking about the first few years, here, the years when she first got sick—something that was making it worse. For one thing, her voice got shaky the minute somebody called. She'd be talking to me in her normal voice, just fine, then she'd pick up the phone and all of a sudden she was on her deathbed— "Hellooo . . ." She'd drag out the *O* like she was pulling a lifeline . . . it didn't matter who called.

My mother was fat by then. After she was diagnosed, all she did was eat. The doctors told her she'd get thinner. I think she was trying to fight it, stock up.

I think she got fat, too, because my father never came home. And the more he stayed out, the bigger she got.

I can't pinpoint a time when this started, when he started going out more without her—I just know it happened. There was my beautiful, thin mother one day—and you have to keep in mind that I don't mean thin like today: a little padding was in style. Then came the news from Dr. Janislovski and everything stopped. *Bang!* There was this big lady who always stayed home.

And she'd spring up like a jack-in-the-box when my father walked in—I can tell you that much!

"Where the hell were you!" she'd holler.

There was no shake in her voice then—no trouble moving if he tried to switch rooms.

"Look who it is." *Spring!* She'd be all over him. "You still know the address?"

"Oh, Lena, I just came home to check in on you. You know I'm at the club."

"Well, you did your duty," she'd tell him. "Get the hell out."

"Get out?" he'd yell back at her. "This is my house too!"

"Did you hear that, Mary?" She'd point her head toward me like she wasn't sure I could hear them—like I could ever hear anything else. "This man here says he lives here, Mary—you've seen him before?"

And she'd dig in: "What's so special about that band, anyway? You never made it before—you think you're gonna make it now?"

This didn't seem right—she'd always been so proud of his playing before.

"Lena, you knew I was a musician when you married me."

"I thought I knew a lot of things then."

I used to feel sorry for him—for my father. I didn't understand any of it: I knew she was sick, I knew he stayed out more. But he was always out before that—I couldn't see how this was worse. And I suppose it's natural to blame the other one when you're married—to blame the one who's not sick. I didn't know about Judy—like I said—and when I found out, I felt much less sorry. By then I was married; I had my own troubles to think about. To tell the truth, I had no sympathy for him at all.

Those years flew by so fast. (Not easy—but fast.) I'd been so close with my mother; she encouraged me. Not just with the singing, but with everything. And I don't know where I got the idea that I could be a movie star: It was usually a teacher I used to play with her . . . first a gypsy, then an Indian, then a crossing guard—that was a short-lived one—and then a teacher.

I was a good reader. Right from fifth grade. I used to check out a book a week from the Jersey City Public Library—the Miller branch, right on Clinton and Bergen; they had every book you could want. I had plenty of schoolwork—the public schools were good in Jersey City then—but I'd read extra books. Books about Russia—the tzars, Catherine the Great . . . I was very interested in Russia for some reason—the royalty. Books about a girl named Heidi—they were popular: she had lots of adventures.

And then I'd give a class at home. I'd give the class to my

mother; she'd pretend to be my pupil, and I'd ask her to spell out the words—"t-z-a-r," I'd say. "The *t* is silent."

She even bought me a small blackboard that I put up in her bedroom—my father's bedroom, too, of course, but when was he home?

And we had breaks, my mother and me—yes—but that was fine: I got to go downtown, see my grandparents, my aunts, Charlie, the men at the saloon. . . . I was happy overall. I'd had such a good childhood.

Then this!

The bathroom was the one place I had to myself then—the one place where she wouldn't interrupt. Where I could sit and think. I'd get fifteen minutes—a whole half-hour if she was having a good day.

And I'd try not to be resentful—I tried not to hate her, even then. It wasn't her fault she got sick.

I never went downtown anymore—hardly ever. I never saw Charlie, to boot. She was always in bed or on the couch lying down. Either that or she'd sit up in her "special" chair—the green one with the blue leaves. And she always needed something—a pill, her slippers . . . an ear.

By the time I was a junior at Snyder High, she was in and out of the Pollak Hospital—the Sister Kenny Floor, #5; they named it after some nun who got polio and worked with other polio patients.

It was a boarder hospital—you'd stay the week, come home on the weekends—and when she was boarding, I'd ride the Montgomery and West Side bus after school to Baldwin and Montgomery, get off near Borden's Luncheonette, pass the Medical Center. . . . It was one big complex; Frank Hague built it that way: the Medical Center itself, the Margaret Hague Maternity Hospital that he built for his mother, the Pollak (this was originally for tubercular patients), Murdoch Hall, where the nurses slept. I'd pass the Medical Center, go to Baldwin and Clifton Place, walk down the big hill past Murdoch Hall and the Margaret Hague, and head over to the Pollak. I did this all after school. I enjoyed the walk, the break, the time to myself.

My aunt Dot was always trying to fix me up. My grandma Angelina died when I was fourteen, so Aunt Dot had full reign downtown.

"You're a beautiful girl," she'd tell me, "I can do things for you." And she was drinking a lot then—drinking and dialing—otherwise she wouldn't be so direct . . . wouldn't go around my mother. "Come here after the hospital," she'd say. "We'll go out."

I was about sixteen by the time she made these calls. I knew my father would kill her. (Kill us both.) My mother would too.

"Then keep your mouth shut," Aunt Dot would say. "Just tell them I'm doing your hair."

"What about school?"

"All right." She'd give up. "Call me in the summer."

I didn't call, though. I knew the kind of men she was offering—Mafia men, some famous, some married. But I can't say that bothered me. If anything, it excited me. (What did I know about that life? I was so damned bored.) It was something else that held me back. And this is the part I can't leave out.

I'd think about my mother—that first mother—all the energy she used to have, racing back and forth from the curtain store, waking up early to cook, going out late with my father to dance . . . and sometimes, when I was staring in that mirror, pretending I was in a movie, listening to her yell for her pills, wondering if she was pretending, too, I'd try to remember how I'd looked forward to seeing her each day, how I'd wanted her to stay home—how I'd wanted to rush home and stay there myself.

And I must have thought I could undo it, bring her back—I must have thought I could wait her out. I must have thought, *Maybe . . . maybe if I go to the hospital enough, stay close.* So a part of me wanted to stay home. A part of me wanted to hold tight. Volleyball and swimming were fine. I never felt guilty about those because I'd done them before, back at #24—and I knew I'd be home in two hours, three tops. But the rest—the other things you do when you're in high school—I paused before I did them. And I have to put this in because, yes, I wanted out. I wanted her to leave me alone, let me breathe. But at the same time I wanted my mother back. Both things were true.

I was never one for female friends, no, but Peg Roman was my one big exception. Thank God for her!

We met at Snyder High—the first day—and I liked her attitude . . . the way she walked with her head up, didn't apologize for her chest (she developed so early). At school Peg talked when she had something to say, and in between she stayed quiet. Unless there were boys around, and then it was giggles, chatter, doe eyes all the way.

We used to smoke together in the basement, pluck each other's eyebrows in the girls' room, pick a boy and have a contest, see who could get him first. Mind you, we never did much with these boys—no matter what the other girls said—just a few kisses in the locker room, a walk home, and some rubbing in our parents' vestibules; we'd talk on the phone afterward—after I made dinner (I took that over too) and Peg, at her house, watched TV.

Those girls I mentioned earlier—Judy Scerbo, Stella Schilizzo, Carol Salerno—they weren't much in the looks department, and they made a real clique. Homely girls who stuck together, started trouble—and I should have been nicer to them. I should have been the better person. But I wasn't. I walked past them like Peg did, my head held high—*snub!* They liked to spread rumors about us, what we did with those boys, whether we wore underwear—all kinds of nonsense. And I knew that—they never did this to my face, mind you; I'd never tolerate that . . . but I knew. I was busy, though. I kept to myself, save for Peg. And what did we care? We knew who got asked out on dates and what we did on them.

It was Peg they liked to talk about more, and it hurt her feelings. They'd say she stuffed her bra, make stupid-Polack jokes.

Peg's father was a milkman, and her mother wasn't too bright. Poles, right from Poland, with a shortened last name.

She never got good grades, Peg—it's true—but then, she didn't try. I always thought she had a good head on her shoulders, but she liked to act dumb. It went with the image: blond hair, blue eyes, a full breast from the time she turned twelve. This was the fifties, remember—the time of Marilyn Monroe and Mamie Van Doren. . . . If you had blond hair and a certain bra size, the program was set.

Me, I had a little more leeway, I had the dark looks and the dark hair: people never knew what to expect of me—the boys *or* the girls. I was used to people talking behind my back, anyway—in my family, you got used to it early. I can't say I liked it, I just never expected anything else.

But Peg I could trust. Peg was my one big exception. And I was lucky to have her. I didn't need a pile of friends at school. We made friends fast, Peg and me—real friends—and we stayed that way.

Chapter 7

## MARRIAGE

I met my husband on a Ferris wheel. The Jersey Shore—Seaside Heights. This was the early sixties, before the trash took over—the white trash with the sandals and bandannas and long hair: men with long hair. And those radios—in their hands, in their cars, on their beach blankets . . . It wasn't the blacks who ruined the shore. People say that—stupid people. It was the whites. White trash.

Back then, the Ferris wheel had the big rocking carts. You could fit three, maybe four people in them—if you were thin. And I was thin. I had an athletic figure long before it was in style—like a gymnast, my husband said.

You'd think Peg would grab all the attention because she was a blonde, but no. We made a good pair. We never went down the shore with more than five, six dollars in our pockets (save for bus fare—enough for a boardinghouse, maybe). We'd lie to our parents and say we were staying with somebody's mother.

Peg and I never paid for a meal, and we certainly never paid for a drink. Yes, we drank. Everybody drank back then. With

our short, wavy hairdos and makeup we looked—God knows—
twenty-five, maybe. We were sixteen and a half, seventeen years
old. Only the dogs paid for themselves.

And Peg loved the rides. Those, we had to pay for—the Ferris
wheel was the only one I'd go on. Peg would go on them all—the
Whip, the bumper cars—but I was dressed nice; I wasn't there to
go on rides. I would play the stands, though—shooting the water gun till you filled the clown's head, tossing the ring over the
shot glass, the little mini-bowling stand. The stands we could get
the boys to pay for, and besides, a crowd would gather at the
stands. On the rides, a boy could get you alone, just the two of
you. Or maybe four of you: two couples. But the stands were
out in the open; you could play and stroll. We were the play-
and-stroll kind of girls.

Bobby was in the cart below me one night, way up on the
Ferris wheel. Peg and I were rocking. We were rocking and making eyes—her at Bobby's friend, Paulie, me at Bobby himself.
My shoe fell off and Bobby caught it. A tough catch, but he did
it. Bobby was a good ballplayer. He still is.

"She did it on purpose," he said to Paulie. Voices carry when
you're up that high, out over the ocean—either that or they dis-
appear. But Bobby had a deep voice. It caught the wind, carried,
came right to me and Peg.

When we got off the ride, I wouldn't talk to him.

"Thank you," I said, and I took the shoe from his hand, put
it on, started walking.

"You always wear high heels on the boardwalk?" he shouted
after me. He was laughing, so was Paulie; I could hear them. Peg
was walking next to me and she started laughing, too; she was

wearing flats, as usual—Peg is five foot eight. I didn't turn around, and Bobby didn't follow, though I figured he would.

We met a few hours later at the diner—the same diner Peg and I ate at every night: Pat's in Belmar. (We'd hitch a ride from somebody we met—you could do that back then, a lot of kids snuck down the shore.) Bobby saw us and walked right up.

"So, you still have both shoes," he said, looking down at my feet. "If you want, you can throw the other one; I'm even better on the ground."

His friend Paulie was standing near the cash register, watching, grinning like an idiot.

"Cute," I said. "You're very funny. But we're *very* hungry, and your friend is waiting, so why don't you—"

"Listen," he said. He was looking at me first, but he turned to Peg when he finished (he did this so he wouldn't seem obvious). "You wanna get a booth?"

"I don't know," Peg said.

"Come on," he told her. "The four of us. We're harmless—I promise."

Peg looked at me, and I shrugged my shoulders.

"Paulie's paying," he said.

Peg looked at me again, and I shrugged my shoulders again—so, finally, she said, "Sure, fine, why not?"

"You positive?" Bobby said—this time to me. And again Peg answered: "It's fine, really. Why not?"

We found a booth, and Bobby made sure Paulie slid in right across from Peg; that left me to talk to him.

"Where you from?" he said.

"Jersey City," I told him.

"What block?"

"Mallory."

"I live on Roosevelt," he said, "the lower part."

"Wait," I told him. "That's two blocks from my house."

"I know," he said, and he told me that he'd seen me before. "I see you on the corner sometimes. West Side and Williams. At the bus stop. Waiting."

"So why'd you ask where I'm from?"

"I was just making conversation."

"Okay," I said, and I looked at his face, tried to see if I could recognize him—but no. I asked him for a cigarette—I only smoked when I was out of the house—and he said he didn't smoke at all, never, because he still "played ball," but he bummed one from Paulie, gave it to me, anyway.

"So, you've been watching me?" I said. I put the cigarette in my mouth and leaned in, over the table, so he could light it. "For how long?"

"Hold it," he told me. "I said I saw you; I didn't say I was watching."

"Fine," I said, and I leaned back in my seat. "So you weren't watching."

"That's right," he said, and he leaned back too, crossed his arms, got quiet.

"And you're not interested?"

He didn't answer right away. He just looked at me—almost through me—and I looked back. Finally, Peg butted in. "He didn't say that, either," she said, which made her and Paulie crack up. To tell the truth, by this point I'd forgotten Peg was next to me. I was just sitting there, staring. And Bobby was staring back.

That's the way it happened with him—it never happened that way before, and it never happened that way afterward (I'd like to think it happened for both of us). Everything else slipped away—and fast.

He asked me how old I was—which seemed natural enough—and I said, "Well, how old do I look?"

"I don't know," he said. "I need to see you with your face washed."

"Jesus," I said. I looked at my reflection in the mini-jukebox window—back then all the diners had mini-jukeboxes at the tables—and I did look a little overdone.

"All right," I said—he and Paulie were laughing—"knock it off," and I rubbed my hands across my cheeks, smoothed out my rouge.

"I graduated a few months ago," I told him. "Early!"

I was wearing my mother's charm bracelet that night, and there were only a few charms on it (I didn't ask before I borrowed it, so I had to grab it the way it was), but one of them was a heart with a half-carat diamond in the middle. "Pretty nice," I said, when I saw Bobby was looking at it, "huh?"

"Nice." He nodded. "What does your father do?"

"For a living? What kind of a question is—"

"Look," he said, "if it's something you can't talk about . . ."

"Can't talk about? What? Because I'm Italian?"

"I didn't know you were Italian."

"What'd you think I was—a gypsy?" We had a big gypsy community in Jersey City—a whole family (maybe twenty or thirty people) lived just a few blocks away on Communipaw Avenue—so I saw how they looked. I knew what they wore. And

I used to like to play one as a girl, like I said, with my mother. . . .
I'd told Peg my stories. She got it. She laughed.

"I thought you were Italian!" Bobby snapped back at me. "I
just said I didn't *know*."

I liked the way he kept up with me. "Well, I am," I said,
"more or less."

"And so you can't tell me . . . ?"

My heart was pounding; I could feel my temples starting to
twitch. I wasn't mad, mind you . . . oh, no, not at all. If my skin
were lighter, I might even have blushed. "He's a musician," I
said.

"Oh?" Bobby said. "What instrument?"

"All instruments," I said. "The guitar, accordion . . . He plays
by ear."

"Where does he play by ear?" Bobby asked, and the left side
of his mouth lifted, the beginning of a smirk.

"Newark," I said, "mostly in Newark. What does your father
do?"

"Still?" Bobby said, not answering me. "He still plays in
Newark?"

"Sometimes," I said. "The clubs that are left."

"And he makes a living that way?"

"Sometimes." And I repeated my question: "What does *your*
father do?"

"He has an office job. He works for a security company."

"Fine," I said. "My father drives a truck when he's not playing."

"Which is when?" Bobby said.

"During the day," I told him.

"Every day?"

"Yeah," I said, "every day. He plays at nights and on weekends, at Club Rendezvous and the rest of them."

"So he's a truck driver?" Bobby said.

"No," I said. "He's a musician and he drives a truck on the side. What the hell do you do?"

"I'm a truck driver," Bobby said. And then he smiled. "Same as your father."

He'd never taken his eyes off me the whole time. Not one comment slid by. It was push and pull, sure, but I liked it. . . . By now he'd slipped his hand across the Formica table, put it over mine. He had a tight grip about him—nothing subtle—the kind you can't squirm out of, not that I tried. His foot, under the table, was pressing against the heel of my shoe—the same shoe he'd caught.

I'd been lying to my mother pretty regular by this point: saying I was over Peg's house—"I need to use her typewriter" (we took secretarial courses the last year at Snyder); saying I had extra shifts at the Blue Ribbon—I'd taken a job there after graduation and I was a good waitress—just fine. The money was good too. My own money! But I wasn't looking for a career in waitressing. I'd had enough of that at home.

And the lying came easier than I'd expected. I should have done it earlier, really—it got me out of the house—but I'm not a liar by nature. It's just not me, and I got tired of it. I got sick of making up girlfriends at the diner and fake baby showers, wrapping empty boxes like gifts. By the time I met Bobby, something inside me just said, *Stop*.

"I've got a date," I told my mother flat out the first time he rang the bell.

"A date!" She said it like it was the craziest thing in the world. She sprang up from her chair. "With who?"

"Doesn't matter," I said, "just a guy from the neighborhood." (She didn't need to know where we'd met.)

"What street?" she asked me, like it mattered. "Do I know him? What's his name?"

"He's just a guy from the neighborhood!" I said. "He lives on Roosevelt—you happy?"

"Does your father know about this?"

"It's just a date, Ma. One date! I'll be back in two hours. Don't start."

But it wasn't just one date. I knew it wouldn't be. He picked me up the next night, and the next night . . . and the one after that. Bobby and I were an item fast.

"Is it the same boy?" my mother'd ask before each date. "This Bobby?"

"He's not a boy," I'd say, because Bobby's six years older than I am and—who knows?—maybe I wanted to get her goat a little. Then again, maybe I just wanted her to know this was serious. "He's twenty-three years old."


He used to take me to Lincoln Park, Bobby did—it's the biggest park in Jersey City and we'd go for long, long walks.

He took me for a few dinners, too—Robinson's Steakhouse on the square (it's closed now), Jule's near the cemetery on West Side. And he took me to some movies—at the Loew's, the State, the Stanley; they were all still up and running.

He would've taken me to more, too—more dinners, more films—I'm sure of that; he was very attentive back then. But for that we needed more time—for that I needed to lie. I'd have to get picked up and dropped off at Peg's house, make excuses, sneak around. And I was feeling good about myself—I felt I had no reason to be ashamed.

"It's a date, Ma," I'd tell her. She used to hover by my bedroom door while I did my makeup, fluffed my hair. . . . (Peg had convinced me to cut it, and I liked it that way—short and wavy. I'd arrange a big curl on each cheek.)

"Who with? This same boy? This Bobby?"

"I like him, Ma—don't start."

"So why can't I meet him? Why can't you bring him up the stairs!"

I was in no rush to show Bobby my house, mind you—none at all. I was in no rush to put him up for twenty questions, have him see my mother in that house smock—see that furniture that was wearing away.

"You'll meet him soon enough." This went on for a couple of months, these conversations. "Just give it time."

And she'd try her old route: "Mary, I don't feel so hot. Maybe you should stick around."

"Oh, Ma, you never feel well." I wasn't gonna cave so easy now.

"Mary! I'm your mother. What a way to talk!"

"All right, all right," I'd tell her. "I'll be home before you know it. Two hours—no more."

So it was usually just the park . . . and we usually didn't have much time.

\* \* \*

There was a lovers' lane in the park back then, right behind the Casino—the Casino-in-the-Park. Bernie, the owner, named it that when he thought gambling would spread across New Jersey. But it didn't. So it's a banquet hall with a downstairs bar and restaurant.

There's a lake right across from the Casino, and granted, it's a man-made lake, but it's pretty all the same, and even then the Casino got a lot of weddings, so it was nice—especially in the spring or the fall when it wasn't so hot—to watch the brides getting their pictures taken in front of the water.

If you visit the Casino now, you can see a storage yard in back, and in the middle of that storage yard is a shut-down water fountain. On either side of this fountain there used to be benches. Stone benches. Bobby made a lot of promises to me on those benches—*I'll buy you this, I'll take you there.* . . . in between, he'd give me a kiss on the neck or the mouth.

A lot can happen in two hours—a lot of big talk, anyway.

I think the fact that I was never too available, that I always had to run home . . . I think this added to the attraction for Bobby—an incentive! It added for me too. And Bobby was never one to hold back—he was never one to take things slow.

As for me, I'd never even had a boyfriend before.

We couldn't do much on those benches, mind you—not on those walks, either. We were in public, no matter how tall the trees. That didn't stop his mouth from going, though—*You shouldn't have to work in a diner, Mary. . . . You're too young to stay home.* I told him a bit about my mother, not every detail, but enough. That didn't stop him when he was ready to propose.

It was a Sunday in October, that day he asked me—

October 8—barely three months after I'd met him. And this was fast, sure. Even then it was fast. But that was Bobby's way—still is—very impulsive, jump right in. It was a different world then—I should say that—it wasn't like you dated four, five guys, waited till you were thirty . . . but still it was fast.

That night was warm for October—it was early and the sky was still light. We were sitting, talking, watching—the usual: there was a wedding party right in front of us, maybe fifteen feet away.

"She looks beautiful," I said, and I remember pointing to the bride. Back then the veils were so long—yards and yards of white tulle—and she had hers fanned out on the grass behind her.

The wind was blowing and, right in the middle of all the photographer's clicking, her veil blew straight up. It got caught in a branch and stayed there; one of the bridesmaids had to run over, jiggle it free. After that, the bride threw it at her mother—"Just hold it," she said—and she went back to posing, this time with just a headpiece.

"A real brat," Bobby said.

"She still looks beautiful," I told him. "It's a beautiful dress."

"Yeah . . ." Bobby said, and he paused a few seconds, then, out of the blue: "But you'd look better, Mary."

"You think?" I said.

"I know," he told me.

"Oh," I said—and not much more; I could tell where he was headed and, to be honest, I was shocked. Not that it happened—I knew it would happen (I was hoping). I just never expected it that day.

"And what about me?" he asked. "How would I look in a tux?"

"I don't know."

"You wanna find out?"

"Sure," I said, and I smiled, tried to pass it off as a joke. I didn't know what else to do. But he wasn't kidding. I knew he wasn't. It was just like I thought. He had the ring out and everything.

My father liked Bobby right off the bat: Bobby kept quiet around him and he had manners. He knew how to eat. This sounds small, I know—but some of my uncles (my mother's side especially) . . . Eating chicken with their hands—you can talk until you're blue in the face, and then keep talking, but still, it's the chicken in their fingers, the piece of napkin stuck to their chin. After a while, you give up—at least my mother did—you find out they're coming and you boil a pot of ziti. Macaroni, you can't pick up.

Bobby was the first boy I ever took home for dinner (the first man—he was twenty-three, like I said earlier), and, for my father, this stood out.

"I'm impressed," he said, when Bobby left. "Must come from a good family."

"The Nolans," I said, "over on Roosevelt Avenue." He already knew the address, but I was trying to make them sound familiar. "You never heard of them?"

"No. Can't say I have."

"Well, they're fine," I said. Bobby's father was dead already.

He had four brothers who seemed nice enough. His mother was very aloof the one time I met her (she had us in for coffee—no dinner—a store-bought ring cake on the table), but I wasn't gonna let that hold me back.

"He's not Italian, true," my father said, "but times are changing; that's not the end of the world."


My mother was a different story. My mother didn't like Bobby at all. Nothing against him personally, so she said—but the job.

"It's just as easy to love a rich man," she told me. She was on her best behavior that night, too; she'd even gotten up early from bed, helped me make veal chops. She waited until both Bobby and my father were gone (my father ran out to the club, as usual), then she kept calm while she laid in: "Mary, you'll do better than this one. There's just no other way to put it. I think you should wait awhile—you'll see I'm right in what I'm saying. Just wait."

And who the hell did she think I was gonna meet in Jersey City? Me, with my hot two hours, my stolen trips to the shore? Some millionaire?

"What if I don't wanna do better?"

"Oh, Mary"—she laughed in my face—"you're so young."

"You just want me home," I told her.

She put her hand on her heart, crestfallen—an act. "You shouldn't think that; it's not that simple."

"No?"

She saw she was getting nowhere. "What about college—huh?"

It's true, I was supposed to register at Jersey City State College for that January—but I'd already put it off a semester because, let's face it, where was college gonna get me? Four more years at the diner? Four more years at home with her?

"Can't you just be happy?" I said, holding up my ring. It was half a carat, pear shaped, very elegant—Bobby's older brother helped him pick it out.

"You're rushing, Mary . . . you'll be sorry."

"What rushing?" I said. "I'll be eighteen in March."

"You're rushing, Mary!" She couldn't stay calm long. "You're rushing because of me!"

"Right, Ma—it's all about you."

"And what about him?" she asked me. "Why's he in such a rush? Is this the way he does things"—she threw her arms up—"this man?"

"Worry about your own husband," I said.

"Mary!" If she had the energy she would've slapped my face.

I knew that was out of line. "I'm sorry," I said.

"Keep the ring," she said finally, and she got calm again. She forced herself. "You don't have to set a date yet. Just think about it. Keep the ring. Tell him you'll think about it. Just wait."


I married Bobby quick, though—just five months after that night on the Ferris wheel. I didn't care what anybody said.

I had a proper wedding: Our Lady of Victories, the Hi-Hat in Bayonne for the reception. Peg was my maid of honor. It wasn't like I had to get married. I just didn't waste any time.

Peg said I was marrying Bobby just to get out of the house . . . to get away from my mother.

"Come on, Mary, is she really wrong on this?"

And I'm not saying I wanted to hang around—of course not—but Peg *was* wrong. They both were. That wasn't the only reason. I thought about it, sure . . . and it's true, sometimes Bobby wasn't so easy to get along with: he had a nasty way about him (I'll get to that), so you could look from the outside and say, *She must've had a reason.*

But that was only sometimes.

He could be sweet, too, Bobby could. He was smart. He'd been in the army, he worked hard. He wasn't some goof-off like a lot of the guys on the corner . . . like most of the boys in my class—though, granted, they were younger.

And there's no denying it: the man was handsome! It wasn't just the blue eyes, the wavy hair—he had the teeth, too. Irish teeth. Big and straight and white. And they get bigger when he smiles. An overbite, really. Like the Kennedy boys. When Bobby was young, he was something to look at: the blue eyes and the black waves and the big white teeth. Sweet. Like an altar boy all grown up. Especially in the summer when his skin would turn pink. Bobby doesn't tan like I do. Just burns and then peels. A good candidate for skin cancer—not that I'd wish it on him. And, sure, maybe I did want to get away from my mother. Maybe I did want to start my own life.

But that doesn't make any difference—none at all—because my father had other ideas. I no sooner moved out, got my own apartment, than he was right there, my father, dropping off my mother. Every morning he would drop her off! My own father. And he'd pick her up every night, washed and changed and fed by me.

"It's just for a few days," he said the first time he brought her over. He even left the motor running like he did when he dropped me off at school when I was a girl.

A few days was a few weeks, a month, a few months—then it was every day that she wasn't in the hospital.

He never batted an eye—I couldn't believe it.

"Daddy, I'm married," I told him. "It can't be like this."

"She's still sick," he answered. "I'm so busy. Just a few days more, Mary. She's having a bad week."

"You can't pitch in?" I asked him. "You can't come home early, go in a little late?" (I knew he'd already used up all his sick days for my mother, for the band.)

"I don't make my own hours on the trucks," he told me. "It's not like when I worked construction."

My father'd left trucking before my mother got sick—he'd opened his own construction company, set himself up as the boss. It was a good two years for him, too—the business was taking off. But then she got sick, he needed the benefits; had to go back to the trucks.

He shrugged his shoulders. "And the band can't play without me. You know how that is."

"Then hold off on the bookings!" I snapped back at him. I had a lot at stake here—I wasn't backing down so easy.

"Mary, it's almost winter." He kept his voice calm, boxed me right in. "The money's good. We're lucky that we're busy. We take what we can get."

And busy he was! I should have known then it was more than work and the band!

I never even took a honeymoon. Bobby didn't have the money at first—the man never saved till he met me—and by the time we saved up, I had my mother in the living room. I felt too guilty to leave. It would've been one thing if I didn't have to see her every day—that was the plan—but I did.

I'd quit my job at the diner; Bobby kept that promise. "You don't need to work—just fix up the apartment, make it how you like." So it was the two of us—me and my mother—together, alone. I felt too guilty to go back to work, too. It was just like Mallory Avenue.

I got pregnant right away—I never planned this (I never planned against this, either)—and even then, she was there.

*I had this under control,* I'd think, when I had a minute to myself. *I was on my way, what happened?*

I think Bobby was shocked too. He'd come home—he was always working late—and he'd see us. This was a small apartment, mind you—just three rooms on Winfield Avenue, right across from the kiddy park, about twenty blocks from my parents' house (we found it quick; it was just enough to get us started).

"Where's your father, Mary?"

"He'll be over in a minute," I'd lie. "He just called, he's on his way," I'd lie again.

"You want me to drive you home, Mrs. Marelli?"

"You trying to get rid of me?" she'd say.

*Oh, God,* I thought. There was tension right away between the two of them—she never even gave him a chance.

She was getting sicker every day now. The illness slowed down for a few months when I got married, almost a remission. But she was wilting now . . . fading fast. And she didn't even try to be pleasant—I can only imagine how she treated my father at home.

"I never said you weren't welcome, Mrs. Marelli."

(This was when he still made an effort.)

"Then what *are* you saying? Huh?"

"I'm saying you shouldn't put words in people's mouths. . . . How's that for a start?"

They'd get going from there.

"I notice you come home late a lot, Bobby."

"Yeah, I work for a living . . . so what?"

"I thought maybe you forgot the address."

"Oh, Ma!" I'd jump in. "Knock it off. That's just not right."

My husband would bite his tongue.

"I better go out," he'd say, and he'd run to meet his friends at the bar. "I'll be back later." The door would slam.

This was a tough spot for me, really, once he went out—that hour or two before my father came to get her was a real stomach turner—because I was loyal to my mother. Always. No matter what. But I needed to be loyal to my husband now too.

"You let him go out to the bar." She'd start in on me.

"Oh, Christ, Ma—you haven't caused enough trouble already?"

"He's late a lot, Mary."

I wouldn't answer. I wasn't giving her any ammunition.

"Just tell me. Is he late a lot? Or is it just me?"

And I'd keep my silence, hold my ground, but she'd plant the seeds, you see: she'd make me wonder. I was very naïve then— too naïve. I never even knew which bar he went to—but I began to wonder: *Why does my husband get home so late from the trucks?*

\* \* \*

I can't say I blamed my husband for coming home late. I can't say I blamed him for running out when he saw my mother, either—it was that or a fight. But my father worked for years in trucking and he always got home around five-thirty, six o'clock. And like I said, my mother kept planting these seeds. I was pregnant and I wanted him home.

So I decided to ask him. I didn't want a fight of my own, didn't want to sound like my mother. So I asked him, very calm, when he got home from the bar one night, after my mother was already gone. I said, "Bobby, how come you're always getting in so late?"

"From the bar or from work?" He was good at dodging a question.

"From work."

"It's overtime" was the answer I got. "Why's your father always so late?"

And this made me suspicious.

"My father stops off at the club, Bobby—he has to, he's in a band." (I *still* didn't know about Judy.) "But he's done before that on the trucks. He's done by five, six o'clock . . . tops."

"Your father works for a different company," Bobby said. "Don't listen to your mother. We just work late at American Can."


The next day my mother was right back in her chair. (My father made Bobby bring it over. Bobby was very respectful to my father—he did what he was asked.) It had the green, nappy upholstery with worn-out blue leaves. She wouldn't let us buy a new one. Nothing new—not a housedress, or slippers . . . not even a comb.

She'd start tapping her foot around five-thirty. "It's getting late, Mary. . . . Did your husband call yet?"

"Lay off, Ma. . . . Did Daddy call you?"

"If this is the life you want, Mary . . . I told you not to rush."

The way she spoke to him—so surly, so suspicious right from the start.

Bobby never said he hated my mother. He never pulled me aside and said, "Mary, I hate your mother—she's bitter. She's a troublemaker. Keep her out of my house." You can't say that about someone who's dying; someone who's fading a little each day; but you can watch her shrink and hope she shrinks faster.

And it wasn't only him who had those hopes. No, I'd be a liar if I said it was. Sometimes, when I'd be helping her up the stairs to the apartment—maybe it was morning and my son was crying, crying for me, and I was already pregnant again—I'd wonder what would happen if she just fell; if I just let her go. *No one would blame me,* I'd think. They wouldn't say a word. But they wouldn't have to. They'd think it. They'd think: there she is, she dropped her mother down the stairs. Or: there she is, she let her mother fall. She wanted her to fall. She murdered her own mother and got away with it.

And I'd try to stop thinking like this! I'd try to remember her—my first mother—the one my husband never met . . . the one who didn't dig, snap, start trouble.

I'd look at her in that chair and I'd try to find something, anything, to remind me. . . . I'd see her in one of those old smocks she wore—just cotton with a faded check pattern, red and white, and I'd think, *Oh, how she loved to shop.* . . .

My mother had an old boyfriend, Fred, who owned a store on East Fourteenth Street in Manhattan, and she used to take me on the train to shop there.

"The Jews know fabric," she'd say.

And she wasn't prejudiced. No, not her. Freddy was Jewish, and he was her first boyfriend, the only one before my father: "Freddy the Jew." And again, this was not to be prejudiced. That's just how they called you: one detail, and you got your name—just like "Limpy," or "Specs," or my uncle, "Tony the Horse."

She wasn't a spendthrift, either. She worked in a store; she knew value; she knew how to make a deal.

My mother dumped Freddy right away when she met my father, but they stayed friends.

"You pick the coat you want," she'd say. "Let him show you them all, but don't say anything, just give me the eye."

She was heavy then: not too heavy, not the way she got. I'm talking about maybe 1952, 1953. She was short-waisted and she had a big chest, so she never wore skirts and blouses. Only dresses. She knew how to look good: it's not just about fashion or price tags. It's about knowing your body. She liked floral prints. Dresses that showed off her legs, her bosom—all her strong points. She had the black hair and the white skin—not dark like mine—but pretty, just the same. And how she looked in those floral prints! With the bright red lipstick! Yes. All the salesmen in all the clothing stores used to smile when she walked in the door. Not just Freddy, but all of them. And they'd smile at me too. We were quite a team.

And then, when we'd find a coat, she'd pretend she didn't like it at all: make a face, click her tongue, shake her head. She'd ask about three or four others, pull them off the rack, examine them with her fingers, say, "Oh, that's too much, how about this one?" and then finally, reluctantly, she'd point to the coat I wanted.

They'd tell her the price and she'd roll her eyes, no matter what they said—maybe shrug, lift her arms in the air.

"I don't know," she'd say. "We've already settled . . ."

In the end, they'd come down. We'd get the coat at a discount. Sometimes at cost.

She used to go to New York alone, too, sometimes, or with my aunt Dot—they got along here and there—and I'd wave to her from my grandma Angelina's window as her train passed by.

The train tracks were on top of a hill, right behind my grandmother's house, so I'd sit at Grandma's back window, almost eye level with the tracks, and wait. When the train went by, the whole house would shake and the silverware in Grandma's drawers would make a racket. Who knew if my mother could see me, but there I'd be—shaking and waving, with the knives and forks going *clinkclinkclink*.

When we rode the train together, my mother and me, I'd stare hard out the window and try to find Grandma's house. "There it is," my mother would say. "See Grandma? See Grandma waving." And you could see the tar roof, the shape of the house . . . a few window frames even, but a hand—impossible.

Then, maybe a few days later, I'd be at my grandmother's house again, waving to the train, pretending that my mother could see.

All this pretending, all this waving . . . I used to think that if I stopped—if I didn't wave—then something terrible would happen. So I'd wave hard, lean out her kitchen window, make sure Grandma saw what I was doing. Even then, when I was practically a baby, I was trying to save my mother; trying to protect her—and always in some stupid, impossible way.

Chapter 8

## ONE AFTERNOON

"I look at myself now and I think there are two Lenas," she says.

My mother got morbid around lunchtime—even more morbid than usual: "Two of you," I repeat what she's said—"I know. Believe me, I know."

I've just put my first son, Tommy, to sleep on this day—this one that stands out (I'm jumping ahead—I'll get to my sons). It's his nap time—what a restless kid my Tommy was!—and I finally have a moment's peace. I finally get to rest. So I sit down in the living room, across from her. She's been alone in there; she's been working herself up.

"Ma, please," I tell her, "don't start. I'm getting a headache."

But it's too late. Her eyes fill up fast—the way they used to when she laughed: "There's the Lena who had you, Mary—the one who married your father and worked and went to Florida and cooked for all those people, and then there's this Lena"—she points at herself with her stiff, skinny finger—"the Lena who gets carted around, washed and dressed in the morning, delivered like a package nobody ordered. And that first Lena, she's gone. I know you see that, Mary. She's dead already."

*So she sees this, too,* I think.

"And Dom. I think he misses that woman."

"Of course he does." I say this before thinking about it—it only makes her feel worse.

"That's why he has her."

I'm shocked and I don't answer.

"Oh, Mary, don't look at me like that—you think I'm stupid?"

We've never discussed this. She's never said it straight out—and now that she does, I realize that I know. I've known for a long time—in my gut, maybe, just not in my head.

"She works at the ShopRite. I made Beta take the bus to see her."

"I don't need to know this, Ma." My voice gets firm, which surprises me.

"She looks like *me*"—my mother pauses—"like I used to."

I sit on the arm of her chair. I touch her shoulder, rub her back.

"He looks at me, this stranger." She starts crying. "I'm a stranger." Again she points to herself. "He's still healthy," she says. "He's still young."

"Oh, Ma." I don't know what to say. My own eyes are filling.

"He looks at me, this old, angry woman—I can't help it, the way I yell at him . . . I really can't—and he's mad at me because I took her, I replaced her—but I didn't take her, Mary—and he loved that Lena, the first one, but so do I. I miss her too."

I slide my hand up to the back of her head and touch it. This usually calms her. But I can't calm her down today.

"I didn't mind the other women. We had time then."

"It's okay," I tell her. "Let it out." I rub her back again. "Just keep your voice down." (I don't want her to wake the baby.)

"And the two of us—we're stuck together. We should be friends, really. We've both had a loss. But when he combs my hair in the morning he looks at me like I'm a murderer. And it's not this Judy that I hate him for—I hate him for that."

"Her name is Judy?" (I didn't know her name until then.)

"Mary, listen to me!"

"I am, Ma. You don't *hate* him." I'd like to kill my father, but I stand up for him—for them . . . my parents—I don't want to make it worse. (I don't want to take this on, either.)

"You don't understand," she says. "We had time together! *They* did—those two people . . . this other Lena and my husband. And he was out, gone, never home. And we still have a little time, now, yes. . . ."

"You do," I say. "Maybe more than a little."

"But he's so angry. He's so angry—you don't see him at home!—and so am I."

I pull out a tissue from my pocket and hand it to her.

"And now she's the one who's never home," she says. "Oh, Mary, I could go on forever," she cuts herself off, wipes her face, catches her breath. "And I know it's hard on you. But it's such a pleasure when he drops me off."

I didn't see this coming. I didn't know she was headed for this place. "It's not so hard," I tell her—and I mean it! On this one day, I mean what I'm saying. "It's good he brings you over." *She's not gone yet*, I say to myself. *She's still in there, still thinking.* It's a good day all considered—a good day for us—and I know it won't last, but I'm glad for it anyway. I put my hand back on her shoulder. "It's good he brings you over, Ma—it's good you get to see my son."

## Chapter 9

## THE KIDS

I'd had Tommy in August, '63, and by the end of that October, I knew Bobby Jr. was on the way. I wanted a family moment—I thought we needed one—and that's exactly what I got!

"Irish twins," my mother said, when we gave her the news. I'd made sure Bobby was home when I told her—a mistake, really—and she went straight at him.

"My daughter's not a baby machine," she said.

"Oh, yeah?" He told her, "Well, neither am I."

My mother wasn't expecting that answer; she didn't know what to say. She paused for a moment—Bobby was the only one who could make her do that—and then she got up from her chair. "Good," she said, "then you agree: something should be done!"

"Something?" he said.

Bobby's nostrils were flaring, bright red, the way they get before he screams. And my mother . . . this was the amazing thing: when they fought, her whole body would straighten up. Her back would arch, her chin would go up, and she'd practically smile. It was like the old days with my father. Even then, just months before the end—maybe eighty-two pounds, curled up and shriveled, almost in a ball—a fight with Bobby could take ten years off her.

I'd been standing between them. Not on purpose—it just usually happened that way—but I backed up, let them at each other, face-to-face.

"I'm a Catholic woman, for God's sake," she told him. "Not something *now*. Something after."

"Okay, then maybe you could tell me what you mean exactly by *something*," he said, "you being such a Catholic."

"Oh, Bobby," she said, and she looked away, disgusted. "You know what I mean. You should talk to the doctor. There's a lot he can do."

Now I couldn't stand back any longer. I stood back a lot at this point in my life—I admit it—but not this night.

"Like what?" I said, and I stepped toward her. "There's a lot he could do like what?"

"After the baby," she said. "Not now. After this baby . . ."

"Like *what*?" I said.

"He can close the baby shop, for Christ's sake. He can make sure you don't have five more."

Then Bobby blew. "You want me to have her tubes tied?" He was screaming now; he swung his hand, knocked the phone off the wall. And there I was, right between the two of them . . . again. I'd just put Tommy to bed. He'd been sleeping before they'd started. I could hear him now, starting to cry.

"You want me to have my tubes tied?" I said softly. I put my hands over my stomach. It was almost flat, just a tiny bulge: left over from Tommy, just starting from Bobby Jr. . . . Who could tell?

My mother turned to me. "All right," she said, over Tommy, over Bobby, over everything. "Maybe you should have them tied. How many kids can he support, anyway? You want them all to wind up driving a truck?"

My husband ran out to the bar that night. He didn't come home until midnight. My mother went back into the Pollak the next day.

The guards at the Pollak Hospital were so nice to me that winter—nicer than ever. That was one good thing. The elevator operator, too—his name was Peter, a young guy, Irish like my husband. I think he had a crush on me.

"Another on the way?" he said, when my belly got obvious by the following spring. He'd waited, I'm sure—he didn't want to insult me. I thought that was cute. He said it one night while I was just getting on the elevator.

"Yeah, I keep busy," I said, and we both laughed. I didn't mind joking with him—I'd known him since I was a girl.

(It was times like this I was glad I was married—times like this when I knew I'd moved on.)

The kids on the Sister Kenny Floor were happy to see me, too—"You're like the Pied Piper," my mother would say, because sometimes I'd have two or three kids waiting for me when the elevator door opened (they knew I came around seven-thirty). And I swear, my mother was happier in the hospital. She was sick and in pain—she was really dying this time—but her mood lifted in the hospital, all the same.

I think it was all the attention—the nurses, other patients . . . me without my husband. I'd lighten up, too, in the hospital. (She looked terrible—true—but I tried to act hopeful. . . . I hardly mentioned Bobby at all.) I brought Tommy up there a few nights, and all the nurses made such a fuss. But most nights, I left Tommy at home with Bobby. Most nights, we took our shifts.

I thought there'd be less tension in the house with my mother gone. I was wrong, though. We were fine in the bedroom—at least until the eighth, ninth month. Looking back, I should have appreciated it more.

But Bobby was always so aggravated. Always so easy to set off. Jealous, too . . . he was jealous of everybody. I told him about Peter, the elevator operator—how sweet, how pleasant he was to me—I thought maybe he'd see this as an example . . . maybe he'd remember those long, long walks.

But no. He said, "Peter? Who's this Peter? How come you know his name?"

"Oh, Bobby, I'm going there for years," I told him. "He works the elevator—that's all."

"That's not what it sounds like."

"You're absurd."

And Bobby threatened me: "Stay away from this guy, Mary. . . . Stay away or I'll come up."

"You wanna visit my mother?" I thought I'd inject a little humor.

"Don't play with me, Mary. I'll punch him right in the face."

And he was still staying out late. Most nights it was seven o'clock, but sometimes it was even later than that. The bar made sense when my mother was home with me every night (at least that's what I told myself), but not when she was up at the Pollak.

Bobby'd call me from a pay phone at the end of the day and say he'd "stopped off for one," or was about to. I didn't want to nag him—I didn't want to be like my mother. . . . But then again, she had a point—he didn't play in a band like my father did (she was quick to point this out, just like I did).

"So what's with the bar?" I said, finally, when he strolled in at eight-thirty one night. I'd just had to call up to the hospital, send a message that I couldn't see my mother. I was five months pregnant, too—my second kid—I'd let this build. "You forgot you were married? You forgot you had a wife?"

"I have friends," he said. "I'm not a loner like you."

"A loner! You leave me home alone and then you call me a loner?"

"Ah, Mary . . . you're always running out, anyhow."

"My mother's sick," I said. "She's sicker than ever—what do you want me to do?"

"Your mother, your mother," he said, and he turned it around on me. "It's always your mother."

I knew this whole situation was tough on both of us, so I tried to be reasonable. "If you want, I'll stay home a few nights." This was a big step for me—but I meant it. "I'll see my mother tomorrow . . . we'll talk."

"Fine," he said, "you do that."

I couldn't tell if this was a relief for him, or a burden.

"Bobby," I said. "You wanna be with me or not!"

He didn't answer.

"I'm pregnant"—I was practically crying now—"I've got a

mother who's dying, another kid in that crib." I pointed over to Tommy (we kept the crib in the living room). "What the hell do you want from me?"

"Mary"—he pulled me close to him, tried to calm me down—"you don't have to tell me you're pregnant. That's my kid you're carrying. You forgot?"

I leaned in close to him, right against his chest. "I'm not forgetting anything," I said. "You're my husband. I just want you home."

"All right." He patted me on the back. "I'll come straight home tomorrow."

"You promise?"

"All right!" He got impatient—it didn't take much. "I'm not late every night." (He was.) "Don't nag."

## Chapter 10

## A WAY ABOUT HIM

On the night I went into labor with Bobby Jr., I stayed home until the last possible minute—just like Dr. Carter told me to do.

We had company—our friends Nicky and Barbara Jean were over for dinner. Nicky was Bobby's friend from childhood—a real hothead; I never liked him, but Barbara Jean was sweet. I liked to invite them over for dinner. . . . The dinners made Bobby stay home; I liked the company, too.

My labor started in my back around eight o'clock, like it did with Tommy, but it was two in the morning when we finally got into the car. Barbara Jean and Nicky had gone home; we'd dropped off Tommy with Irene, our upstairs neighbor. My contractions were three minutes apart, but I knew my body; I knew I had a few hours to go.

"Calm down," I said. "You'll give yourself a heart attack."

But Bobby was fit to be tied. He kept cursing the car (it was stalling), cursing the doctor, cursing me: "We should've left hours ago."

"Look," I said, "knock it off, already. You're not helping. The hospital's ten minutes away. You're worse than the labor pains."

Bobby insisted on a shortcut. I told him, "No, don't bother," but he turned off the boulevard, went up Bergen—right through the black section. There were black men with their shiny, slicked-back hair, screaming (this was before Afros), giving our car the finger. The crowd got thicker as we drove ahead. By the time we got to Monticello Avenue, we drove right into a police line. One of the cops broke away. . . .

"Where you going?" he asked.

"She's having a baby," Bobby said—loud and fast, like the cop should have known.

The cop bent over and leaned in the window. He looked past Bobby over at me, my belly, my face. I looked back at him. He was young, nice-looking—not red and bloated like most of them—and he had his nightstick in his hand.

"This road is blocked," he said. "You can't go through. Too much trouble at the other end."

"It was her idea to wait," Bobby told him.

"I told him to stay on the boulevard," I said to the cop.

"I don't know." He pulled his head out of the car, stood up straight, hooked his nightstick back on his belt. "I don't know what to tell you, mister." He was talking to Bobby, but his eyes were on me. He shrugged his shoulders. "Is she that close?"

"Close enough," Bobby said. He turned around and looked: there was a whole line of cars behind us. "So now what?" Bobby asked me. "I can't back up."

The cop was still looking my way—even as pregnant as I was, he kept staring at me: at my face, my arms (it was hot that night; my maternity dress was sleeveless).

"Well?" Bobby said to me. " 'I know my body. I know my body.' So now what?"

"I'll tell you what," I said. "I don't care *what*, Bobby. . . ."

The cop leaned in the window.

"You stay out of this," Bobby yelled, then he turned to me. "You wanna call Dr. Carter now?"

"Don't start," I said. "Just don't start, Bobby. I want to get to the hospital. I want to have this baby. I'll go with *him*, if I have to," and I pointed to the cop.

"Oh, you will?" Bobby said.

"Yeah," I answered. Then after a second: "He can pick me up and carry me, for all I care."

Bobby looked in the cop's face. The cop smiled, tried to look friendly. "You'd like that," Bobby said to him, "wouldn't you?"

The cop backed up. "Wait a minute," he said.

Bobby turned, looked back at me. "And so would you, probably."

"Why not?" I said. "He's a lot nicer than you are."

"Why not?" he repeated. "Because I'm your goddamned husband."

I had another contraction before I could answer. I grabbed for Bobby's hand, but he pulled it away. I closed my eyes, tried to stay calm, and dug my nails into the seat.

"Great," Bobby said. He punched the steering wheel. "Have it right here in the car, why don't you?"

I was still squeezing, still digging.

"I guess your mother will blame me for this, too."

I took a deep breath. "You fuck," I said through gritted teeth. My nails broke through the vinyl. The pain stopped for a minute.

"Listen, lady," the cop said, leaning over again, "I can get you an escort."

"Just drive me," I said, and I unlocked the door, started pulling up on the door handle.

"No, ma'am," the cop said. "Stay where you are. It's too dangerous."

I looked over at the police line. There were about ten cops with their backs to us. We could hear the demonstrators off in the distance, and the sound of police sirens.

The cop blew his whistle and backed away from our car. He waved over two squad cars, gave them both instructions, and their sirens went on.

"Follow the first car," the cop said when he came back. "The second one will follow you."

This was 1964: there'd been fires and "demonstrations" and my city was in trouble. . . . Those race riots that started in Newark, they were spreading . . . my whole town was in an uproar. Mayor Whelan was in office, and by now he'd called in the National Guard. There were soldiers with machine guns holding back the crowds. Somebody threw a rock, anyway, and it hit the window next to me. After that, Bobby got quiet. He held my hand and I held my stomach. Bobby Jr. kicked the whole way.

"Everything . . ." Bobby started, as we pulled into the driveway at the emergency room. "With you . . . everything's a drama."

"Oh, Christ," I said, too tired to argue. "Bobby, you can't blame a whole riot on me."

"I suppose I can't," Bobby told me, and again—maybe for the second or third time in his life—he was quiet.

* * *

And that's the way it always was with my husband by then: fights. Nine times out of ten. There was no holding back, now—not for him, not for me. I tried to avoid them, mind you, but he was always so quick with the dig, the comeback, the comment that would send you spinning. Sure, maybe I should have known what I was in for, right from the beginning. Maybe I saw it with that little push-and-pull in the diner. Maybe I was even drawn to it—look at my family. But these fights—he enjoyed them, you see. And he'd get you going—I have to put this in—he'd get you so that you were enjoying the fight, too, at least for a while.

A real mystery, that man, my husband—through and through. We married fast, but I figured I'd get to know him. I figured it would all unfold—normal—but I was wrong about that too.

He'd been in the army: stationed in Japan; pictures in uniform—all of it. He had good stories, so I figured—but he never told them. The most he ever did was show me an old Dutch Master cigar box with his memorabilia—a brown overseas cap with yellow braiding that folded flat like a pancake, an arm patch, one epaulette. . . . He'd spent time in Hokkaido, the place *Life* magazine called "sin city of the East," and he'd smile whenever I asked about it . . . but that's all he'd give, a smile. And that made him all the more interesting. At least it did back then—it was bait.

Intense, too. Intense when he talked and even more so when he listened. He was like this in bed, especially those first few months after we married—that whole first year, maybe—late at night, after my mother was gone. When the apartment was quiet. Just a dim light shining through the window (our bedroom faced the street lamp on the corner). When you talked to Bobby, he looked right at you. Like it was the first story he ever heard. And you felt like it *was* the first story: the first one you ever told.

I'd tell him about the saloon, the singing, and he'd try to picture me in front of all those men, but he couldn't. So I'd sing a few lines for him—he was egging me on, really. I'd sing them soft, as low as I could, and he'd smile, say, "Yeah, now I can see it."

He'd grab me. We'd get going again.

When he got drunk, it was another thing entirely—just the wrong puff of a cigarette could start him yelling: "You think you're a movie star?" or "Don't blow that in my face."

Or maybe I'd cross my legs and a man across the restaurant would look at me. (With my mother in the hospital more, we went out more. I was pregnant, sure, but I never gained that much weight . . . I still looked good.) And Bobby would start to fume. He'd turn colors, stop looking my way, get quiet. Not peaceful quiet but stern, stare-right-through-you quiet, like his mother got. Like a priest. There's a lot of power in that Irish-Catholic *hush:* like everything you've ever done and will do is wrong. All without a word. Or worse, if we were at a bar, say the Casino in the Park, he'd tell the guy to watch it.

"Watch what?"

And I can't tell you how many men said "watch what?" before Bobby hit them right in the face. He'd always been easy to rile—right after we married, before that even . . . maybe a few dirty looks at Jule's Restaurant if somebody looked my way (this would set him off). But this was a lot more than I'd bargained for. He'd never actually swung a fist.

He got away with it, though. And he had friends to back him up if he needed them. He'd hit these men, and they'd hit him back sometimes, but the next day it was over. He was never afraid to walk down the street. Nobody waited at the corner for him. In my family, things were different. An enemy was an enemy. You had to watch your back.

*　*　*

My mother died two days after Bobby Jr. was born (her in the Pollak, me in the Margaret Hague). She never even got to see him.

But she meant what she said about having my tubes tied on that night she fought with Bobby. Meant it so much, she cried like a baby afterward—and those weren't fake tears; she wasn't putting on a show. *"You want them all to wind up driving a truck?"* I can still hear it now.

She sat down, reached over to me, turned my face with her hand so my eyes looked at hers: "Please," she said. She talked as if Bobby were gone, not just two feet away. She saw something in him I didn't—something *worse*—and she didn't care who heard. "Your grandmother loaded grapes the day I was born. She was out there, on the street, both her arms full when she felt me. Aunt Beta had to run like a lunatic to get Aunt Sadie. The next thing was the screams. My screams. I heard that story all my life. Grandpa told it like it was a tribute—his wife and the grapes and the baby. 'A good worker,' he'd say. 'Not like you lazy kids.' This is a different world for you," she told me.

"Ma," I said, "you're upsetting yourself."

But she wouldn't let go. She wouldn't stop talking. "You graduated in January, for God's sake. Six months early. You were supposed to go to college. You have ambition, Mary."

My husband walked over. He peeled my mother's hand off my face—not rough, but deliberate. He pulled me next to him so we were both facing her—the two of us together, me and him, both on the same side. That's when she started to cry.

"For Christ's sake," she said. She held her hand over her mouth so her words were muffled. Still, you could hear her: "For Christ's sake, have your tubes tied."

Bobby walked right out the front door. Didn't even close the door behind him. I had to run to close and lock it. Tommy was bawling his head off by now. I walked back through the kitchen, started heading for his room.

"He'll be fine," my mother yelled. "For God's sake, Mary, it's just the noise that's got him going. You checked him two minutes ago. You can check him for the rest of your life. Get over here and listen to me."

*This is it,* I said to myself. And I was angry, sure, but they were her last words. Her last words or close to it—you could see that in her face—and she was using them on me. It was no surprise that she went into the hospital the next day. (She never brought this up after—even on the nights I was alone by her bed at the Pollak. She'd said her piece . . . she never took it back, either.) I stood there that night and waited. She leaned, almost fell, against the kitchen table. She was panting, reaching for air. I pulled out a chair so she could sit, but she wouldn't.

"The day you were born your father threw a party," she said. "Three days and nights. He worked as a bartender then, in between jobs with the band. I was in the hospital. He came to see me—once, maybe twice. But then it was back to the party, me all alone."

"Please, Ma," I said. "A million times I've heard this. Keep quiet. Let me get you a drink."

"But that was progress!" she yelled. She crunched her brittle fingers together, made a fist, and punched the table as hard as she could. It barely shook; she looked disappointed. "Me alone and my husband out drunk! I never wished him a bad time, Mary. I wasn't that kind of wife. But he didn't wait. I wasn't invited. And that was progress. It was progress all the same. Do you see what I'm saying? Move up, Mary. Move forward. Stop it, Mary. No more kids."

*　*　*

I never had the operation, but my mother got her way. After my second baby, Bobby hardly came near me—not for years. He'd push off any man that came near me—that never changed. At home, though, he had no interest at all.

# Chapter 11

## AUNT DOT'S STORY

People say Italians stick together. One big happy family. The families are big, all right, and you hear it right away if you don't invite one second cousin to a wedding; if you miss one christening or send one cheap gift. . . . But stick together? Maybe years ago, maybe when they all first came over, when they spoke no English and had no choice.

I made my mother's funeral arrangements right from my hospital bed at the Margaret Hague—no help from anybody.

My uncle Birdie offered to pick up the tab, then changed his mind. My father finally had to step in—which he should have done in the first place—and Uncle Birdie gave in. Or almost. He sold us the coffin at cost.

And all those other relatives—my aunts, cousins, great-aunts, uncles: "Just call if you need anything. Really, Mary, just call." Well, let me tell you, I called: I was exhausted from my mother—young, sure, but exhausted—I had two baby boys, a husband and a father on the road. I called my aunt Beta (though what help could she give, really?). I called my aunt Loretta (I'll get to her), my uncle Birdie, his wife. . . . I called my cousin Josie, who'd moved to Carteret (she became a teacher, like I was supposed to). I even called my nosy aunt Delia.

When Aunt Dot finally pitched in—the only extra hands in the lot—my father made fun of her. "The old whore," he'd say. "Look at her; out to pasture."

This was right when I came home from the hospital, right after the funeral; I could barely hold my head up.

"Oh, don't even," I told him. "Don't you dare drive her away. You've got something to say, you go home and say it."

And what a sight she was changing diapers, too: the glass of ginger ale in one hand (she was sober by then), the ice cubes clinking—she always used ice; made her feel like it was Scotch— the box of Johnson's baby powder in the other hand, a cigarette dangling from her mouth.

"Please," I'd say. "Don't smoke so close to the babies."

"Don't you worry about me," she'd answer. "I'm changing diapers since I'm five years old. Changed your uncles' diapers and I changed yours too. I'm the oldest, Mary—the oldest of the second batch. . . ."

My grandmother had kids in batches—that's how Dot put it—a few miscarriages in between.

And she'd go on: "What? You think your grandpa Louie lifted a finger? You think your father ever pitched in?"

"All right," I'd say, because once she brought up Grandpa Louie there was no stopping her—and once she got started on my father . . .

"There's always one, Mary," she'd tell me. "One daughter who takes over. In your case it was easy, Mary . . . you're the only child."

"I know," I'd say. "It was easy."

"But that's not the truth," she said one day, thinking better of it. "No." She corrected herself, put down the powder. People like Aunt Dot—people like my mother—they're like that: they repeat themselves over and over (it's no wonder they fought), but each time it's a fresh conversation for them, and one day, out of the blue, the story changes, or at least the ending does, and you realize that there's thought behind this, and you've been yes-ing them to death or smiling along, which is your job, definitely (Dot got more talkative the less she drank)—but there's a point, maybe, too.

"You were—what?—eleven when your mother got sick, twelve?"

"Twelve," I said.

"So, twelve. If you fell apart, Mary, somebody would have stepped in. Somebody would have had to. It might have been me."

"But I didn't."

"No, you didn't." She could tell I was getting irritated. "So we didn't." She paused. "I didn't." She paused again, this time for emphasis. "Nobody did—not even that father of yours. He could have hired somebody, could have asked his brother Birdie for a loan."

"All right, Dot . . . maybe. Maybe. But I really don't want to go over this right now."

"Ah, maybe," she said, disgusted that I wouldn't jump on my father. "In my family it was me: Mama had Philly when she was forty-two—the tenth kid, twelfth if you count the two she lost. . . . She was tired, Mama was—worn out. Women get that way. . . ."

"I know," I told her. "Believe me, I know."

"No, you don't know, Mary. Mama wasn't like you. You're just tired. Mama was different—a different woman altogether. It built up with her—this was still the thirties, but now you'd call it 'depression'; and I'll tell you"—she pointed a diaper pin like a warning—"it runs in the family. For two years Mama could hardly get out of bed. Somebody had to help. Your mother was already married to your father. All the normal sisters were gone, married, settled in Elizabeth . . . in Rahway. And Beta's no use to anybody."

"Oh, Dot," I said. "It's such a big family, if you're gonna go straight down the line . . ."

"I love her, Mary, but my sister Beta—singing while she walks, church five times a week, shoplifting on the avenue; it's all she could do to count pencils at the Dixon factory. And God forbid one of the boys would have stepped in. I was the valedictorian at Ferris High; did you know that?"

"Of course I knew. Everybody knows."

"I had a job in New York," she said, "an accounting firm, Touche Ross. I was a file clerk, but I was up for a secretary job. I even had a boyfriend there. A normal guy, especially for me, an accountant—Danny—not short, really, but not tall either. My height. The job got me home late, though—what with the commuting—and so did Danny. Papa got me work at the labor union here in Jersey City, the one down on Brunswick Street: it was a block away from the house."

"I know where you worked"—by now she'd stopped working there—"my father belonged there too." He did construction (extra day work) for a while. . . . He worked so many jobs.

"That's right," she said. "Papa got him in too. And that's

where I met Bobby Manna—your father introduced us—and Bobby Manna's friends. You know what I'm talking about, Mary."

Bobby was the local Mafia king. My father knew him from the card games he used to cut—just a matter of protection, really, protection for "the house." My father knew Bobby's father, too—he hung out a lot downtown, he had good connections. Bobby didn't get Dot started with this circle when they first met, but he had tie-ins to the Genovese family, which certainly gave her a jump start.

"Well . . . yes," I answered.

"People said, 'Oh, Dot, how could you? How could you?' But what the hell else would I do? I was always ambitious, Mary. I always bored easy. I was up at five-thirty in the morning getting my brother ready for school; I was back home at five-thirty at night to make him and the rest of us dinner . . . and around all those men all day in between. None of them worked; nobody works out of that union. It's a front, Mary. . . . And I was still young, mind you. . . ."

"You were very young, Aunt Dot, I know that. . . ."

"I'm not making excuses, Mary. I know what I am. I was still young and I looked even younger than I was, and Bobby's friends noticed that—that's all I'm saying. You do what you have to do. I had a kid brother who called me Mommy—he still does when he gets drunk or excited, and he's forty—I had a stupid, boring job. I liked those men. I liked the clothes they bought me, the few hours out in the city—and the extra money. Extra money is good, Mary."

"You were very pretty," I said, because I wanted to make her feel better.

"No. You're pretty, Mary. Your mother was pretty. Your grandmother was pretty. I was just young. Young and I had brains. Better than average, maybe," she added. "And valedictorian! Ferris was a good school then, too—not just a bunch of lazy Puerto Ricans."

"Don't start on the Puerto Ricans," I said. Aunt Dot's neighborhood eventually went Puerto Rican just like my own went Filipino, so that was all you heard from her.

"This was before the public schools turned into prisons, is all I'm saying—prisons with the drug dealers in the classrooms, and cops with guns in the hallways. Those men at the labor union liked me because I was young and because I made good conversation. And I liked the men, plain and simple. . . . I would have shot myself, walked right into the Hudson, without them, that's the truth of it. I'm like Papa; I'm very extreme."

"You did a good job with Uncle Philly," I said. "He's a very good man."

"He's all right," she said, and then she put down the baby, took a drag of her cigarette, came toward me. "I'm sorry I didn't step in, Mary. I know how your mother could be; I grew up with her—and I know how sick she got. . . . As for this, though." She pointed at Tommy and Bobby Jr. on the changing table. "You've got two cute kids, Mary; don't get me wrong. And I never say a bad word about your husband—not like the rest of the family . . ."

"The family?"

"But this"—she talked through me—"this you got into yourself."

"Oh, Dot, please!" I had to make her stop—that was the last thing I needed to think about, my whole family talking about me behind my back. "Just don't blow smoke near their faces," I said.

And she listened, I'll give her that: she'd turn her head when she exhaled.

After that first year, though—the year after my mother died—even Aunt Dot bailed out. Even from her it was *Call if you need me*. Only she was different. She meant it. Even the way she said it was different. No bullshit. "Mary," she said, "I got you over a hurdle. Enough, now! You have my number: use it if you need it."

And I did use it—believe me—because one thing about Dot, you could trust her. But she had her limits; I made sure not to wear them out.

# Chapter 12

## PEG

My girlfriend Peg got lucky: two years as a secretary and she'd married her boss. He was a lawyer named John Glavin—Irish, but his family were practically Pilgrims, they'd been here so long. John was an older man. Bald, with little hands. But he was crazy about Peg and he couldn't keep those little hands off her.

Peg was one true girlfriend back then—still. Just like in high school. She was loyal, honest, funny—all the things you could look for. She was there if you needed her . . . she did what she could.

Peg and John got married in '66, four years after me and Bobby, and I used to go to their house up on Gifford and Bergen whenever I got the chance.

I had no car then, not while Bobby was at work, and Bobby Jr. was still in the stroller. Strollers make a real scene when you're getting on a city bus, so I'd walk along Kennedy Boulevard. Bergen Avenue would have been quicker, but by the midsixties Bergen Avenue was a mess. Not up by Peg's house, or even so much by mine—but in between, forget about it. Very spotty. And it was a shame, really, because I can't tell you how many walks I took along that avenue when I was a girl—long, window-shopping walks with my mother and my aunts past the custom-made dresses at the Peggy Lee shop, the fur coats at Kreps. . . . But that strip, those stores, were gone by then, or going . . . just like the whole avenue. If you were white and you walked too long on Bergen, you took your life in your hands.

So I'd push along the boulevard, the stroller in my left hand, Tommy in my right—you needed a good grip with that kid because there was a lot of traffic and that boy always loved cars—movies and cars—and you never knew when he'd squirm loose, try to run after one. It was a long walk, over an hour, but once we got there, it was worth it. Gifford was a beautiful block, one of the last nice blocks to hang on—nothing but doctors and lawyers on Gifford Avenue—big houses with front lawns on either side and old, tall trees whose branches touched each other in the middle of the street.

Peg's house had a stone front and a wraparound porch that we used to sit on—big enough for Tommy to play with his brother, run, even ride the old scooter John would leave out for him. John grew up in that house, and he saved everything. He even had the same maid, Margaret, who took care of him as a kid. Margaret's old face would light up when she saw my two boys. She'd shuffle them right off to the kitchen for cake—she had one of those big glass-covered cake plates that you see in diners and it was always, always full . . . soda bread, pound cake—plain stuff, but she made it herself, fresh. Sometimes she'd let them play hide-and-seek on the first floor (let them burn off all that sugar); Peg had so many rooms, she didn't know what to do with them.

"It's a good thing John won't let me redecorate," Peg said. "I told him I wanted to, just because . . . well, I figured I should show some interest, but he said, 'No, no, this house has been the same for years.' The rugs [they were hand-loomed], the piano [a black lacquered stand-up], the tables and chairs, the plates [gold-leaved and they ate off them nightly]: John grew up with these things. Even the bed we sleep on [a big, knobby, mahogany thing]—it was his parents'."

"Maybe you should make that one change," I told her.

"Maybe," she said. "But it's funny, don't you think? I met John's mother once before she died—the woman hated me."

"I'm sure she didn't *hate* you, Peg."

"My father delivered milk, for Christ's sake. Of course she did. And John's father would have hated me, too—don't doubt it."

Peg was wearing falls by now. She always had thin hair, and she used to have it puffed up at the beauty parlor—the same place I went before I stopped going, Vincent's on West Side Avenue. But by '66 or '67 she would just comb it back, hook on the fall, and stick a headband over the line where the real hair met the fake. With the long full blond hair and her thick black false eyelashes, Peg looked like a centerfold.

"Oh, Peg," I said, "when's the last time a man hated you?" and she laughed.

"Or you?" she said, still laughing.

Some women blow up after childbirth, but I had no time—if anything, I got even thinner. Almost bony. Fine, if you liked that look; not so fine if you didn't. I still had my legs, though, and I was sitting with them crossed. All the same, I didn't answer: Peg knew about Bobby and me; she was just being nice.

"Either way," Peg said after a few seconds, "here I am, up and down on their bedsprings."

Peg and I both had a good laugh over that one—no matter how many times she brought it up.

"Still," I said, "there's something backward about it—you and him in the same bed he was made on."

"Oh, never mind about the furniture," she said. "You know I'm not one for that stuff, anyway. Besides . . ." And I remember this conversation clearly—it was either June or July 1968, because it was hot and we were drinking iced tea, and I remember that she took a big gulp before she said this. . . . "Besides, John wants to move."

"Oh, no," I said, and I almost grabbed her by the arm. "Peg, you wouldn't."

"Mary," she said, and she shrugged her shoulders, lifted her arms to say, *What can I do?* "Face it, Mary. The city's going down the tubes."

And Peg was right. Jersey City was going down fast. It was falling apart—the race riots, the fires in the housing projects.

And Jackson Avenue was even worse than Bergen: Lovely Lady Frocks, the Rainbow Shop for lingerie, the Lucky Spot for curtains and slipcovers, where my mother worked—all closed and boarded or well on the way. Even the Blue Ribbon diner, the first place I worked—gone. There were stabbings on the street; you name it. You couldn't walk down the street, let alone go shopping. A shame, like I said . . . no, more of a shame, because Jackson Avenue was *the* avenue when I was a girl—even more than Bergen Avenue, which had the prettier houses (all boarded up too; boarded or split into apartments—welfare apartments usually). And downtown—the heart of the city, the place we all got started—it looked like a ghost town. You could look at Newark Avenue and cry: the Fabric Center, the Italian delis and butchers and the big A&P . . . the Adorable Shop for kids' stuff—it wasn't as bad as Jackson Avenue, but it was falling, slipping, fading away fast.

People were leaving; the young couples, white couples anyway, were all moving away. Running to the suburbs. Running to "get out." That's what you heard everywhere: "Get out. We need to get out." Like a fire drill.

Bobby thought maybe we should do the same, but I said, "Oh, no." For me, things were bad enough on Winfield Avenue, lonely enough in Jersey City. . . . What would I do out in Nutley—worse yet Totowa or Paramus?

By the end of '68, Peg was gone. She didn't move to any New Jersey suburb, though—no, not to Clifton or Upper Montclair or even Short Hills. John wanted a clean break from the city, a clean break from the whole area. He got himself a transfer—a transfer to San Diego, California, no less—and so it was *Merry Christmas, I'll see you soon* . . . and we all know what that means.

Peg was there when I needed her, though—like my aunt Dot. At least on the telephone. She made sure of that. "Just call and let the phone ring twice," she told me before she left. "Then I'll call back."

"You don't have to," I said.

"I know you can't afford it, Mary. Please, you're like a sister."

"All right," I said. "I'll see."

"Remember, though, exactly two times," she told me. "Three times and it's my niece Suzanne."

Suzanne was her brother's daughter. She was twelve. Her mother drank too much and her father drank more. Between the two of them, the girl was practically on her own.

Peg's offer made me feel like a kid, pathetic even—and Peg liked that, just a little—the upper hand. Who's kidding who? But then again, so did I a little—the idea I'd get taken care of . . . and what did it matter anyway? She was right: I *didn't* have the money.

"All right," I repeated. "I'll see."

## Chapter 13

## DISAPPEARING

After my mother died, I used to dream about her. Even years later. She'd come to visit me and she'd sing. It was like in the beginning, the two of us in the kitchen, the radio playing in the background. She'd have a suitcase in her hand, and she'd lay it down on my kitchen table. "I'm living in Chicago," she'd say. "Don't tell your father." Or sometimes it was Baltimore, St. Louis, Miami. One night, after I read a book about Christopher Columbus, it was Madrid. And she'd open the suitcase, singing all the time, "Gonna have a hot time . . . in the old town . . . tonight." She'd pull out a dress, her makeup bag, a wig, and she'd start getting dressed, start tucking her hair into the wig. She was old in the dreams. And shriveled. Like she was at the end. But she'd put on the makeup, the wig, a dress—always with the pretty flowers—and she'd transform. She'd pat on her rouge, tiny taps with her little hand pad, and her cheeks would puff up. She'd take out a tube of lipstick—bright red, still—swipe it over her lips, press them together, then fill in the places she'd missed, press again . . . make a popping sound when she was done. A quiet pop, the way she used to. Her back would straighten.

Sometimes in the mornings I'd tell my son Tommy about the dreams before he went to kindergarten. This was four, even five years after she'd died. . . .

"Like a movie," Tommy would say when I told him about the dreams, because even then he loved movies—and Bobby Jr., he'd nod along, repeat after his brother: "A movie, a movie." Then they'd run out—Tommy to #33 school, Bobby Jr. out front to play—and I'd go back to bed.

I don't know why my husband lost interest, but after Bobby Jr. was born it was two years before he touched me again—and even then it was once in a blue moon.

I'm sure what my mother said didn't help. I'm sure that didn't help him warm up to me! I'll tell you one thing, though, it was her words that got me on the Pill. I thought I might leave him. . . . I had two kids already—and, sure, he hardly came near me, but what about when he did? I knew I couldn't be walking out the door with nine mouths to feed.

I went to see Dr. Carter, who gave me good advice, as usual: "Don't tell him," he said. "So what if you're Catholic? Hide the pills. Take them when he's not home. You think *he* cares how many kids you have? He works the same hours no matter what."

This was all before we moved, left the apartment on Winfield (it was only supposed to be for a few months anyway) for good. 1968. The year Peg left Jersey City and Tommy started school and, for me, things started to hit bottom.

I'd spend all day in the apartment alone, Tommy at #33 school, Bobby Jr. out front playing Wiffle ball, handball, kick ball (it was usually kick ball, and he had some set of legs on him;

I can't tell you how many windows I paid to replace), my husband out driving God knows where.

Bobby would call from a pay phone, and that was my big chance—my three minutes—until the operator cut in.

"I'm running out of change."

"Should I call you back?"

"Never mind, I'm working."

Sometimes it was easier just to fight.

I was disappearing.

I stopped wearing makeup. I stopped buying new clothes.

I cleaned the house, though. Always. I never let that go. Sometimes, I'd be dusting, and I'd lean over, catch my reflection in a silver ashtray, or maybe in the mirror at the back of my china cabinet—no makeup, my hair pulled back—and I'd scare myself. I looked almost like her: my mother, near the end. I'd have to lie down, take a nap, then get cleaning again.

That goddamned linoleum: the white floor with copper specks. "Flecks," they called them—you could open any apartment door in the building, any door on Winfield Avenue, and that's what you'd find: a white floor with copper flecks. The same with the countertops—though those were Formica. They last forever, those linoleum floors and Formica countertops, but you can never tell if they're clean. And I'd wipe and mop, wipe and mop, until I was seeing circles—circles and flecks. Even the kitchen table had them—my Formica table with the aluminum edges: sharp, ribbed aluminum that always caught my nails. But the table had green flecks, too: copper and green flecks on a white background.

I'd sit down afterward on my aluminum kitchen chairs—aluminum to match the edging; everything matched one way or another—with the flat, hard, vinyl cushions. The seats had a pattern when we bought them (when my *mother* bought them, just like the couch, and she never let us forget it) and the pattern on the cushions was green and orange—a dark orange, the closest she could find to copper—but color on vinyl wears fast, and the vinyl cracks in places, too, so I'd have to patch them up with duct tape. And the cushions wear fast, too; right down to the aluminum. A blurry green pain in my ass, those chairs became. Blurry green and faded orange, some silver duct tape here and there that would stick to my dress, my underpants. And the boys loved to peel that tape—of course they did—which would only pull up more vinyl, and I'd say, "Bobby, we need new chairs," when he was home—if he was home—and he'd say, "Of course, of course," and then he'd smile and flash those teeth and tell me that new chairs were "bound to fall off the back of a truck sooner or later," like that "fine roll of linoleum" that was covering our floor. "And you really should call it Congoleum, Mary, if your friends ask, because that's what it is, and Congoleum costs a lot more, because it has much better color, a much nicer pattern—just look at the edging," and I'd yell, "What friends, Bobby, what friends?" and Bobby would shake his head and say, "It's not cheap, Mary, that Congoleum. I don't bring home cheap things."

And what the hell did he care about broken nails or shoddy, worn-out seat cushions? It wasn't my hands that were touching him—not like I wanted them to, I'll admit that, even now. It wasn't his ass those chairs were sticking to. He wasn't home for dinner anyway, and even when he was, he'd slip off to the living room and slurp it up on the couch, TV blasting all the while.

*Christ,* I'd think, *even the manners are gone—is this what it's come to? Is this what I bargained for? He's as bad as my uncle Archie (God rest his soul), bad as my uncle Birdie, my uncle Philly . . . Freddie—all my uncles put together.*

Either that, or he'd eat standing up—talking on the phone.

Truck drivers don't talk on the phone, they holler: "Yo, John," at the top of their lungs, like they were backing up an eighteen-wheeler, yelling directions, calling for help. "Yo, John," and his voice would boom across the kitchen; I'd put my hands over my ears, punch the table, tell the boys not to laugh.

"Yo, John," or "Y'ello," and no conversation, just loud barks of information: "Pick you up at seven. Wait in front. The fron-a-tha-building," all one word. Hang up. No good-bye.

"Who was that?" I'd say.

"That was Charlie. Charlie Doyle. He needs a ride in the morning. The wife wrecked the car."

*"Yo, John . . . the Wife,"* I'd repeat, disgusted, dropping my voice, making fun of him so he could hear how he sounded.

"It's just an expression, Mary. . . ." And he'd pick up his burger, chop—a bowl of spaghetti even, lean against the counter, inhale.

"Call him by his right name," I'd say. "He's a person—just like you, just like me. And his wife: her name is *Helen.*"

"An expression, Mary, like 'Hey, Mack.' I'd do the same if it was Paulie—you know that, Mary." He'd roll his eyes, maybe turn, show me his back, disgusted too. "The same if it was Nicky or Sean."

"Use their names, Bobby." I would soften my voice, try to reason with him. "If it's Paulie, then say it. If it's Charlie, then say that. Even if it's Nicky. I want the boys to know you have friends, Bobby, friends with real names—real wives. Except for

Nicky and Barbara Jean, they never meet a single one of them. They hardly even see *you*. And I want you to talk in normal tones, like a normal person; my head is spinning, Bobby."

"It's the way we talk, Mary. Take an aspirin if your head hurts."

"My father never talked that way. Never," I'd tell him. "He never ate that way, either."

"But your father's not a truck driver," he'd say. "Your father's a musician, Mary—remember?"

The boys would watch his tricks and try to pull the same thing: The "Yo, John." The smirk and then "Oh, Mary." The "Take an aspirin, take an aspirin." Good little mimics they were, too—the feet on the coffee table, the toothpick in the mouth. Even the standing and eating. And that was the last straw! Neither one of them could even reach the sink, mind you, but they'd stand on their chairs and eat, talk, yell. Bobby Jr. had the nerve to pull up a chair one day—right up to my sink . . . me sitting like a dope at the table, still talking to him . . . Tommy already laughing, instigating . . . he leaned over, took a bite from his sandwich.

"Oh, no," I said, "no you don't," and I ran over, scooped him up, slapped his hand and ass, sat him right down in his place. "The buck stops here," I said, and he just looked up—didn't say a word, didn't dare cry—ate his sandwich in quiet little chews.

"And that goes for you, too," I told Tommy, my hand up and ready to go if it had to. He did the same.


My breasts got bigger on the Pill, which I didn't like—the extra weight hurt my back. I was so thin then, it made the straps on my new bras—I had to buy "C" cups—dig in. But Bobby loved them. Loved them so much that for a while we were up to two, three, four times a month.

During this time he'd come home early some nights. He'd see me in the kitchen, leaning over the broiler, maybe—I never baked and I still don't—or my head half inside the refrigerator. I'd pretend not to notice and he'd sneak up behind me, slip his hands around my waist. We'd go at it right on the kitchen floor.

"You should come home early every night," I'd tell him.

"Oh, come on," he'd say. "I'm working overtime, it's time and a half."

And I wonder, still, who he thought he was talking to. . . . Who he thought he was dealing with. I'd look at his paychecks— I deposited them at the bank, for Christ's sake—and they were always the same amount.

Being cheated on, left alone, ignored—that's one thing. That's bad enough. But to be treated like a fool . . .

"Just stop lying," I told him one night. I couldn't take it anymore. "If you wanted to be home, you'd be here. I'm not a dope," I said. "And if you want a dope, then you can marry one. I'm not like my mother; I won't look the other way."

"Oh, Mary," he said, and he grabbed my head in his hands. "You spend too much time with the kids. You're making things up."

"I'll divorce you," I told him. "I mean it." But then I lost hold of myself; I started to cry. All that crying I did—I cried and slept and cleaned through the sixties. The women's movement— hah! I'd see it on the TV—I'd look at those freaks and think, oh, those raunchy women, burning their bras. But who was I to talk?

Bobby would wrap his arms around me after a fight; he'd slip his right leg between my two, and it was business as usual—just not usual enough. His face would be flushed from a day on the trucks—all that wind blowing in the window against his white skin. Bobby had strong forearms from all that lifting, all that loading and unloading. My knees would shake when he touched me—when he snuck up behind me, turned me around. The waiting helped, no doubt about it: all day alone, cleaning, thinking. And then the buildup: the door creeping open, the squeak of his workboots with every step. Rubber on Congoleum— Congoleum that smelled and sounded clean even if it never looked it. I'd collapse into him like a rag doll.

"He's a liar," I'd tell myself. "This is a rotten husband, a dishonest man." Sometimes I'd say it out loud. But before long we'd be on the floor, kissing, grinding. (We'd gone from famine to feast.)

Tommy saw us once in the middle of this—our clothes still on, thank God; I thought he was out front with his brother, playing—and he said my face looked like I was drunk.

"When have you seen me drunk?" I said. What else could I tell him?

After that, we held out till the bedroom. I made sure of it. And it was hard, believe me, after all that waiting in between.

I never told Bobby about the pills. I got a diaphragm just to distract him and he'd fight me over it. I'd say, "Okay, let's just forget it," and then I'd pull it out, we'd get going. He never suspected a thing.

*　*　*

It took Bobby maybe six months, a year, tops, to get used to my new breasts—and then it was back to once in a blue moon.

I was a young woman, not even twenty-five yet; I had needs. It got to the point where I was practically begging. Then it got to the point where I did beg. My father overheard me one night. We were in the bedroom . . . and who knew he'd slipped into the apartment? He had his own set of keys, but he rarely used them. He used them that night, though—he was sitting at the kitchen table and he heard every word. I came out, saw him. He looked away, put on his hat, left.

I'd spend hours—all day sometimes—at that kitchen table . . . my boys at school or out playing, my husband out driving, my father not talking to me. He didn't say boo for months after that night he overheard us. He must have been ashamed of me. He stopped dropping by.

I'd sit down on those hard, blurry, sticky chairs after I scrubbed them, mopped the floor, scoured the sink, dropped coffee grinds down the drain (it cleared the pipes). I'd close my eyes, put down my head, breathe in the sharp-sweet mix of Comet and Pine Sol (I used them on everything). But then I'd open my eyes and there they were again—the flecks—white and the copper and a little gray or green thrown in every two inches or so, which is why I picked the green chairs to begin with—to match; and then at night, she'd visit me, my mother. The red lips and the frosted blond wig: sometimes she looked beautiful; sometimes she just looked dead with a lot of makeup. But she was always singing, always having a good time. And I was disappearing.

## Chapter 14

# TWO-FAMILY HOUSE

By 1970 we were living in a two-family house. It was just off Mallory, a block from where I grew up. Aunt Dot helped us get a construction loan and we had it built from scratch—like a lot of couples in my neighborhood. "You need to change *something*!" Dot said. "This will help." And I wanted to believe her. She also said I should never rent to cash-only tenants, but Dolores Mulryan showed up when we were in a pinch. Irene, our first tenant, came with us from the apartment building on Winfield Avenue, and then—out of nowhere—she met a man. It was late in life for Irene, forty-seven, and she got married fast. I was happy for her, but her husband was a military man, and she had to move out, follow him to Virginia. She was gone before the year ended.

"My son" this, "My son" that, Dolores kept saying when we interviewed her, so we'd think she was a family woman. She had fiery red hair and a good figure, though she must have been forty-five years old. And she told me she was about to open a checking account.

"Tomorrow," she said. "Unless they call me in at the restaurant; then my next day off."

She blew air up her face—"whew"—and her bangs lifted, like some TV actress, as if to look busy, harried . . . always working hard.

Dolores paid the first month's rent in cash. And then she kept paying the same way. By the end of August—three months later—there were still no curtains in the front window, and her son *(my son, my son)* came to visit twice, both times stoned, both times with a different girl on his arm.

"I thought he was married?" I asked her when I saw her in the hall, after his second visit.

"Oh"—she laughed, rolled her eyes, practically shooed me away—"he is."

I asked her about the curtains, and she said, "Come on . . . is that in my lease, Mrs. Nolan?"


My own boys were growing so fast. Tommy in the second grade, Bobby Jr. in the first. Some mothers carry on when their kids go to school, especially with the youngest. You see them in the courtyard at Our Lady of Victories, tears running down their faces, a son or a daughter hanging from their house smock, crying too—like it was wartime and they'd never see them again. I never wore a house smock in public—no matter how low I felt—and I certainly never cried. But it was no party going home by myself, let me tell you: no party in those empty rooms.

Both my boys were good students, and they both got noticed right away: gold stars, penmanship awards, trophies for bowling and spelling. Tommy has my father's name (his middle name—

my father liked it better), but he's got my husband's face—handsome and furious. Bobby Jr. has my husband's name, but my face. People stop to look at Bobby Jr. He's not as dark as I am but he has the eyes. The eyelashes too. With Tommy, it's the voice that hits you first—all those big words, right from the beginning: "television," "ricochet," "a-u-t-o-m-o-b-i-l-e." But with Bobby Jr., he just walks into the room . . . like my mother, but even more so: people listen even before he talks. I don't play favorites. I don't love one more than the other. And, for me, it's a little of both—I like to look good, I like to use my mouth. But I think it must be nice for Bobby Jr.—nice to talk without speaking. And either way, for both of them, it was a pleasure to go to parent-teacher's night. Right from the first grade, Tommy got straight As. Bobby Jr. did the same thing a year later. And it was nice to get out of the house.

Their first-grade teacher, Miss Hughes, was an ex-nun. The Sisters of Charity pulled out of Jersey City in 1970 and the nuns at Our Lady of Victories had a choice: they could either stay in Jersey City and leave the order—try to make it as regular teachers . . . regular women—or they could move with the Sisters to Montclair, New Jersey. But the times were changing; most chose to try it on their own. They were homely, really. Each and every one of them. No makeup, long faces from years of praying . . . mustaches on their upper lips. I had to teach Miss Hughes to pluck her eyebrows, and she was twenty-nine years old.

"Oh, Mrs. Nolan," she said, when I suggested it. She'd been over my house twice by that point: once to bring homework (Tommy was sick); this time just for coffee; but she could never bring herself to call me Mary. "Wouldn't that hurt?"

"Of course it hurts," I told her. "But you get used to it."

"Really?" she said.

"Look at mine," I told her. "Plucking since I'm twelve."

"Twelve?"

"I matured quickly," I told her.

"I'll think about it," she said.

"Oh, no," I said. "Whatever you do, don't think about it. It's like cutting a cuticle, waxing that hair on your upper lip—if you think about it, it'll never get done. If you want, I'll do it for you, get you started—but don't think about it."

"You wouldn't mind?" she said shy—even more shy than usual. "You're sure you have time?"

"Me?" I laughed. "I've got nothing *but* time. Come on." She didn't move. "Come on," I said again. "I'll show you. Follow me."

Miss Hughes downed her coffee like it was a shot, then she stood up and walked my way—just a few steps, really, but she walked them like the plank. We stepped into my bathroom and I turned on the spotlights around my new medicine-cabinet mirror. Then I slipped the tweezers out of their holder in my old cuticle case, while Miss Hughes stared wide-eyed like I was about to do surgery. I stuck my face up close to the mirror, spotted one stray hair on my left side, arched my brow to meet the tweezers, and plucked.

"See," I said. I made sure not to flinch. "It's nothing."

Miss Hughes pursed her lips and tensed her shoulders like she'd caught a bad chill.

"I'll do it for you," I told her, then I sat her down and put her back to the mirror.

She carried on for the first few hairs, and I figured she'd calm down, but she didn't.

"Maybe we should stop," she said, but by then we'd made some progress.

"Now it's uneven. If we stop now, you'll look worse than when we started."

"Excuse me, Mrs. Nolan?" she said, very huffy, very nunlike, and you could see, in that moment, that Bobby, the way he huffs and scowls—the way his mother does too—is just a measly imitation. When you see a face like Miss Hughes's, a face like Sister Eucharista's (her ex–mother superior), or a face like Monsignor O'Brien's (the head of OLV parish—the one who fired and re-hired her)—you know that huffiness is Irish Catholic. (Not Italian Catholic—wrong mixture.) And it comes right from the top!

"Look," I had to tell her, "you're a nice lady, but nobody's perfect. Your eyebrows were a mess. That's why we started this. If you give me five more minutes, I promise we'll be done."

She was much quieter the second time around. She flinched a lot and the polite little smile she put on kept twitching, but all in all, she hung in like a trouper. Those nuns, ex or not—and you can say whatever else you want about them—have a lot of back-bone: it's all in the training.

When we were finished, she asked me for a drink. Vodka. I poured it, joined her, didn't ask any questions. Her brows were red and swollen, but I'd plucked some pretty perfect arches.

Miss Hughes started coming over pretty regularly after that. Sometimes she'd bring her friend, Miss Warnock—another ex-nun. They'd come over for spaghetti, a little wine. They used to go to singles bars to meet men—"fern bars" they called them, because they always had those big green hanging plants and wood paneling. They'd focus on the Upper East Side of Manhattan, because—and they never said this, but I knew a thing or two about the city myself; I read the papers (the *Jersey Journal,* the *Daily News* sometimes, the Newark *Star-Ledger* on Sundays)— I knew they wanted men with money.

I'd try to pull myself together when they came over. Sometimes I'd comb out my hair, iron a skirt—or culottes; they were just coming into style—and put on some lipstick; never red like my mother's: I'd stick to pinks, maybe orange, even light brown . . . softer, more modern colors (a mistake, to be honest, with my dark skin). It was almost like a date. After dinner, they'd fix up their hair, their makeup—which I'd help with, most times—and they'd head out for the night. Miss Hughes would wear silk scarves around her neck to hide her double chin (my idea). Miss Warnock wore one tied around her head (she had very weak hair). I don't know what they feed nuns in the convent, but the two of them—both Warnock and Hughes—had to lose a lot of weight to wear pants. And they did it—I'll give them that. It was a pleasure to watch them shrink and grow.

And these were good nights—no doubt about it—good nights in my new house. Nights I felt like myself, a good sketch of myself . . . maybe me on the boardwalk—excited and all dressed up!—on those long walks with Bobby . . . as a girl in the saloon! Most nights, though, to be honest, it was just like in the apartment: the boys asleep, my husband out . . . me at the table, reading the paper, listening to the radio—WNEW, William B. Williams and his trivia, some watered-down Muzak turned low so I wouldn't wake anybody. I liked that—the talk and the Muzak, no real songs . . . soothing—my head would be down by the end of the night . . . my face against my new round wood table. My mother stopped visiting once we moved: she'd show up from time to time, but the dreams were cloudy now—

cloudy and quiet, like the Muzak; even when she talked or sang it was in a muffled voice, a slow echo—like she was fading too. . . . Or like she was too far away . . . Like I'd left her behind with the move. (A relief, really.) And I'd sit there—different kitchen, same position—and just wait. Waiting for Bobby, waiting for Bobby.

Then even my father left town.

He'd stayed on the trucks after she died, held on till he could get a decent package—but by 1971, he was ready to retire.

"You're only sixty," I told him—I knew there was a move in store—"You're so young!"

"Mary," he said, "I'm working since I'm eleven. Don't question me."

After that he took a powder. . . . He bought and sold houses in Upstate New York—and who saw him? He kept his house on Mallory, but when he came back he practically lived with Judy—and he knew better than to bring her over.


Some nights, I just couldn't stay in the house . . . this house that was supposed to change everything . . . and I'd get in our second car—an old blue Buick, gigantic, big as a Cadillac, and roaring loud. . . . Bobby bought it used and never, ever fixed the muffler. . . . the boys in the back (I'd wake them if I had to), and I'd drive. I'd drive along Mallory. Along West Side. Through Lincoln Park. The lovers' lane was gone; they'd expanded the Casino (not that I'd seen the inside in years). You didn't dare stop the car in the park at night. You didn't dare get out and walk.

I'd drive along Route 440, sometimes across the city line to Bayonne, through Bayonne Park, take a stop off at the walkway (you could still walk in Bayonne at night) near the water just to think. The Hackensack River's a sewer—even when my father was a kid he'd get terrible rashes, flus, you name it, from swimming in there—but at night, even that water looks pretty. And then I'd drive some more. The boys had their little turntable, some battery-operated thing that their father brought home, and they'd play their singles, yell if I hit a bump—Cher singing "Half-Breed," a song by a man about some "Afternoon Delight." Annoying songs, the same words over and over again. Sometimes I'd hit the brakes, make a sharp turn sharper—try to scratch the record, make the needle jump, at least; give me a break.

On the way home, I'd stop for rice pudding at Al's Diner—that's where I used to see Charlie . . . still with the black suit, the black hat, always at the pay phone. We'd just wave, usually; wouldn't even say "hi." We'd lost touch: he'd gone his way, I'd gone mine. He'd been in the papers a few times already: arrested for booking numbers, helping with this robbery or that, a bad check run, some talk about a murder—just talk, though, no convictions. He was always on the pay phone or standing next to it, waiting. Always waiting too.

"You gonna be long?" I'd hear him ask if someone else wanted to use it.

He was sleeping with Ruth by then. Ruth Manganaro, a girl from my neighborhood. She even went to Snyder—but she was five years ahead of me; I hardly knew her then. Her husband was a cripple. Not when she married him—it was all from a car accident. And, oh, the things that man would say to her. . . . Ruth and I got friendly from the diner—just "hello" and "good-bye" really, but I'd see her during the day at the bank (she worked at First Jersey on the boulevard), and she'd chew my ear off: he was numb from the waist down—impotent; he would call her a slut, accuse her of being with this man and that one—all his friends, her boss at the bank, anyone. Finally, she gave up. She stopped coming home. Somehow—I don't even remember how—she wound up with Charlie. She'd tell me all about Charlie too. He was good to her, very understanding. She didn't mind that people laughed at him; that they called him a hood, a second-rate hood at that. She didn't even mind his name. She told me he was good in bed. I never asked for this information, mind you, and I didn't want to hear. I'd made my marriage.

Bobby and I rarely had sex by this point. And I wasn't about to beg—not again. I was getting older: not calmer, but better at acting calm.

"I could run around on you too," I told him one night. "It's not like I don't get offers."

"From who?" he said.

I told him about a construction worker named Mario, for one—a cement layer who was doing the new sidewalks at the Hudson Shopping Plaza.

He was digging up the old cement and he saw me coming; he saw I had open-toe sandals on—a little bit of a platform, worse yet—shoes Peg had sent me as a birthday present (Bobby forgot my birthday completely). He offered to carry me across the rubble.

" 'I'm heavier than I look,' I told him." (I said this to Bobby.)

"You were flirting."

"I was telling the truth. I'm no feather, Bobby; I'm sturdier than I look."

"And did he pick you up?"

"He tried."

"I'll kill him," Bobby said.

"Good," I said, "kill him. Just like that. Find his address and kill him. But what about you, then? How many people should I kill? How many women?"

"Don't change the subject," he said.

"Oh, no," I told him. "Don't even try it. This *is* the subject."

"I wanna talk about this Mario."

"I wanna talk about these women."

"Mary, I never said there were women."

And then I lost control all over again, started stamping my feet, screaming, crying as usual. I threw in Charlie's name. I wanted to scare him.

"Mary, I think you're losing it. I thought the move would help you. You have to get out more."

# Chapter 15

## AL'S DINER

"I grew up in an age of virginity," I told Miss Hughes one night—Miss Warnock, too, since she was sitting right next to her. "A real fool: one man, and not until you're married."

"Oh, stop it," Miss Hughes said. "You've got a very handsome husband," and then she caught herself, looked away.

"Yes," Miss Warnock added, "a very good provider."

"Besides," Miss Hughes jumped back in, "what do you think we do at these bars?"

"You never mind about my husband's looks," I said, because that was never in question—it's still not—"and don't play dumb. I watch television, I read the papers."

Miss Warnock just laughed. She was the quiet one, but sly—you could tell she'd do just fine outside the convent . . . at least in *that* way.

"Maybe I should get a baby-sitter, come out with you girls," I said.

Miss Hughes changed the subject before we got any further; that was her style.

If you asked me when I was a little girl, when I was singing for those men . . . or later, at the shore with Peg; working at the diner; on those long, necking nights with Bobby in Lincoln Park . . . if you asked me where I'd be on a Thursday, even a Friday night, in 1971—and if you asked me *with who*—I don't know what I would have said. And maybe that was a problem. Probably. And a big one. But I'll tell you one word you never, ever would have heard, and that's *nun*. Ex or otherwise. Not in a million years. But it was nice to have those ex-nuns at my table. Nice to hear their stories, to help them get dressed.

And it's ironic, too, that around this time, all those girls I went to Snyder with—Carol Salerno, Judy Scerbo, Stella Schilizzo, the ones I'd pass by in the hallways without even a "hello"—got so friendly toward me. This started slow, even before Peg moved, but it picked up fast after she left, and later, after Bobby and I bought the house.

And it was nice to bump into those girls at the ShopRite—sometimes I'd take Barbara Jean with me (she had no license)—or the Two Guys down at the plaza on Route 440. They'd meet for coffee almost every day: mostly at Stella's, which was right next door, and more often than not I let them know up front that they could count me out. I wasn't looking for a hen party. Even at the supermarket, I'd cut them off just before the gossip. It was the same thing if I bumped into them on the corner. I'd stay for a few tidbits—a few jabs about Helena Malvesi's weight; a comment or two about Nicky and what an animal he was (when I wasn't with Barbara Jean), how he lost this job or that—I'm only human. But I never kept on with it; I never forgot where I knew them from—and back at Snyder, I was the one who got talked about.

I never made any apologies for my looks back in high school—I was just like Peg that way. And I'll bet they loved seeing me the way I became—my hair in a kerchief, ten pounds underweight, my skin broken out, and blotchy, dark circles under my eyes.

Poor Barbara Jean: Nicky used to hit her—half the time, she had a swollen jaw or a black eye. She was always in sunglasses—big ones—and so I'd put a pair on myself to make her feel better: "They're good enough for Jackie O," I'd tell her. "They're good enough for us."

And God forgive me, but when Barbara Jean put on her glasses, all you could see was that nose. I love Italians and I am one, more or less, but—sometimes, that's a definite drawback, and all I can say is, thank God I got my mother's nose instead of my father's.

I started to go to the Woman's Club on Tuesday nights—Stella Schilizzo convinced me to join. She said it was "a big club, hundreds of members, different women come to different meetings; not the same old faces." So I gave it a try.

The Jersey City Junior Woman's Club—that's the full name. Over a hundred years old. And some of those women, you'd think they'd been there since the beginning. There was supposed to be an age limit, but it didn't look that way. They kept busy, though—we all did. We were always raffling off something—a bucket of Cheer, a trip to Florida, a new blender—so there was always something to shop for during the week, and I'd volunteer.

The money we raised—and we always raised *some*—would go to some Catholic orphanage, some Catholic hospital, a Boy Scout field trip to Wild West City. We'd have tea, maybe something stronger, we'd talk—not real talk, just chitchat, the kind that usually drives me crazy: talk about the kids, the teachers. . . . The new mothers and grandmothers (they'd always find each other) would talk about diapers and Pampers and which was better and how breast-feeding was back and they were "relieved," "disgusted" . . . or who the hell cared? It was better than sitting around Stella's kitchen table—I still said no to that—and it got me out of the house, got my mind off Bobby, off me . . . off Bobby and me.

A few times, though, when I got home, I noticed that the door to Dolores's hallway was unlocked. It didn't hit me the first time—but then it happened three, four weeks in a row. You could tell because her door shook when I opened my own (we had separate entrances)—and it wouldn't if it was bolted.

"Why is this open?" I asked Bobby one night—he was on the couch, our new corduroy couch—when I walked in; he was eating his dinner.

"I don't know," he said. "Why don't you ask her?"

"I will," I said. I was still in the foyer and I turned toward her door. But then I thought about her—that smug face, those smart-ass answers. It was late . . . who knew what she'd be doing . . . or with who? "Oh, never mind," I said. "Who cares? The front door's locked."

"Yeah," he said, "the front door's locked, so don't worry."

"And what would she care, anyway? There's nothing to steal in that apartment; it's not like she's wasted any time decorating." I stepped inside our living room.

"You shouldn't snoop," Bobby said.

"Who's snooping?" I said. "I was up there looking for the rent. She's a month behind."

"Did she give you the money?"

"No. Not yet."

"Don't worry," he said. "I'll take care of it."

The next Tuesday, Dolores's door was locked. And the next. And the next. After a few more weeks, though, it was open again. Again with the shaking.

"She's at it again."

"What?"

Again he was eating on my new corduroy couch.

"It's open," I told Bobby.

"So?" he said, like he couldn't be bothered.

"So I wanna know why. I wanna know where she thinks she's living. Next she'll start leaving the front door open too. Did you talk to her about the money?"

"Look," he said, "I wanna watch this game," and he turned on the TV. It wasn't on when I came in. "If you've got questions, go ask her."

"All right," I said, and I turned around. "I will." And this time I meant it. I put my purse down on the living-room floor. I'd already closed and locked our own door behind me, but then I turned around and started to reopen it.

"Wait," he said, as my hand hit the doorknob. Now, all of a sudden, he could give a damn. "It was me. I had to go up and help Dolores with something. I forgot."

"You forgot?"

"I forgot. I'm tired. Shoot me."

"Help with what?" I said.

"The sink," he told me.

When there was something wrong with the sink upstairs, I could hear it. It made a whistle. And there was a leak. But there was no leak. No whistle. And Bobby never asked me to call a plumber.

I took a good look at him. His hair was damp. You can always tell with wavy hair—it looks longer . . . flatter, too: the waves hadn't puffed up yet. And I'd gotten pretty good at looking at that head of hair, because that's the most I'd see of him, usually: late at night, asleep next to me, the covers pulled up to his neck. I'd touch it, play with it—he'd get annoyed if I tried to do that with the boys around. I'd try to count the grays if there was enough light coming through the window (Bobby grayed early like his mother, like a lot of Black Irish). And he usually took a shower when he came home—true—but right away. He'd been home since before I left. Hours ago. And now that I thought about it, it was the same the week before . . . and the week before that. . . .

"Did you just take a shower?" I said.

"Sure," he said.

"You've been taking them later and later, yes?"

"I guess."

"Especially on Tuesdays."

He didn't answer.

"On Tuesdays when I'm out."

Dolores was already two months behind on the rent—two months behind and Bobby wasn't saying anything; not to me, anyway. I felt a little like I might vomit, a little like I might collapse. I turned to lock my own door back up, to rehook the chain, and I broke it; it was never a strong chain anyway, and it broke off in my hands.

"Mary!" he yelled.

I fell against the door. My head was spinning. I needed to lie down.

"I'm tired," I said.

"Jesus. How hard did you pull it?"

"I was leaning, Bobby. . . . I'm tired and I was . . ."

"Don't worry," he told me. He walked over, took the chain from my hand. "I'll get a new one tomorrow. So long as the front door's locked. . . . Maybe you should go to bed, Mary." He rubbed my back a little, nudged me away from the door, faced me toward the bedroom, in the opposite direction. "Really, Mary. You look like you could use some rest."

"Yes," I said. I turned away from him, I started walking.

"I'll come in when the game's over. Don't wait up."

I'm in the parking lot at Al's Diner one night, rice pudding in my hands, the boys in the car, waiting. We've just gone for a long ride, and Charlie grabs me. He pops up out of nowhere and gets hold of my arm.

"Jesus . . . Charlie," I say, and I almost drop the two cups of pudding.

"Never mind," he says.

"What's wrong?" I ask him.

"I can't stand back anymore."

"Stand back?" I say. "What are you talking about, Charlie? Let go of my arm."

"I know you since you're a little girl. You look terrible."

"Oh, Charlie," I tell him, "it's nice to see you too." I hold up my left arm—it's dripping with milk from the pudding and I make sure he can see it. Charlie pulls out his handkerchief. He's still carrying white handkerchiefs . . . monogrammed, always—and always somebody else's initials. He hands it to me.

"What's he do to you, Mary?"

"Who?" I say.

"Who do you think?"

"Charlie, don't start."

"He hits you?"

"Oh, Charlie. Nobody hits me."

"Be honest, Mary. . . ."

"Don't try to be a hero," I tell him. "You're not my father, Charlie."

"Jesus Christ," he says, "I know I'm not your father. Who the hell said I was your father?"

"He doesn't hit me," I repeat. "You satisfied?"

"Then what's he do? What's wrong with you, Mary? I see you with that sad face, the scrawny arms, a bag of bones, out night after night. . . . And what happened to your hair, Mary? It used to be so beautiful, now you wear it in that kerchief, like an old lady."

"It's in style," I lie.

"I know clothes, Mary. That's not in style. Maybe for a grandmother . . . Why aren't you home, Mary? Tell me! What's he doing to you?"

"Nothing," I tell him. It's been at least two weeks since that night with the door.

"He does nothing to you, so you stay out all night. . . . You get in the car, you drive, you eat all that pudding and still you lose weight, you cry. . . ."

"The boys eat it."

"You cry . . ." he repeats.

"I'm not crying."

"You were, Mary. I saw you on the highway."

"Nothing," I'm yelling now. "Nothing, not a thing. He does nothing. Don't spy on me, Charlie."

"I'm not spying."

People in the parking lot are looking; I almost *do* cry, but catch hold of myself. "Not a goddamned thing. Not with me, Charlie. You understand what I'm saying? Nothing every night and nothing every day."

Now Charlie is embarrassed. He even blushes. But he recovers fast. "Mary," he says. He takes the cups of pudding from my hands. "You wanna go inside? You wanna get a booth, talk for a while?"

"I can't," I say. "I've got the boys in the car; they're waiting."

"So let them wait a little longer," he says.

"I can't, Charlie. This is a parking lot. It's late. . . ."

"I can watch the car through the window. Nobody's gonna steal his boys, Mary."

"My boys, Charlie."

"Your boys."

"Oh, Charlie." I look at his face, almost handsome now: he's gained some weight; it's filled in. The skin is still dark but less blotchy. His eyes are dark too—small and dark—like always. And like always, they're staring right at me—he hardly even blinks. "Still? You're still like this? Even after all these years?"

"I can't help it," he says. "I'm sorry. . . ."

"Where's Ruth?"

"Home. She had to go home."

"I should go home, too, Charlie. So should you."

"Just for a minute." He's almost pleading. "Really, Mary . . . they're fine in the car. You look a mess, I'm telling you—not just sloppy; I wanna know what's wrong."

"Charlie, I just can't talk now. You can't just leave kids in a car. Thank God you're not a father."

He doesn't answer, of course, just looks down, hurt. . . . He's never married; his girlfriend has a husband; he's been in and out of jail—and now I feel awful: for him, for what I said, for myself.

"Look," I say. "I'm sorry, too, Charlie. But you push. . . ."

"You want me to talk to Bobby?" he says.

"No," I say. But then I think about it for a second, and Charlie can see I'm still thinking, still considering, which makes me nervous. "I mean that," I say, and I make sure I sound definite. "You stay away from my husband."

"I just said 'talk,' Mary."

"I mean it, Charlie."

"Fine," he tells me. "I'll stay away if you want me to."

"I want you to."

"Fine."

"Charlie," I say, "I have to go," and I start to walk away. But then I feel rotten just leaving him there—Ruth home, his friends in the diner staring. "If you want . . . you can walk me to the car," I say.

"If I want?"

"I'm inviting you."

"I can't, Mary."

"Like a friend," I say. "I'm inviting you like a friend. You've never even met them."

When we get to the car, I open the back door to where the boys are sitting.

"Boys," I say, "this is your uncle Charlie."

"Uncle?" Tommy says. "Whose brother is he?"

"Oh, Tommy," I say, "don't cross-examine me. Just say hello to the man."

"Hello," they both say, in unison, very singsong.

"Not like that," I tell them. "Not like brats." And then Charlie butts in.

"Pleased to meet you." He puts the pudding cups on the roof of the car, wipes his hands, takes off his hat, and offers his hand for shaking: "Name is Charlie. Charlie Cupacoffee."

The boys start laughing as soon as he says it, and Charlie's face drops. Again he recovers quick, though: he's tired of being laughed at, you can see that—who wouldn't be by his age?—but he's used to it too . . . used to handling it.

"Cute kids," he says.

"Thank you," I say. Then I get in the car.

"You call if you need me," he says. He hands me a piece of paper with his home number on it. "Or just ring up the diner."

"Great," I say, "just what I need—more phone numbers."

"What?" Charlie says.

"I said 'great,' Charlie. Now I have both numbers." And I drive away.


My mother was wrong about the money; about Bobby driving a truck. The money was fine—good benefits, too—the Teamsters were in power and going strong. That wasn't the problem at all. But the rest of it . . .

And it's funny the things you fix on, the things you remember when you're alone, when you're in a state, but sometimes, alone in the house, or out driving with the boys, I'd think about Tsa Delia. Tsa Delia was the mother of a man named Jake—a man at my grandfather's saloon: Uncle Jake, I called him. He was there, at the bar, every time I went to visit. We lived near my father's side of the family by then. (My first two years, we lived on First Street—I don't remember that.) We'd already moved up to Mallory Avenue, and Jake's mother lived in the house behind mine. *Tsa* means aunt—it's an Albanian word, or Italian, or maybe a little of both, because that's what those men spoke, a mixture. But you don't use *tsa* for a young aunt, it's for an old lady, an elder. I thought her name was Sadelia—which sounds the same, anyway—and I thought that was a beautiful name. I'd say it over and over for this man, this Uncle Jake, because, like the other men, he loved the way I could put on an accent: "Sadelia, Sadelia," and he'd give me a penny for every time. Then he'd get drunk and cry.

And then, when I was back on Mallory Avenue, I would talk to Tsa Delia. She'd tell me that Jake never came to visit, that his wife was a horrible woman—a horrible woman with "the evil power" (Tsa Delia still believed in the *Malook*). She'd say that "the wife" was keeping her Jake away from her. I used to tell Tsa Delia that I'd seen him—that I saw him all the time, and he asked about her; that he asked me to say her name.

"When?" she would say. "When did he ask you?"

"All the time," I would tell her.

And then Tsa Delia would cry too. I could do this: I was only six, maybe seven years old, and I could bring them together, a few seconds on either side, and I could make two people cry—one for happiness, one because he was so sad—and all with a few words. That was a power too. Not an evil power, no, but a power, and I liked to use it.

My grandma Angelina couldn't even write her name. Not in English, hardly even in Italian. Any hopes she had to learn, to get better, were shot the day she got on the boat; she left so young. And if they weren't shot then, they were shot the day she got off it. All those days alone in the house—alone besides a million kids. Cooking, cleaning . . . her mind going numb.

"You'll wind up just like her," my mother said. She said it the night of her big finale.

But you don't lose power—she was wrong (just like with the money). You can misplace it, forget how to use it—but if it's there, it's there.

Chapter 16

## WAITING IT OUT

      I met Merna by a fluke. I was at the parent-teacher's night, in late October. There was one Jewish teacher at OLV—Mrs. Shimshack, who taught social studies. She'd gone to Israel for her honeymoon and came back with photo slides. The school made a real event of it, and Tommy wanted to see the slides, so I took him along—took Bobby Jr. too. My husband had promised to come home early, to go with us, and I'd waited: we got there late, no Bobby (needless to say), my eyes a little extra puffy. There was only one seat in the back of the room. Miss Hughes and Miss Warnock were supposed to save me a place, but neither one showed up—they both found last-minute dates.

Merna was Mrs. Shimshack's sister-in-law. She wound up sitting next to me. She stared at my face, and I'll never forget it, because she kept on staring. Nothing polite about it.

"Is that your son?" she asked me, pointing at Bobby Jr.—he'd found a seat right under the projector and his brother had crawled in next to him. With the light beaming over their heads, they looked like two little angels. I was feeling sensitive, like I said; and for some reason, her question made me start in again: my eyes filled up, started pouring.

"He's one of them," I said, sniffling, wiping my face.

"How many do you have?" she asked me.

"Two," I said. "The other one's right next to him."

"Oh," she said. "Oh." Not *Very nice,* or *I have two myself,* or even *Where's your husband?*

"Why the 'Oh'?" I said, rummaging through my purse looking for a tissue. Back then, you could've saved the world with what I kept in my purse—Band-Aids, Tic Tacs, aspirin, Yo-Yos, a fold-up umbrella, extra shoelaces and a roll of Scotch tape. I found everything but a tissue.

"I'm sorry," she said, "but you look very young."

"I'm twenty-seven," I said. And then I took a good look at her through my sniffling. "Not that it's any of your business."

"You look even younger." She smiled.

"Younger? Well, thanks; I'm not wearing any makeup. . . . Who are—?"

"I don't have any tissues, either," she interrupted. "Would you like my napkin?"

"Thank you," I said. I took her cocktail napkin—the teachers had put out wine and beer that night—and wiped my face.

"Are you married?" she asked me.

"What?" I said. "Of course I'm married!"

"I'm sorry, I meant . . . 'married still.' "

"Who are you, anyway?"

"My name is Merna," she said.

"Who're you here with?"

"I'm David's sister. I apologize. David Shimshack. I'm being too forward, yes?"

"Yes."

"I thought maybe you were . . . you came in alone . . ."

"I'm still married," I said.

"Listen, Mrs. . . ?"

"Mrs. Nolan."

"The movie's about to start," she said, "and I don't—I mean I *do not* usually do this . . . but here." She handed me her card. It said: Merna Sheps, Ph.D., Licensed Psychotherapist.

"What?" I said, when I looked at the card.

"I do marriage counseling," she whispered.

I didn't answer. The lights were going out, one by one, and I didn't know what else to say, so I said, "It's not a movie, it's a slide show."

She rolled her eyes and pointed to her head, like this was the kind of mix-up she was always making—which for some reason made me like her.


A few nights later I showed Miss Hughes and Miss Warnock the card with Merna's name on it. I could never get used to their first names, Irene and Julie—there was something so formal about them; they'd taught my sons.

"You should go," Miss Warnock said. "I've heard she's wonderful."

"Yes. You said she does marriage counseling," Miss Hughes added.

"Then Bobby should come, no?" I said.

"Will he?" Miss Hughes asked me.

"Never!"

"Then you better go by yourself," she said.

"If you want, we'll go with you," Miss Warnock offered.

"Four women?" I said. "No. Thanks, but no thanks. The last thing my marriage needs is more women going to work on it."

"I still think you should go," Miss Hughes said. She didn't even crack a smile. "Things aren't getting better." Then she added something that tipped the scales. "This woman's a professional," she told me. "She'll never repeat a thing."

Merna had a ground-floor office on Avenue A in Bayonne . . . right in the fifties. I did about ten loops around Bayonne Park before I could bring myself to park—and parking is a bitch in Bayonne, always has been. I wound up fifteen minutes late.

"I thought you'd changed your mind," she said, when she opened the door.

"No receptionist?" I asked her.

"I'm not a dentist, Mrs. Nolan."

I knew that was supposed to be a joke, and I didn't get it, but I really didn't care.

"Listen, Merna," I said as I sat down on her couch—it was black leather, very plush, but very severe, I thought. "Before we talk, I just want to know, are you married?"

"That's not important," she said. "And I'd rather not . . ."

"Look, if you can't answer that one simple question, then . . . well . . ." I stood up.

"All right . . ." she said. "Not currently."

I sat back down, thought for a second. "Divorced, then?"

"Mrs. Nolan, don't worry about my life, we're here to talk about you."

"How many times?" I said. "I just want to know."

"Twice."

"Two times divorced, and you're gonna help me with my marriage?"

"I'm a professional," she said.

"I see that," I told her, eyeing the two framed diplomas on the wall.

"Listen," she said, and she pressed her hands together like a little Catholic girl—which seemed strange, all considered. "We need to set some boundaries here." She took a deep, stagy breath to calm herself. "How long have you been married to your husband, Mrs. Nolan?"

"Call me Mary," I said.

"Fine," she said. "And if you want, you can continue to call me Merna."

To make a long story short, I left there with a prescription for Valium: five milligrams, a two-month supply. She didn't write it herself; she had the man in the office next to her do it—they shared the floor.

"I never do this," she said, "I mean I *do not* typically interrupt a session. But you seem, well . . . worked up." She slipped out, knocked on a door, came back in with a man. His name was Dr. Shapiro, a psychiatrist—a tall guy with a comb-over and a friendly face. Her boyfriend, I decided. He talked to me for a half hour and started writing on his pad.

"Your insurance will cover this prescription, I trust."

"Probably," I said.

"Good. Dr. Sheps will keep me posted."

* * *

On the second visit, I got a little more friendly with Merna. I told her about the Jewish girls in my high school, how they were the only ones who went to college.

"I can imagine," Merna said. Then she caught herself. "That's quite a shame."

"And some of them were very pretty," I told her.

"You sound surprised."

"Me? Oh no, not me. But I thought you might be."

"Mary, are you saying that Jews are not usually pretty?"

"Of course not."

"What then? That college girls don't usually have good looks?"

"Merna," I said, "I'm not saying anything. You're a very smart woman. You can figure out anything you need to know. All I'm saying is that maybe you should do something with that hair."

She had that ironed look—long and dry, the kind that got so popular with Jewish and Italian girls, the ones with curly hair—and it didn't suit her.

"Maybe you're right," she said. "I've been thinking of having it cut." And then she looked at her watch—she was always looking at her watch. "But you're a smart woman yourself, Mary—are you saying the two are mutually exclusive?"

"The two what?"

"Intelligence and good looks."

"I never said that."

"What then? Good looks and a career?"

I liked that she kept on track and stood up to me. Then again, I had no answer—and this bothered me . . . she could tell.

"You don't have to answer these questions right away," she said.

"Good."

"Just think about it." She looked at her watch again. "Our time is up for today, Mary. But maybe next time we can talk a bit more about *you*—yes? A bit less about me?"

"Okay," I said. "Next time."

"Good. I'll take that as a promise. In the meantime, take your medication. I think it will help."

The Valium didn't bring Bobby home—but it gave me a nice, warm, sort of woozy feeling when he wasn't, almost the way I'd felt those nights in the kitchen, back in the apartment, those nights when he'd sneak up behind me.

Two months had passed since that night I broke the lock. I stopped going to the Woman's Club. I made sure all my Merna appointments were during school hours so I never had to tell a soul.

I can't say I got much from Merna besides those pills, but she tried.

I'd walk in and start bitching about Bobby—what I thought he was up to, how he rarely came home—and she'd turn the conversation back to me.

"I can't tell you what your husband's up to, Mary. He's not the one in my office."

"Well, he's the reason I'm coming."

"No, you are, Mary." She was very consistent. "Let's talk about you."

And I'd try to play along with her. "Tell me what you want to know."

"For starters, you can tell me what you do all day."

"Nothing." I was honest. "That's the problem!"

"Then tell me what you want to do."

But again I didn't have an answer. And it wasn't Merna that I wanted to talk to. She knew this. (At home, Bobby barely said hello. He knew what I wanted to talk about. We were both waiting now.)

Merna'd ask me questions about my mother, my father, my school days, my kids.

"I'm here to talk about my marriage!" I'd snap at her.

"We are, Mary—you're half of your marriage."

I'd get frustrated and stop talking.

A few more months went by. I cut back on the appointments (what was the point, really?), but I kept taking the pills. Sometimes I'd forget things on the Valium, and the boys said I repeated myself, but for those first few months, anyway, I'd say it was an improvement. At least I wasn't so nervous. My mouth was always dry, though, and I'd forget entire trips to the grocery store. I'd wind up with two of everything—two cans of Lysol, two bottles of shampoo, dish detergent, pancake syrup—even things like milk that could go bad, so I'd ask the boys to try and drink it fast, and they'd say, "Ma, what's wrong with you?" And I know I shouldn't have been driving around—especially at night, and especially, *especially* on the bad nights when I'd double up on those little yellow pills (I could never tolerate that much now)—but I did. I liked the movement. I had a beautiful kitchen for the time: a nice round wood table, lots of room around it—with the middle slab in, you could seat six—and I had a separate dining set, but that was mostly just for show. The walls were papered with bright orange-and-yellow sunflowers on white; the floor was still linoleum, but none of those flecks: it had a brick pattern. Orange brick to match the sunflowers on the walls. And my avocado-green stove and countertops: I had nothing to complain about in that area. But like I said, I liked the movement. I'd drive down the block nice and slow, out for a cruise. The boys would be in the backseat—they always liked to sit together, even if it was just to fight—so I felt a little like a chauffeur.

Sometimes I'd pretend that I was one; the Valium made me playful: that's an upside. . . .

"Where would you gentlemen like to go?" I'd say . . . and Tommy would say "Al's Diner." Or "The parks, madam: both of them."

We had a lot of fun . . . and sure it was dangerous and I wouldn't do it again, but we hardly ever drove on the highway, and even then, it was just Route 440—less than a mile. The cars whizzing past me, the lights—I never liked to drive fast—and my mind could really wander during those drives.

It got bad at one point, though; Tommy would have to look for the traffic lights. "Brakes, Ma!" he'd yell, and I'd slam down my foot. (God forgive me!)

I talked to Judy Scerbo years later—she was on Valium too, not to mention Stella, Carol, and the rest of them (though Stella was on Librium)—and she said it's a wonder she got anywhere in one piece.

I got cheap for some reason. A couple of more months went

by, and I got very tight with my money. And I started hoarding things. I'd stock up on food, even when I wasn't forgetting things. I even bought new linens.

If the boys really begged me, I'd give them a few quarters for candy. But nothing else. I watched every penny. I was stocking up on that, too, I suppose—on my money. I'd ask Bobby for cash—for a new dress, a movie, whatever—and I'd stash it away.

After therapy one day, I went to see Ruth at First Jersey and opened my own savings account, in my own name—the first time in my life. Merna encouraged me—I'll give her that—but it was my idea. I was saving up for *something*.

Chapter 17

# FINALLY

It was Miss Hughes who spotted Bobby with Dolores. She'd been out the night before in New York at one of her fern bars, and she called me the next day. She started with an apology. "I'm sorry," she said, and then she told me about the kissing, lip wiping, standing close, touching—the way the bartender knew them both by name.

"Is this the first time?" I asked her.

"The first time I've seen them?"

"Yes." I repeated: "Is this the first time?"

She swore that it was.

"And Miss Warnock? Did she see?"

"Yes," she said. "It was the first time for both of us. A new bar, our first time, I swear."

*Evidence,* I thought. And somebody else saw it. Somebody I know. God knows how many other people saw and didn't say anything. People I didn't know . . . and people I did.

"Thank you," I said, and hung up the phone. I went right upstairs and knocked on Dolores's door.

She had a baby in her arms when she opened it, her grandson.

"Put him down," I said.

"Mrs. Nolan?" she said. "You can't just barge in here."

"What'd you call me?" I said.

"Mrs. Nolan."

"That's what I thought you said."

"Oh," she said, and she paused, backed up. "I see." She walked over to the portable crib in her living room and put down her grandson.

"So you know?" she said. She crossed her arms across her chest and stared straight at me.

"Yes . . . I know," I told her.

"And?"

I took a step or two toward her and she didn't back up this time. Instead she stepped toward me . . . and I don't know what she thought she was walking into, but I'll tell you what I saw, right there, between her and me—I saw the distance between what I thought I'd get and what I settled for. And that's a big distance, maybe, but sometimes it's a very short trip. And I thought about Bobby on the park bench the day he proposed: how I looked in his eyes—they were shiny with tears; at his hand, the ring pressed between two fingers and shaking. And how I thought about my mother and that house and those curtains and that stove . . . how I said "Sure, why not?" like it was the most casual thing in the world.

And I thought about how Dolores called the night before my ad ran in the *Jersey Journal,* how she knew all about the apartment.

I'd been driving all day, so my blood was already pumping. I didn't say another word. I grabbed her by her dyed-red hair and pulled her toward me. The next thing I knew, her face was against the wall.

"You wanna eat off my plate?" I said.

It's true I'd taken an extra Valium that day—and another before I came up the stairs. That helped . . . it made me a little looser. It helped her, too, probably, because—big as my tolerance became—I was a little slower than I would have been. I could feel her old, whore-y skin move as I pressed her harder— the cheekbone against the wall, the chin. She didn't even scream; I think I grabbed her too fast, threw her off guard; she just whimpered . . . like a puppy, a dog. I didn't know what to do next . . . what to do now that I had her. . . . And then it came to me: *I'll throw her down my stairs.* And I wanted to hear myself say it, so I did: "I'm gonna throw you right down," I told her. "Right down those stairs. Right back in the street."

"You'll go to jail," she said.

"We'll see about that."

I'd never closed the door behind me, and with my foot I pushed it open the rest of the way. I pulled her arm behind her back the way Charlie and Grandpa Louie used to at the bar. The way they used to when a man got too loud, when he started trouble, wouldn't pay up on a bet—when they threw a man out.

"Please," she said, and she whimpered some more.

"For how long?" I said. "I just wanna know how long?"

"He loves me."

"He loves you? He *loves* you?" I spun her around and slapped her across the face, good; then waited to see if I felt bad, if I'd gone too far. I didn't. I hadn't. So I slapped her again. Then I slapped her a few more times. Her mouth was bleeding. The mouth she'd kissed him with.

"Years, then? Just tell me and I'll stop. . . . This started before we moved?"

She didn't answer.

"You moved into my house, my own house, my kids right downstairs?"

Again she didn't answer. "He loves me," she repeated—and that was it. She was kneeling now, almost sitting, right at the top of the stairs; my left leg was between her two. She would have fallen if I'd let go. Just rolled down the stairs, backward, broken her neck. Or maybe she would've grabbed hold of the banister, caught herself, crawled down the stairs, away from me. But I wasn't taking any chances. I didn't let go. I felt my fingers tighten in her hair. I felt my right foot move, slide back, take aim. Then my leg bent, got ready. I pulled on her hair one last time; some of it ripped off in my hands. I kicked her three times, got right to the heart of the matter. She screamed the first two times. I let go of her hair, she turned sideways, and I watched her roll. She only fell a few steps, then she curled up in a ball. I stepped down, stood over her.

"You'll be gone by tomorrow," I told her.

She nodded, didn't say a word.

"You call the police and I'll call your restaurant. The owner. You hear me?"

She mumbled a yes.

"I grew up in this city." I said. "Not one person will eat where you work. . . ."

"Please," she said—who knew what she was begging for? She probably thought I'd hit her again.

"And Bobby knows all the cops—you know that. If he doesn't, his friends do. Don't make him pick between us: you'll be sorry."

And then I thought about Bobby. I ran down the rest of the stairs. I closed my door and locked it. I fished Charlie's number out from my makeup case and picked up the kitchen phone. Those extra pills were kicking in fast now—that's what happens after a hurdle—and it was hard to dial. Charlie wasn't home; it just rang and rang, so I called up to the diner. He wasn't there either. And that was good luck for Bobby, very lucky. . . .

I don't know how I got to my bed, but that's where I woke up. My boys had crawled in next to me—something they hadn't done in years. Tommy had his face against the back of my neck, his body spooned around me, asleep. Bobby Jr. was curled up in front of me, his face against my stomach, crying.

My husband was across the bedroom, just standing there.

"I'm sor—" he started, when he saw my eyes were open.

"Is she gone?" I said.

"Mary," he said, and he gestured with his head and eyes toward the kids.

"Is she gone?" I repeated.

"She's gone, Mary. Her son took her hours ago. He'll be back in the morning to pick up her things. You'll never have to see her again."

"And you?"

"I'll leave if you want me to."

"You do what you want, Bobby. You do exactly what you want."

He walked toward me and leaned over. He sat down. "I'm sorry," he said, and he started to cry. "I'm so sorry." I thought he might put his arms around me, around all of us. Instead, he put his head on my chest. He found a nook between my breasts and Bobby Jr.'s head. They were all crying now. Everybody except me.

I closed my eyes and thought, *Three of them. That's the offer. Whatever you hoped for, whatever you planned, you've got three of them. Take it or leave it . . . but that's what you've got.* And I fell back asleep.

Chapter 18

## GOOD-BYE

The morning after my night with Dolores, Bobby made us breakfast. Pancakes. "Hotcakes," he called them. He'd been a cook in the army and never learned to scale things down; he made about sixty of them. Bobby Jr. ate about twenty and Tommy was close behind—the two of them were moaning and groaning afterward. Me, it was all I could do to get out of bed, all I could do to take in the scene: Bobby at my stove, busy in a puff of steam; the boys opening and closing cabinets; plates passing hands, landing, somehow, on the table; forks and knives clunking next to them—glasses, too.

Bobby'd put the newspaper out on the table for me, the spot right in front of my chair (I always sat right under the wall phone; he always sat under the radio), just like I used to do for him when we first married. But I was still bleary-eyed, still woozy from all that Valium the night before. I just pushed it aside. And it was a good thing I didn't open that paper in front of him. A good thing, indeed—but I'll get to that.

My spatula was working overtime. Bobby flipped each pancake up and over and onto a stack. He thought he'd impress me, no doubt.

The boys were ready to be served—they didn't care by who.

"Be a good boy," I told Tommy. "Pour your mother more coffee." And I held out my mug.

"Oh, no," Bobby said, his hearing sharp as a bat's now. "I'll do that." And he walked over with the pot, my shiny silver percolator for special occasions, and filled me back up. His head was down the whole time, his eyes on the coffeepot, avoiding mine; even when he was right in front of me he didn't look up.

He wanted to stay, you could see that—all this pouring, cooking, folding (he'd turned the napkins into perfect little teepees)— he wanted to stay all right; and he wasn't at all sure I would let him.

"You like the coffee?" he asked, waiting for his pat on the back. "I made it extra strong; you looked like you needed it."

"It's strong all right." I took another sip. "I'll be up till next Tuesday."

"How about the hotcakes?"

They were delicious, light as a feather. "Fine," I said, "just fine. You think you made enough of them?"

He looked at the four stacks on the countertop next to the stove—four stacks on four plates, plus God knows how many on the serving dish. He'd covered each stack with a paper towel to keep them warm.

"You're like my grandma Angelina in that respect," I told him, and I took another slow sip while he listened. "She cooked for an army too."

He smiled, shrugged his shoulders—very cute—and then he

turned on his foot, actually gave me a salute, walked back to the stove.

Nothing would change. You could see that much. He was trying to dazzle me—scraping low this time, yes, but trying to dazzle me. Just like in the beginning—all those promises, his manners . . . that perfect, pear-shaped ring. Just like every make up along the way: a hand reaching out when you least expected it—maybe to catch a shoe on a Ferris wheel, maybe to sneak up behind you while you were cooking and send you trembling with excitement to your knees. And then afterward, where was he?

And now that hand was pouring coffee, flipping pancakes. . . . If things were about to change, he would have talked to me— quiet, alone, sensible—but, no: the only thing different was that he got caught.

"The hotcakes were very good," I said, when I was finished, and I dropped my little teepee onto my plate—I'd never even unfolded it, just used the corner to wipe my mouth. "You'd better keep an eye on these boys," I told him. (Tommy'd barely finished and already he had his hands over his stomach, his bottom lip turned downward: trouble was on the way.) "I'm going back to bed now."

"Bed?"

"Yes, bed," I said.

"You want more coffee?" He had the percolator up and ready to fire.

"No," I said.

"More hotcakes?"

"I'm full, Bobby."

"How 'bout the paper; I ran out early to get it, Mary."

"What I want is my bed," I said. "Our bed, Bobby." And I stood up, blew a hole in his *nice-nice*. "My back hurts, Bobby, and so does my arm. Your girlfriend gave me quite a workout."

"Mary!" he said, and he shot his hypocritical eyes toward my sons, as if to say how dare you? How dare you in front of the boys? The naming it was the sin with Bobby—never the doing it, just the naming it—and I was supposed to keep quiet, play along, act grateful for the crumbs like his mother would (that woman let a lot of things slide—a lot more than I knew at the time). I was glad I'd caught him by surprise, glad I let my mouth open—my sons were no fools; they knew what was what.

"My back hurts," I repeated, more quietly this time, "and as you can just imagine, Bobby, I have some serious thinking to do. . . ."

"Well then, good," he said, rising to the occasion—rising to his feet as well—and this was a big deal, mind you, because for him it was no small occasion to talk in front of the kids; to yell, that was one thing, but to talk openly, that was a different story. "I think you *should* get some rest, Mary. I think you *should* do some thinking. And maybe, now that I flushed those damned pills down the toilet, you can even think clearly."

"Oh," I said, "you wanna start on that one, Bobby?"

"Yes, I do, as a matter of fact."

"You flushed *my* pills down *my* toilet?"

"I flushed your pills, Mary, yes. And I called *your* doctor."

"Oh, you did, did you?"

"Yes, I did, Mary."

"And what did you say to her, Mr. Big Shot?"

"Her?"

I realized he must have called Dr. Shapiro, the name on the pill bottle. "Whatever," I told him, "her, him. . . . Don't change the subject, Bobby; my head is cloudy. What did you say?"

"I told him you wouldn't be needing his services anymore. I told him he could keep his little pills to himself too. I'm not gonna have any wife of mine—"

"You said it," I interrupted him. "You're not gonna have any wife, period, if you don't watch your step."

"You want me to tell the boys what kind of a doctor he is, Mary?"

"Oh, Bobby," I said, "look at the calendar, will you? What year do you think this is, anyway—1950? It's 1974—so what if their mother goes to see a doctor when she needs one?" I was bluffing, mind you; I certainly didn't want to explain to my sons that their mother was seeing a psychiatrist. And I certainly didn't want Bobby using it against me anywhere else—to my father, his friends . . . anywhere. "You tell them what you like," I said.

"I may, Mary. I very well may."

At this point there was no going on; Bobby was back in his element—a fight—and if there was one place he felt comfortable, it was deep within the loop of an argument.

"I'm tired," I said once more. "I'm going to bed. Just don't forget what the point is here, Bobby, and who did what to who."

I kissed each one of my sons on the head—they were looking a little scared, to be honest; they'd had quite a night and morning—and then I headed for our bedroom. "And whatever you do," I added, "don't you dare come near this room."

I walked down the hall, went inside our bedroom, shut the

door, locked it, and lay down. But there was no sleep to be found for me that day—none at all. I was still a little light-headed, true, even after all that coffee, but still, there was no keeping my eyes shut. I picked up my copy of *Reader's Digest,* the copy I always kept next to my bed, but I'd already read everything in it—every recipe and advice column . . . some ridiculous story about a man who went "back to the wilderness" and got mauled by a bear— and finally I had to storm back out to the kitchen and get the newspaper.

I picked it up just as Bobby was about to open it.

"This was for me, wasn't it?" I said.

"It *was,*" he said.

"Then thank you," I said, very politely, and I took it, went back to the bedroom to read. And thank God I opened that paper when I did. Thank God I was alone and not in front of Bobby, because considering the surprise that awaited me, there'd be no way to contain myself—no matter who was in the room.

As it turned out, my friend Charlie had a very good reason for not being there when I called him. I'd no sooner turned past the front page and there it was, right on page three, top right-hand corner: CHARLIE CUPACOFFEE HAS HIS LAST CUP.

The *Jersey Journal* had quite a good time with my friend, I can assure you. The reporter went on about how he'd died in the coffee heist, how that last cup was a bitter one, how maybe Charlie didn't want to sell that trailerful of coffee at all—maybe he just wanted to drink all two thousand pounds—and maybe *that,* the reporter said, was why Charlie's partners had to shoot him.

"Charlie died for his cause," the reporter wrote, nice and sarcastic, and then he named a few suspects, talked about how, with his dying grip, Charlie had ripped a piece of flesh from a man—

probably from the man's forearm—and so that man would probably not be hard to find.

I was a little surprised by the fact that nobody'd called me; but then, like I said, I'd lost touch with him and he'd lost touch with everybody—even me, as far as anybody knew. I tore out the article to save—to hide from the boys, also, in case they went through the paper (they'd met him just that once, but I didn't want them talking)—and I thought about the fact that on the one night I should call out to this man, after all those years of him offering, he was killed. And I can tell you it made me feel pretty sorry for myself. Another woman might have been sad for Charlie, I mean sorry for Charlie *only*—a better woman, I grant you that. A better woman would never even have stopped to think of herself at a time like this, but that was not me. I had a good cry, it's true—my face in the pillow, my body curled up like a baby's on the bed—and I'm glad I didn't open the paper in front of Bobby, because the crying didn't stop so fast (who knows, maybe Bobby heard me from the kitchen and thought I was crying about him), but as far as I was concerned, I always knew Charlie would end up this way, it was just a matter of when. I had to think about myself now—the message was clear. All those years as a girl when I had Tony to look out for me: a guardian angel—one with a gun, no less. And then, in the back of my head—way back in my head—there was Charlie after that. And now it was clear, those days were over; it was just like I figured in high school—when I got tired of waiting for that first mother to come back—and I never should have lost sight of this: I was on my own.

And I wasn't going back to Merna, either. Talk is nice, and she did all she could for me—but at the end of the day, we came from two different worlds. She could sit, *talk,* collect all the extra degrees and ex-husbands she wanted . . . she had family money (I got that much from her), a big salary, no kids.

Me, I needed action. I needed a plan. I was done with the Valium too—I was through feeling numb.

Ruth called the next day and asked me to drive her to the funeral. I should have called her first, really, to offer my condolences—I knew nobody else would. I tried to get out of it, but in the end, she had nobody else to take her. She knew I cared about Charlie, at least—and I knew the same about her. Besides, it would have been cruel to let her go by herself—a married woman, alone and sobbing at the funeral of her boyfriend. She made a terrible scene, I can tell you. Crying, wailing, walking up to the hole in the ground, throwing dirt in like she was the wife. People say she threw herself in the grave, refused to get out—but I was there (it was mostly the old ladies from downtown who came, and they love to talk, love to invent and then pass it along as gospel)—it never happened. She just made a scene, embarrassed herself. Very understandable, really, though when her husband found out, he didn't see it that way.

Me, I stayed in the background. I was quiet. I had my own melancholy to deal with. I kept thinking about that day in the saloon, the one day I told you about—the day I ran home and told my mother about Charlie: about how he was looking at me when I sang; about how I caught him looking and my voice went up high, so much higher than usual, and still stayed on key. "And that must mean something, Ma," I told her, because these things—I couldn't have explained this then, but I could feel it— things like this, they sneak up on you, they happen a little each day, and then by the time you notice, there they are. And that was my day—our day, Charlie's and mine, the day things added up. . . . And I thought about how she ruined everything, my mother—for Charlie, for me. Everything. And maybe she saved me a little bit too. Maybe she was right. But nobody asked her. Nobody asked her to butt in—things might have turned out different. And now Charlie was dead. Charlie was dead, my mother was dead, Tony and Grandpa Louie were dead too. As for me, I'd never sung in public once after that last day in the saloon— never, not once, and I was getting better too.

But as I said, I had no time to linger on Charlie, and I'm getting ahead of myself again. Charlie was, for me, the road not taken, as they say—he knew it himself. He watched me marry Bobby from the last pew at OLV, right next to Grandpa Louie . . . even bowed to my father as we walked down the aisle. And now I had to worry about the road I did take. I had to worry about Bobby, the boys, what to do about them.

## Chapter 19

## AUNT LORETTA

I was never a dishonest woman. Honest to a
fault, really. Even that lying to my mother bothered me—I was
good at it, I could do it; it just never felt right.

But the fact is, I needed money. I'd decided to leave Bobby . . .
no more to think or rethink on that subject—but first I needed
money. Money that was extra. Money that was my own.

I wasn't gonna be one of those pathetic women in some one-
bedroom apartment. Not me. I didn't hold on this long for nothing. I wasn't gonna move down.

Oh, sure, he would have let me keep the house. But who was
gonna pay the mortgage, the taxes, and the boys' tuition? And
who'd watch the kids if I went to work? Besides which, I had no
job skills. It's a shame when you consider what you're worth in
the workplace, when you take some time, think it over, add it up,
and get zero. I'd taken typing and stenography in high school—
Snyder was a good high school for that. They had two tracks—
the college track and the job track (which for girls meant secretary).
I was on the college track, but I took extra classes here and there.

I took them instead of gym, and they let me because I was on the volleyball team, I swam—at least for the first couple of years—I'd built up credit. I took typing, steno, *and* shorthand, and could hold my own, still, in all three (at least with a little practice, I'm sure). But as for a job, I only ever worked as a waitress. And I wasn't going back to that.

Mind you, there's a lot of numbers you deal with in being a mother—a lot of charts and organization. The vaccines and doctors' visits alone could keep you in circles if you didn't keep track, if you didn't keep a system: certificates of immunizations and tests, records of childhood diseases—I had sheets and sheets from Dr. Cardiello's office: legal-size papers with columns that I made with a ruler. Columns that I filled in like so:

Chicken Pox (severe case)—4/68
(Separate forms for both boys. And you had to keep track of all the shots.)
Diphtheria—1/19/65
Tetanus—2/27/65
Pertussis (that was whooping cough)—1/3/65

It's a wonder the boys could walk with all those germs swimming around inside them, but they did, and the shots worked. Each shot took an appointment, though, and an insurance form, of course, and a filling-in on my home chart.

And I paid all the bills—Bobby had no time for that. No time and no interest. Once a year he'd do the taxes—late always, and always filing for an extension. I paid the bills every month, though—the mortgage, the life, auto, and homeowners' insurance: First Jersey, Prudential, State Farm, Allstate. I had a little metal strongbox that I kept in the back of my closet. It had the big christening bonds for the boys, and all the smaller bonds for their birthdays—my family was very generous with bonds (at least they came through on that front), especially Aunt Dot, which was strange when you think about it, because she hated banks, didn't trust them, kept most of her own money stuffed underneath her mattress or stashed in some cabinet or drawer. . . .

On paper, my boys were worth more than me, and all their bonds had serial numbers and maturation dates, and I kept them all on file—another box, another closet—in case the first one got ruined or lost or stolen. I had three boxes in all: two for papers, one for jewelry.

When crime got so bad in Jersey City and so many people left, I just took out extra insurance. I had the serial numbers for the television, the radio, the air conditioner, the toaster. Even my iron. I had every earring and ring and necklace I owned estimated at the jewelry store and listed on a chart. I had the legal papers for the house and our property; I had the emergency telephone numbers—fire, police, doctors—all Scotch-taped up on the side of the wall phone in the kitchen.

Even the semi-important papers like old tax forms, receipts— old holiday cards and love notes (Bobby wrote a few)—I kept in order, though those I kept in cabinets and dresser drawers. (When we lived in the apartment, before we had proper furniture and extra drawers, I used to keep the papers in a suitcase.)

And I didn't miss a trick.

It's true what I said in the beginning of this book—I was never good with numbers—and if you asked me to, quick, add 48 and 53, or to jot down a telephone number on the back of a matchbook without repeating it, then five times out of ten you'd get a lovely mistake: I'd reverse the numbers; I'd leave one out. But that, you see, is what made me so organized: I checked each number three times because I had to, and then I made sure to write it down.

Even my phone book was a beauty. "A work of wonder," Bobby would call it—one of the few compliments he'd let fly freely. It was metal, too, like my strongboxes—aluminum-cased—and it had a dial on the front, a miniature phone dial. The dial was hooked to a lever that ran up the side of the book, and when you dialed a letter (or a group of letters, I should say)—"G,H,I" for example—the lever would pop open to that letter, and there was your number: Dr. Gardner, Mrs. Gallagher, Gino Brothers' Pizza (The). And again, like with the metal strongboxes, there was no fear of fire.

My grandpa Louie used to have a loose brick in the wall behind the kitchen in the back of his saloon. He kept his secret money there, behind the brick, and he told me that I was the only one who knew about it. He was the one who taught me to stash things. In the 1920s he got swindled by a "savings and loan"—swindled like so many foreigners: he'd put down money for a mortgage and then it disappeared. So he didn't believe in banks. He believed in me, though. Sure, he liked it when I sang, and sure, he told me I was a beautiful little girl—he told me that time and time again—but he knew I had a good head on my shoulders, too, that I knew what to repeat and what not to. And he must have worried about me; he must have known that some-day (who knows if he really knew this, but I think so)—he must have feared that one day I might be on my own. Nobody knew about that few hundred dollars behind the brick besides me. And while a few hundred dollars is not a lot (it was much more back then, say 1951, but still, it wasn't much—just enough to get your feet on the ground), if something ever happened to him, I could always go to that brick, pull it out, take care of myself. He didn't say this, but he knew it.

When he died I was already seventeen, already dating Bobby. I took a visit to the house with my mother—the bar was closed down but still intact. (Grandpa Louie died of a heart attack, very sudden, like my grandmother—I should be so lucky, really—so there was no planning.) I said I wanted to take a walk through "for sentimental reasons," which was more than half true, and my aunts let me go downstairs alone. I slipped past the tables and chairs: they were all still out, not even folded or stacked— as though there'd been a party and somebody called a fire drill, as though it was still Prohibition and there was a police raid (Grandpa Louie used to tell me about those days, though mostly the police left them alone, drank there themselves)—as though the party could start again at any minute. There were even a few glasses left on the bar, sticky inside from the dried-up whiskey. I walked right past the bar, right to the back, past the kitchen to the back room and the brick—and there it was, $250. I left it there for future reference. When I finally did take it out a year later, it was for my honeymoon, the one I never took but started saving for—which should show you what a fool I was—because I thought, *Now I don't have to worry about such things.* . . . (I spent part of it on a stroller—the rest went bit by bit.)

And it's ironic that I eventually went to work for a bank, but that was later. . . . As I said, all this organization and common sense, while it one day came in handy, counted for nothing in the work world at first—not without "experience," and by that I mean job experience, legal job experience. And I was to get that legal job experience—by hook or by crook, I managed to get it—but not on my first shot, not right out of the gate.

That morning that Bobby made breakfast, I didn't leave my bedroom for hours. I listened to him wash the dishes and enjoyed the sound of the water, the drain, the clink of the plates and glasses—all from another room, a different room from the one I was in—this was a first for me. I listened to Bobby dose out the Pepto-Bismol—like I said, the boys had stuffed themselves—and I listened to the three of them watch the football game. I just sat there, an ear to things, trying to come up with a plan, trying to keep my mind off Charlie, rereading *Reader's Digest,* the *Jersey Journal.* And finally it came to me, my plan.

When the game was over, I heard Bobby turn off the set, and I called him to me. I asked if he could please go to the grocery store, and he said, yes, yes, of course—he saw this as a sign of togetherness, a sign, maybe, that I wanted him to stay.

I made him a nice long grocery list, including cold cuts, so I knew he'd have to wait on line, and I sent him to the Great Eastern—twice the distance of ShopRite or Two Guys.

"The meat is better," I told him, "the turkey, the spiced ham [Bobby loved spiced ham], all of it," and I was sweet as pie.

He was putty in my hands now—truly. I knew it wouldn't last for long, so I took advantage of it. I'd come up with my plan, and I wanted to get moving—fast—before I lost my conviction.

"And take the boys," I said. "They need to get out."

"Good idea," he said. "Some fresh air."

"Yes," I said. "Yes."

They were no sooner out the door than I called up Aunt Dot. She answered, first ring, and I cut right to the chase.

"Aunt Dot," I said, "I need some work."

"Okay," she said. "I thought you were calling about Charlie."

"I'm not," I said, and I nipped that conversation in the bud, put it on hold for later. Aunt Dot kept quiet.

"I was wondering—I've been thinking this over, and I was wondering if maybe you might need help with the loans."

"No," she said, point-blank—which was no small disappointment, I can assure you—"and don't ask again." She followed it up with: "You don't have the backup and you don't have the stomach."

"I could learn," I said.

"No, Mary. When somebody doesn't pay, you have to do things. . . . Look," she interrupted herself, "the answer is no." She didn't go any further, and she didn't ask any questions, either—any questions about why I needed money, I mean: she just paused for a moment, like I did—sheer silence for a full minute, and then she forked up an alternative. "If you want," she said, "you can call Aunt Loretta."

Aunt Loretta was a bookie. One of the biggest female bookies in Jersey City—the most bets anyway, if not the most profits.

"You think she needs help?"

"It can't hurt to ask," she told me.

"We're not close, you know."

"I didn't say you were."

"You want me to just call her out of the blue?"

"I don't want you to do anything," she said—annoyed, clippy. "If it's work you need, then that's my suggestion—you do what you have to do. If it's just a little money, then we can talk."

"I'll keep that in mind," I said. "Thanks."

"Good," she told me.

She was offended, probably, that I didn't ask her for a loan directly—offended, too, that I didn't give her any details. I didn't ask.

Aunt Loretta was my aunt Dot's sister-in-law, my uncle Philly's wife. She'd been a bookie for years. She was terrible with numbers, granted, so she was always broke (she was always making mistakes, always making up the difference).

But that was the part that made sense, actually—the mistakes, the losing money. What I couldn't figure out—what I could *never* figure out—is how she stayed in business at all, how she got the bets to begin with. Aunt Loretta had a rotten personality—moody, short-tempered. One thing about a bookie: you don't have to be a TV host, but you have to know how to work with people. It's not like you're a brain surgeon. It's not like they *have* to come to you. Not even in Jersey City. And in Jersey City, everybody plays the numbers. You have to know your neighborhood, too . . . know who you can trust . . . and you can't be a gossip. Or if you are a gossip, you'd better be a shrewd one. Aunt Loretta shot her mouth off like a loose cannon.

She wore a house smock, always, my aunt Loretta, and she had legs like a football player, which was no wonder: she'd lived in a four-story walk-up since the day she was married. She was always nervous and she was always tapping those football-player legs up and down—tapping her feet, I should say—to the point where she could truly drive you crazy. And no wonder she was nervous: her husband, my uncle Philly, he drank like a fish, lost a job a month and sometimes more. She used to have to phone him down at the bar when dinner was ready. (The bar was on the corner; those days, there was a bar on almost every corner in downtown Jersey City.) And her daughter, Sophia; the poor girl was retarded. A mongoloid—she had her late in life, and what a cross she was to bear. Strong as an ox, though—the more the kids made fun of her, the bigger she got. And no matter what, Loretta ran to church twice a day.

Booking numbers and saying prayers: *Oh, Christ,* I thought, *I'll wind up just like Aunt Loretta.*

Still, I was in no position to get picky. I took out my metal phone book, popped it open to her number, and got dialing.

"Don't tell me," she said, when I told her it was me: "You had a dream, a number came to you. You want me to play it."

I knew this would take some voice time. "Oh, no, Aunt Loretta," I said, "nothing like that."

"Well, you're not usually a gambler, Mary. Did you get a new license plate . . . ?"

"No," I said. "Aunt Loretta, it's not a number."

"Ahhh, then it must be about Charlie; you read that nasty article."

"No," I said, "it's not about Charlie, and it's not a bet, either, Aunt Loretta."

"Good," she said, "because I already called in for the day."

I had to give her an update about the boys, my husband . . . she was full of questions. I answered some and dodged a few others.

"Look," I said finally, "the reason I'm calling is . . ." And now I paused—a little for shame, a little for drama.

"Yes?" I could practically see her ears perk up.

"Money is tight, Loretta; to be honest, I was wondering if you needed some help?"

"Me?"

"Yes, you, Loretta."

"You wanna help me?" And she made a loud, fake . . . I won't call it a laugh exactly, but a laughing sound.

"I wanna make some extra money."

"Mary," she said, "I'm all set up. I'm just fine."

"All right, then. I thought it was worth calling," I said. "I won't keep you. . . ."

"Now, wait a minute, Mary," she said. "Don't be so sensitive. Don't rush off so fast."

"You mean you'll think about it?"

"No, Mary. I said I'm set, and I am, but remember: you're a different neighborhood; you could always start your own little pool."

In my neighborhood, Billy Matches was the big bookie. He had the candy store up on West Side and Roosevelt. (A meeting place, someplace that draws them in—which is very important for a bookie.)

"I can't cut in on Billy," I said. "Even I know that."

"Of course not," she said, "but you don't have to. The women bet too, no?"

"I don't know," I said. "It's mostly men who go into Billy's store." (Bobby was there every morning.)

"Even better," she said. "Make friends with them, the women in the neighborhood, then ask Billy if he'll cut you in: get him on your side. It'll cost you ten percent, but you don't want any trouble. . . ."

I'd never thought of this, but it made perfect sense. "All

right," I said. "Thank you. I'll stop by his candy store. I'll mention the idea."

"Don't be crazy," she said. "You can't just stop in and bring this up: this is not a cocktail party you're planning. You need a phone call, a recommendation. You're my niece. I know him, Mary. I'll make the call."

"You will?"

"Of course. But first, you come watch me: see if you have a taste for it."

I let her keep talking while I was thinking.

"It's a good job—you'll see—you can do it from your own kitchen. You can cook and take bets at the same time, if you want. You don't even have to tell your husband."

She wanted to see if Bobby knew.

"Oh, don't worry about that," I told her.

"I mean it, Mary. Keep it a secret. He'll find out, but by then you'll have the money coming in. He won't complain then, will he?"

I laughed into the receiver, because I could tell she wanted me to.

"Your uncle Philly didn't, now, did he?"

I laughed again, because she wanted me to again—though I'll be honest: I didn't like my husband being leagued with Uncle Philly, not even that night. And then I thought about it: what if Bobby did find out? That on top of the Valium, the psychiatrist: I didn't want *him* walking out on *me*. I didn't want to fight him for my kids.

My wheels were turning—I was thinking in a whole new way.

"I don't know, Aunt Loretta," I said. "Bobby's a stickler, sometimes; he was in the military."

"Come on; he's a truck driver: you mean nothing ever falls off the back of a truck?"

"Not in years," I lied. "Not while he's driving. . . . While his friends are driving, sure, but . . ."

"His friends," she said; now she was laughing. "Oh, Mary, what's he gonna do, yell? Who cares if he yells? Does he hit you?"

She was prying directly now—she wanted something to repeat, something to get off the phone with.

"No," I said—fast, without thinking. But then I thought better of it, and (I'm not proud of this, mind you) I slowed down and lowered my voice. "I mean . . . not really . . ."

"Mary!" she said. "If he hits you, you call your father."

"I will," I promised.

"In the meantime, you come watch me. I'll show you how to take bets. You're very smart, Mary," she said. "I'll bet you have a good head for numbers, too."

"I do," I said. "More or less. I'm not bad."

"You . . . I'll bet you didn't even look up my number before you dialed."

"I didn't," I said, proud, surprised, trying to score a few more points.

"See, and you haven't called me in years."

"All right . . ." I said. "I'm sorry."

"That's not my point, Mary." And then she paused, satisfied. "You're good with numbers. Me, I forget my own anniversary."


I went to see Aunt Loretta work and saw that she'd have five or six women at her kitchen table, the one with the plastic flowered tablecloth, at all times. (Till this day, I don't know what was underneath that tablecloth.) These women were nervous creatures, the kind you meet a lot downtown. Short haircuts dyed to light brown and red, a few blondes thrown in—all of them Italian, all of them natural brunettes turned gray and then dyed . . . loose house smocks made of cotton or rayon, usually rayon, and usually a floral print, like Loretta's, like the tablecloth . . . no makeup . . . and always, always, a cup of coffee. They worried full-time, these women. This was their occupation: to worry. They worried about their sons, and who their sons were marrying. They worried about the weather, the muggings on the streets, the fact that their husbands were getting old and "couldn't work forever—then what?"; they worried because their husbands had "the pressure" (high blood pressure). And still they baked ricotta cheesecakes and deep-fried zeppolis and made meatballs and bracolia for dinner, sausage-and-pepper sandwiches for lunch. Fat men with no moderation, their husbands were, and these women, these wives, they just worried and got nervous, got nervous and worried—and then drank coffee, which made them more nervous.

And they always played the numbers, these nervous women—each and every day. They'd play their new niece's birth date, down to the hour—11/10/1974, 4:55; the number of their crosstown bus, plus the day's date and the bus fare; or their anniversary, if it was coming up. They'd play the number on their sons' old football jerseys that they just found in the back of the closet. And with each bet was the story: "I was looking, cleaning, you know, the usual—and I saw this jersey; it made me think of the old football team, my Ralphie. He wasn't much of a player, but still . . . it's a sign, maybe; here's five dollars, put it on today's date, plus 56."

And then they'd leave, one by one, and get replaced, one by one, so that there were never more than ten ladies and never less than three, and Aunt Loretta would call in her bets in the afternoon, after the last of them, save for me that day, had left, and then she herself would run out, go to church; and for this she picked up about two, three hundred tax-free dollars a week—before mistakes.

I left that day, the day I watched her, and thought, *Oh no, this is not me: my kitchen will be no Grand Central Station.* Still, after a day or so I realized I still wanted to leave my Bobby, though I was softening with each hour in my resolve, and I still needed money to do it, and then the phone rang finally, and it was Aunt Loretta. "I called Billy for you; go see him." And really, in a manner of speaking, things were already out of my control—at least that's what I told myself. So I went, and Billy explained a few things to me, and told me not to use the phone—not yet. "That's for later, when you're off and running and you get lazy," and I didn't completely understand, but he promised not to tell Bobby, which was the main thing, and he said I could stop by every day in the afternoon because the store was empty about three o'clock, and I could turn in my bets, and he'd only take ten percent instead of the usual twenty, and I could drop off the money once a week, and I said, "Okay, how about two-forty-five, because that way, if anybody asks, I can say that I'm just stopping by on my way to pick up my boys at school [OLV was just a few blocks away], and I'm bringing them a treat."

And it began. I was a bookie. A bookmaker. I tipped off Judy Scerbo and she tipped off Stella Schilizzo, and once Stella got her claws around a piece of information she spread it around

like you-know-what, and it was as good as in the newspaper—
and so they started coming over (Carol Salerno'd moved to
Middletown by now). My house was an attraction, mind you,
because I was not one to casually say "Stop over"—not to these
women, anyway—but I was glad to let them in, even more glad
to take their money. I never served coffee, though. I poured
juice. Orange, apple, cranberry. If somebody asked for coffee I
said the pot was broken, and I kept saying it for three weeks, until they finally stopped asking. Nobody lingers over a glass of apple juice, nobody asks for four refills (you'd get sick); so I usually
had them all in and out by about noon.

By this method I took in about $150 a week at my height—
and my height came only five weeks after my beginning, then
went on for another five months after that, until I was able to
sock away about $3,500 into my new metal strongbox, which I
kept at Aunt Dot's. Twice a month I'd take a taxi to see her—I
didn't want to take any chances with my driving (downtown has
such narrow streets), and I didn't want to have to park a block
away (there's so few spaces) and be walking through that rotten
neighborhood with my cash in my shoulder bag. And I'd deposit
it right there with Aunt Dot—in strongbox number four. This
way there was no bank account to trace, not even a safety-deposit
box that Bobby could find out about, and nobody would dare
break into Aunt Dot's. Not with her reputation. And since the
reputation was based on fact, and the protection was real, there
was no chance they'd get far even if they did break in.

But then, at the end of these prosperous six and a half
months, I got quite a scare. Loretta, who was indeed successful
and had become lazy, as Billy would've put it, was calling in her

numbers one day—right from her home phone, as usual, instead of the pay phone (like she'd been told)—to her "bank," and the bank's line was tapped. She found two uniformed policemen at her door less than fifteen minutes later. So did seven other housewife-bookies that day—A STING, the *Jersey Journal* ran as a headline the next day (they were always there for your low points)—and all eight women were called in for questioning.

Before I get to my own reaction—and you can guess it was substantial—I'll tell you about my two aunts. Aunt Loretta, the accused, was asked to name names (so were the rest of the women, probably). "We'll let you off completely," the district attorney told her. "We don't care about you—you're small-time—just tell me what you did, who you spoke to, and that's it: we'll protect you; you'll get off scot-free." Aunt Loretta, though she might have paused a second or two, didn't mull it over for long—in short, she sang like a bird, and was home that night before dinner.

Aunt Dot—not to mention Aunt Dot's friends—got wind of this and hit the ceiling. "You did what?" she said, when Aunt Loretta came over to fess up. (She didn't dare use the phone.) And then Aunt Dot did her own interrogating: "How much did you tell them? . . . Did you mention my name? . . . What am I gonna do with you?"

I just happened to be there that Friday at Aunt Dot's—it was one of my drop-off visits—and Aunt Loretta was shameless. "Let them get mad, I don't care. I even told my kids, Dot. I said, 'Mama made a mistake,' and it was no big mistake, Dot—you of all people should know that, because everybody in Jersey City books numbers, or plays them. And I'm not looking for a career in crime like some people; and now I'm out. I was small-time— all the names I named were small-time—and I'm out."

Aunt Dot was caught between a rock and a hard place. Aunt Loretta left and soon after, Aunt Dot's friend Bobby Manna arrived. "Now, Dot," he said. "If this was anybody else—anybody not related to you—then you know what might happen. . . ."

And Aunt Dot had to say, "Yes, but she is related to me. She's my brother's wife. And it's true, Bobby, I never liked her—but her husband is my brother, her kid is my niece, and the names were small. . . . It's a fact, Bobby; she's right on that one. . . ."

And so Aunt Loretta, with her simple logic, made things very simple for herself. She was still at church two times a day, she had money in the bank account, and thanks to Aunt Dot and the deal she cut with the prosecutor, she had no one looking over her shoulder—neither outside nor inside the law. Sure, her name was filthy in the neighborhood, but even that was halfhearted, because a lot of women in her shoes would have done the same thing, really, and they knew that—besides which, most of them were scared; they'd bet with Aunt Loretta, so they kept their mouths shut. And so, in time, it all blew over for her.

As for me, I took this as a warning. So did Billy. "This is not a business for women," he said, when I stopped by to tell him I was quitting. I resented that comment, because I'd been a very good bookie—I'd taken to it quick, much quicker than most of his male "associates" (he'd told me so himself the week before), but the truth is, I had more at stake because I had a different goal. I needed a clean name, and I figured, though I'm neither religious nor superstitious, that I had tempted fate long enough to get what I wanted.

I called Stella Schilizzo and told her the deal was off, that if she wanted, she and her girlfriends could go straight to Billy from now on, and she said, "Oh, Mary, what do you mean, *my* girlfriends? You mean *our* girlfriends. I'm sure nobody wants to bet anymore—the headline caught all our attention—but we're all still your friends."

*Oh, great,* I thought, *just what I need—more visits and phone calls from Stella.* But to tell the truth, I wasn't altogether unhappy that she said it; in fact, she gave me an idea, a solution of sorts to something that was nagging me. "Yes, Stella, I hope so. But maybe, considering what they said in the article—about how the police were looking for another ring—maybe we shouldn't meet here for a while. Maybe we should keep a low profile for a while—at least not *all* meet at the same time, and not in the same place. Remember," I said, "my husband doesn't know. . . ."

"Really, Mary?" she said, and she tried to play dumb.

"Well, you knew that, didn't you?" I said.

"Well, I figured as much, I suppose."

"And we don't want any of our husbands to know what we've been doing, do we, because I'm small-time, like my aunt Loretta, but they clamped down so hard on her that she caved in, started talking, and once she got talking, well, the line became blurry: a few of her friends got called in too."

"They don't arrest you for playing a number, Mary."

"Oh, sure they don't, but it seems some of her friends played some numbers for their mothers, their kids . . . nothing big, a favor, just the way you did—the way everybody did, Stella, but as I said, the line gets blurry, and for some of them . . . I mean I'm sure they'll all get off eventually—but they were all called in for booking."

"Mary," she said, "you wouldn't give my name, would you?"

"Don't be ridiculous, Stella," I said. "I'll never be in that position. But even if I were . . . you can trust me, you know that. Just like I can trust you."

I don't know what Stella said to her girlfriends once she got off the phone, but you can rest assured, I never heard a word about booking numbers again—and more important, neither did Bobby.

My phone wasn't exactly ringing off the hook, either—nobody nosing around while I figured out what to do next. They were polite, these girls, when I ran into them at the store, on the street, or I made an occasional surprise visit to Helena's, across the street (she'd moved onto the block with her husband, Rich, and her two boys, Dickie and Jim, about six months after me). Helena found the whole thing funny because, for one thing, she'd never made a bet, and for another, she didn't care what her husband thought: she'd already started college by then, and to do that, she took such a stand with him, that as far as she was concerned, there was no more to worry about.

Chapter 20

## VICTORY

After that day with the pancakes, I was very aloof. This seemed to turn Bobby on. No surprise, really; he's a very predictable man in that regard: if it's new—and my aloofness was quite new—and if it's a chase—which is the way I kept it—then he wants it. He started coming at me. I'd say no, and he'd question me. "What's this," he'd say. I hadn't left him and I hadn't asked him to leave—and this is what threw him. He couldn't imagine that I'd just stopped loving him; he took it as a personal affront, a blow to his ego—like he was losing his charm, his power.

"I'm your wife, Bobby," I'd say. "If you want, we can do it. Let's just get it over with."

"There's nobody else," he'd say, and for the first time I believed him. "So what's the matter, Mary?"

And the more indifferent I got, the hornier he grew. Turned on by the challenge, I think, as much as by me. We were up to two times a day—back to our glory days, before the boys, and between them—and I never let on, but I was in ecstasy. Mind you, I never lost my head. I never confused this with a good marriage—I'd had almost twelve years to work that equation out; I knew how those numbers added up. But on the other hand, for most of those years I did without this kind of action, and I was fast approaching thirty: I had a sexual appetite of my own now—and who better to fill it than my husband? His looks were intact, and, to put it mildly, so was the rest of the package. I had no complaints in that area—not for the whole six months after Dolores.

I think that turned him on, too, the fact that I hit Dolores—a very womanish vanity my husband had: the idea of two women fighting over him was such a thrill. In the shower, on the bedroom floor—sometimes we didn't make it to the bed. One time in the garage, another in the yard—the fact that the boys were close at hand made it even more exciting, though I was very responsible in that respect; they might have suspected, but save for that one time on the kitchen floor, they never saw.

I never asked for it, and I never said a word afterward. In fact, we said very little to each other at all during that time. Bobby must have thought everything was perfect. For me, though, there was no emotion in it—we weren't a husband and wife doing this, not for me—we were just two people having sex. Maybe two very good-looking people, at best.

I must admit that Aunt Dot coached me a little in this attitude—but it didn't take much direction. The impulse—and who knows, maybe it was hereditary—was in me.

This lasted—like my stint with booking numbers—for about six months. By then I had enough money so that, even if he gave me a hard time, I could make it on my own for, say, another six months—three months if he took me to court. So, one morning, while Bobby was at work, I called the locksmith and told him I'd lost all my keys at the supermarket. He was over within the hour, and by noon all the locks were new. Next, I slid open Bobby's side of our bedroom closet and pulled out most of his clothes. I pulled out half of our luggage set—his half—and got packing. I was able to fit enough clothes for three weeks— underwear, socks, shoes, and sneakers included—long enough for him to get used to not being here. I even fit in one suit, be- cause I knew he had his niece's wedding coming up, and I didn't want him coming back just for that. With this, I wrote a note, telling him a few things I thought of him, and advising him that if he wanted a fight in the courtroom—over the kids, the house— I was ready; but I wouldn't advise it, because the fact was that when it came to his adultery, I had a few witnesses already and could easily get others; and what's more, the fact that he was hardly ever home for twelve years wouldn't look too good either. I put the suitcases on the front porch, and was about to leave them there, very dramatic, just as I'd planned, but then I realized that they would probably get stolen. I was hard-pressed as to what I should do, and finally I settled upon leaving them with Helena. She was alone when I dropped them off, but from what I heard, by the time Bobby arrived and found my note on our front door (the note that sent him to Helena's), the whole gaggle was there for an after-dinner coffee.

As for me, I'd packed my own bags that day—one for me, and one for the boys. We spent the night at Aunt Dot's, as planned, to avoid any possible scene.

Chapter 21

## THE BASICS

But there was no divorce. No legal separation either. No fighting at all. At least not right away. Bobby surprised me this time . . . just two separate addresses.

He moved back in with his mother, if you can believe it. This was a different time, granted, not like now: people lived at home until they got married—still, he could have found a little place of his own. But, no, he moved in with Mommy. (Just like his friend Paulie—his wife, Maureen, had thrown him out a year before.)

As for me, I decided to get an honest job. There was no way around it, experience or not. One thing was for sure, though, I needed to be mindful of school hours—there was no budget for day care, and there was no grandmother to pick up the slack. The boys were at school, and they were old enough to keep busy during the summer—Tommy was almost eleven, Bobby Jr. was about to turn ten—but no matter what, I couldn't get home much past three o'clock.

I could have asked Bobby's mother to watch them until I got

home, but I still wasn't sure what the two of them might pull—and why stack any odds in their favor?

And this brings me to another concern. I was never sure Bobby wouldn't sue me for custody, because that's the thing about my husband—the thing about a lot of selfish men: they're very good fathers, very kind to their offspring. Doting even. As soon as the boys joined Little League, for instance, Bobby was at every game. Sometimes he'd come pulling into Lincoln Park with the truck—practically right up to the baseball diamond—and he'd whistle, holler from the bleachers, buy them hot dogs and orangeade after the game: he'd even fill them up before the game until I had a talk with him. He'd spoil them rotten, if you want the truth. And it got worse once we separated. You'd think he'd play favorites because Tommy looked so much like him. But then, Bobby Jr. had his name. Or who knows—maybe there are no favorites to be played—two little Bobby Nolans, maybe that's the way he saw it. Me, I was the brood mare. It took him years to appreciate me. Years to come back around. I was just somebody he was in love with—if he ever got to that point; the boys became a part of him, an extension.

In any case, the only job I could come up with that was over by three o'clock—the only decent job—was in a bank, so I picked up the phone and called my friend Ruth. She was still at First Jersey then, and she said that, sure enough, they were opening a new branch down at the Hudson Shopping Mall (they were putting a roof on the plaza, expanding—it was just about to open), just a few blocks from my house. She told me the applications were in already, but if I went over to her house that night, we could type one up, predate it.

"You worked before you got married, right?"

"Well, yes," I said. "I worked in the Blue Ribbon diner."

"But you can type at least, right?"

"Yes, sure," I said, "they made us learn it at Snyder. But I never did it in an office."

Ruth knew I needed help, and she was very eager to help me—she was a kind woman to begin with, and she was really very lonely; she was happy just to get my phone call. Besides which, I was one of her few connections left to Charlie.

"Never mind," she said. "I have a better idea. You'll come here, to my branch: you can start as a teller."

"What do tellers make, Ruth?"

"Almost nothing," she said, "but that's not the point. You can *start* as a teller is what I'm saying. Two of them just quit today, and it's me who's doing the interviews. I'll put your application in that file. I can hire the tellers, Mary, no questions asked. Not technically, but I have some pull at this branch—I've been here six years."

"Well, thank you," I said.

"Then you can start typing on the side," she told me.

"When?"

"Can you type at home?"

"I'd rather not do it in front of the boys just yet," I told her, "I'd rather Bobby didn't find out for a while that I was working."

"You'll type during breaks—during coffee breaks and through lunchtime. Just the way I did. Remember, my husband runs me ragged when I'm home. Always did—even when Charlie was alive. You'll get a good reputation and we'll let you fill in whenever one of the secretaries gets sick. I'm in charge of the substitutes; I'll even call in sick a few days myself. It'll be good; it'll help me, too. Then we can put in for a transfer. The new branch won't ask for experience, they might not even ask for a résumé—you'll be internal, you'll have a track record by then. I guarantee, you'll be a secretary in three months; you'll have a normal salary."

And then she went on: "But take a tip from me, Mary. No more of those sexy little outfits you like to wear. It's taken quite a push to turn my image around. Don't start off on the wrong foot."

"I don't know what you're talking about," I told her. And this brings me to a minor point I've neglected. I'd started wearing very short skirts. Like I said, I had the legs, and I wasn't feeling too good about the rest of me—my face, my complexion, my hair.

"No more," she said. And I knew she was right. "I'd loan you something for the interview," Ruth went on, "but they already know all my clothes at work. Never mind coming to my house tonight, we'd better go shopping."

"All right." I suggested we meet at the Two Guys on Route 440.

"Not Two Guys, Mary. For an interview suit, we need someplace better—maybe Robert Hall."

"I can't afford Robert Hall," I said.

"It's an investment."

I went to pick Ruth up that afternoon at the bank (I hired a baby-sitter for the occasion) and you should have seen her walking through those revolving glass doors that day. She was quite the professional. She had to be: no college degree, a husband with a puny disability check, Charlie dead now. She'd gotten two promotions in the last six months. (I hadn't been to the branch in as long; my numbers kept me so busy I was mailing in Bobby's paychecks.) She'd started wearing her hair upswept. Not a bun, more of a twirl. She wore business suits and silk scarves tied around her neck instead of her old dresses. She'd always liked long nails, but she'd clipped them to a quarter inch and she'd had them French tipped instead of the bright pinks and oranges and reds she used to favor.

We compromised on the stores: first we shopped at Robert Hall and I chose one outfit—a medium-gray gabardine pantsuit with slight shoulder pads (seventy dollars right there). Ruth picked out a similar one (though this one had a skirt instead of pants) in navy blue, and said she'd pay for it, I could owe her—but I said no, I'll get it myself, your help is enough. Then we tried on a few more suits and outfits—her and me both—and went over to Two Guys to look for replicas, something in the same ballpark (though, of course, less well made), along with some little things.

This is a good way to look expensive: you don't buy the little things—the stockings and scarves and hair clips—at an expensive store. Just the basics. Not even the blouses. The belts don't have to be fine leather—not even real leather if you get right down to it—and you don't need real silk for the blouse. (Mind you, silk is nice, and if you're really looking for elegance, that's a good place to start: look for the little things, the belts, the scarves—the socks on a man, or his tie—and if they're quality, then that means something.)

"You should have a good purse," Ruth said. "Nothing big and sacklike—not like a housewife. I can get you one from my sister. It's good if you wear the same purse every day. A lot of women think the opposite, but that's not in style anymore," she said. "You'll look very no-nonsense with just one good leather purse."

"You forget I had a mother," I said. "She had good taste: I'll look through her old stuff."

"Those clip-top things?" she said. "They're ridiculous, Mary. Get with the times. They'll know you've been home for years. Let me handle this: you need a nice, medium-size, shoulder-strap bag, and a simple wallet. A wallet with a built-in change compartment—not a separate change purse like you have now."

"I thought I had the job," I said finally. "I thought *you* were doing the interview."

"I am, but they'll all be looking over my shoulder. There's only one private office at my bank—my boss's—and you can rest assured he won't let me use it to interview a teller. And once you start—because let's face it, unless you make a scene, I'm gonna hire you—once you start, the watching really begins."

"So this is an audition," I said.

"Yes," she said. "But remember, the job you're auditioning for is a secretary—so you better look the part."

Chapter 22

# TUPPERWARE

I enjoyed my first job. My first legitimate job. I never complained about the customers—even if they were rude or smelled or spoke rotten English. (I started that same week I called Ruth, a Wednesday.) I never even bitched when they boxed me in that drive-through teller booth like a prisoner—and that damned metal deposit drawer broke every last fingernail in a week.

Word travels fast in Jersey City—I forgot how fast—so it was impossible for Bobby not to know. I should have seen this coming (it's not like I took a job in a cave), but once I was standing there behind that window—once I had a few days' training under my belt—I got a certain gumption inside of me. *What do I care what Bobby thinks?* I figured. *What do I care what he pulls?*

Bobby's friend Nicky strolled in one morning—I'd been there two weeks at this point—and he wanted to trade his rolled-up dimes and quarters for bills. He walked up, saw me behind the counter with my upswept hair (I just copied Ruth's), and his jaw dropped but good.

"Mary, what the hell are you doing here?"

"How can I help you, Nick?"

"You work here?"

"I'm not volunteering!"

I wore heels every day—we all did—and Nicky's built like a fireplug, so with my extra two inches we were eye-to-eye.

"I need to change these coins for bills," he said.

The coins were rolled, but not neatly, like he did it in a hurry—five rolls of quarters, six rolls of dimes. Nearly a hundred dollars.

"I see you emptied your piggy bank this morning."

"It was time."

"Looks like you rolled them yourself."

"I don't like to bother Barbara Jean."

"That's nice."

"I'm a nice guy."

"Of course," I said, "and here I thought you were buying gifts for your girlfriend."

(God knows he had plenty!)

The next day Bobby came in to see me for himself. It was a Thursday, my drive-through teller day (we all took turns), but they had a problem with the door lock, so I was right behind my regular window, framed like a picture in my new gray business suit.

There was only one person in line, so Bobby waited, foot tapping, then he let the woman behind him go ahead.

"I'm waiting for that one," he said, and he pointed at me.

When I was done with my customer I said, "Next," very casual, and Bobby shot right up to my window.

"Where are the kids?" he said, like he'd caught me in the middle of some drug bust.

"In the vault," I answered, and Jane, the teller next to me, burst out laughing.

"You're not funny!"

"Go back to work."

"Answer my question."

"They're in school, where they always are at this time—a lot you know."

"And what about when they get home?"

"Then they're with their mother," I said. "Now, do you have some banking to do, or not?"

Bobby walked out in a fury. I decided again not to care.

Later, I got worried that he really would try to pull something—that was still my fear: that he'd try to get the boys. So I called Peg in the middle of the night (that three-hour time difference can be a real blessing when you're crawling the walls).

"Be realistic," she said. "What's he gonna do?"

"He could make trouble."

"He doesn't want trouble, Mary. I think he wants you."

Stella and Judy stopped by the bank the next day to get a look for themselves. And after that, they set up camp on Helena's porch so they could see me when I got home, watch and whisper.

I'd just shoot a fake smile, wave, go about my business. I got less worried about Bobby with each passing day.

And it was just like Ruth promised—she gave me my first secretary fill-in spot herself, calling in sick so she could take her daughter for a junior prom dress one Thursday that spring.

They still let me go at three-thirty, even though the real secretaries worked until five. It wasn't three o'clock for the tellers, either, like I'd hoped—not once you added up, proved out, grabbed your things. But three-thirty was close enough, and the boys could fend for themselves for a half hour; most times they had OLV bowling or they'd stop at Helena's to play with Dickie and Jim, and by May they had Little League practice right after school.

If the boys were at Helena's, I'd stop off after I parked my car in the driveway, jiggle my keys, tell Judy and Stella that I had to "get dinner started," was "too busy to talk." Then I'd point to the files in my hand, tell them I had "more work to do." I caught myself blowing my bangs in the air one afternoon to show my exhaustion, my frenzy, like Dolores did that day when I met her, and it made me laugh on my way down the stairs. Helena laughed too—I heard her behind me—she was always in on my jokes.

Ruth had a stockpile of sick days, so she took them here and there—for me, for herself, too. (With me around she didn't have to watch her back as much.) Her boss, Mr. Butler, was a stickler for details—a real pain in the ass, most people said—but he was a good credit manager and his files were in order, thanks to Ruth, so filling in was no problem. He was short, with bad breath, the kind that comes from your stomach and never goes away (he chewed Tums constantly), and he liked to spring things on you last minute.

That first Wednesday, he handed me fifteen contracts at two forty-five. "Can you type these fast? Rush them out today?"

*Christ,* I thought, *is this a test?*

"If you don't mind my mailing them from home," I said. By

then I had an electric portable that folded up—perfect—like a suitcase and slid under my bed. Aunt Dot gave it to me the night before I started. "Don't think like a clock puncher," she said. "If the work's not finished, take it home and finish it." On the inside, she'd rolled in a piece of paper, typed the word *Legit*.

The next time I filled in for Mr. Butler it was a stack of thirty contracts, business letters, triplicate forms—you name it—and all at three o'clock. He just left them on my desk (Ruth's desk), so this time I wrote a note back—*I'll do fifteen tonight and fifteen tomorrow*—and hurried out the door.

On the way home, I got nervous about how he'd react, so I called Ruth that night. (It was nice to have another girlfriend to take my nervous calls.)

"React?" she said. "He's getting away with murder. I'd throw them back in his face. He'll grab you every time I'm out now—if I don't watch, he'll look to have you replace me."

"That's a relief," I said, "but don't worry, I'm—"

"Not worried at all," she interrupted. "I've got my own plans. Just watch he doesn't get you alone, Mary." And then she tried to hang up.

"Wait," I said, "finish what you started."

"What can I tell you?" she said. "He spotted you right away." (Ruth sounded jealous, if you want the truth.) "That first time you came in, he said, 'Who's that you interviewed?' "

"And what did you say?"

"I said you were a friend of a friend, that I met you once."

"He bought that?"

"He asked if you had good references, and I said 'the best,' so he told me to move fast."

"And that's all he said?"

"That's all he *had* to say. We have a shorthand, him and me—I knew he had his eye on you, I knew that meant 'hire her . . . or else.' How do you think I was able to move so fast?"

"You *told* me you could move fast."

"Not that fast. Not the same day."

"So why didn't you tell me?"

"I am telling you. Up till now it didn't matter. Just watch."

After that I tried to avoid Mr. Butler—I didn't want any trouble. But that was until I filled in for the other secretaries . . . the other bosses. Some of these people—these "executives"—you'd wonder how they tied their shoes: files that were lost, names misspelled, important papers in the trash can by mistake. It's not the geniuses that wind up on the bank floor, granted, but I expected better than this—my grandpa Louie with his money behind a loose brick in the wall didn't seem so stupid after all.

Compared to them, Mr. Butler was a prize. And he was where the action was—the credit side. I'd filled in when Maggie, the secretary for the operations manager, was out, and it was all checking and savings, opening and closing accounts . . . the typical nonsense. But Mr. Butler did commercial lending. He went out and got loans. He kept the phones ringing. He could make or break a business, keep the money rolling in for the bank. Mr. Schickler, the bank president, dropped in to eat lunch with Mr. Butler once a week (they ordered turkey sandwiches and ate them at his desk), and what Mr. Butler asked for, he got.

When he got transferred to the new branch in the Hudson Mall on Route 440, he asked for me. And I was the first to put my name in for the transfer to go with him.

Ruth got a half promotion when he left, which meant all his work for half the pay, and no help—they never gave a secretary to a woman back then—but she registered for night classes at Hudson County Community, so they promised to give her a full promotion in two years. Plus she got to stay close to her house and her daughters' school (two smart girls—they both went to St. Al's Academy, right on the boulevard, across from her house).

When Mr. Butler finally made a pass at me, I just handled it. He did it in the safety-deposit room just before the move. I was helping him clear out some personal things—his wife's jewelry, his kids' bonds—and he leaned over (the guard left us alone because he knew us), came close, breathed deep in my face (he was trying to be sexy; I thought I'd evaporate), tried to kiss me on the lips.

"I can't," I told him, and I turned my head away, pressed my hand against his chest. "I've met your wife; she's a nice woman; how could I look her in the eyes?"

He liked that response; it let his ego off the hook. I was glad, because I'd practiced it a million times at home.

He backed up a few inches. "Mary, I understand."

"Thank you," I said.

But then he continued: "If you don't want to transfer with me, I understand that too."

"I have no problem with you," I said.

"Really?"

"And don't worry, I'm no little squealer."

He seemed relieved.

"But no means no, with me."

He stayed quiet for a minute.

"Mary," he said, "maybe I should just find another secretary."

I didn't answer right away. He pulled his safety-deposit drawer all the way out from the wall—I'd pulled it only halfway when he lunged—took out the metal box inside it, and dumped everything into his briefcase on the floor.

"I'll put in a good word for you," he continued. "Don't worry, you'll be fine."

"I don't think so," I said.

"What?"

"I don't think so," I repeated.

Now we were both quiet.

"You're on the prowl," I told him.

"That's none of your business," he said.

"Of course not."

"Then just give me the key."

"Fine," I said, and I held it out for him to take. "But the last thing you need is a girlfriend who picks up the phone when your wife calls."

He couldn't argue. He took the key from my hand.

"Not to mention your kids."

I had his full attention now.

"I've been on the other end of this, Mr. Butler."

"You have?"

"I won't go into it, but trust me, you'll be doing everybody a favor. . . . Keep them separate."

He smirked, put the key in his pocket, then moved closer to give it one last shot. "And if you go with me nothing's gonna happen? You sure about that?"

"Nothing," I said, and I smiled politely, peeled his hand off my ass, pushed his little body against the safety-deposit boxes on the wall, and walked out.

* * *

I enjoyed setting up Mr. Butler's new office from scratch. New file cabinets and carpeting. Even the cement beneath it was new. My desk wasn't real wood, but it was big, and right out on the bank floor. It had a nameplate that read MRS. MARY NOLAN.

Bobby was coming over to the house twice a week for the boys—Tuesday nights and Saturday afternoons—and by now his mother was happy to pitch in. No one in the family had ever been divorced: she thought she could still keep things together, still save face (I got less worried about a custody battle).

And I made damned sure my next tenant was a couple—an older couple with interests of their own.

Lucy and Joe Tener were their names. A Jewish couple— "nonpracticing," she told me. They answered my ad and I invited them over for a nice long interview on my living-room couch. Tommy sat by my side, helped me screen, and Lucy did the talking; Joe nodded along, kept his hand on her left leg the whole time.

*A real weirdo* was my first thought. And I was right. But harmless.

She wore no makeup, and her hair was long and black with thick streaks of gray in it. She kept it in a ponytail that she petted while she talked.

She said she had two Siamese cats, and I got nervous about my wood floors, so she told us she'd had them declawed.

"Declawed?" Tommy said, and he was fascinated, his eyes got big.

"I had to! They'd ruin the furniture."

When she said it, she showed us her own nails—they were

long and clawlike and painted pale pink—and then she dug them into my green corduroy upholstery, just for show.

Joe nodded, and she went on, told us the cats had never been outside in their lives.

"Never, Mary"—she looked straight at me—"not once; if they were let loose on the streets they'd die, literally die of shock—the vet told me! I have to keep them protected."

After the interview, Tommy told Bobby Jr. that she'd taken the cats' nails for herself, inserted them—maybe he even believed it—and from then on the two of them called her the "Cat Lady."

I knew Lucy would keep the boys entertained. And I figured, if she took that good care of a cat, how bad could she be? Plus, I knew Joe had the money—I did a credit check—so I canceled the other interviews and let them move in right away.

Lucy turned out to be harmless—like I figured. Annoying, but harmless. A homebody, like her cats. And she was a real help with Tommy and Bobby Jr.—which I also figured on. She checked in if I was running late, made them lunch if they got bored or lost their keys (they were forever losing their keys). When summer came, I called to check in on them twice a day, but it was good to have Lucy there just in case. A good backup for Bobby and his mother.

Joe drank too much—I spotted the bulbous red nose on the interview—but he was a quiet drunk, and she'd made her peace with that. There was no yelling or nagging that I had to overhear through the ceiling. They had a son of their own—grown up, married but no kids. His name was Mark and he stopped over three, four times a week for dinner, sometimes without the wife. But in between, Lucy still missed him, still worried if he ate enough.

"He's twenty-seven," I told her one day in the hallway. (She'd grab me, chew my ear off, and I could only listen to her so much.) "Don't you think he knows when to eat?"

"Oh, Mary," she said, "you don't know his wife. She's a terrible cook: she'd let him starve to death; you just don't know."

She doted on my sons too. She loved to bake, and they looked forward to her homemade cookies and breads, like with Margaret, Peg and John's old maid—God knows I never made any. She even hemmed their pants (she wouldn't take any money), and no matter how much noise they made, they were "cute."

One day they set off firecrackers in the hallway just to scare her cats, and she never said a word, didn't want to get them in trouble. A good thing Joe told me, because I couldn't let this go on in my own house. And believe me, there was hell to pay.


I think Mr. Butler loved his wife. But he couldn't contain himself—he took a lot of long lunches, and I would talk to Mrs. Butler (Rita was her name) on the phone, make excuses, keep her distracted. I never questioned it; it was part of my job. They lived in one of those pop-up trilevel development houses in Scotch Plains, where she spent all day alone with the kids, chasing them up one staircase and down another, and she called three times a day, kept him on a tight string—or tried to. (She had a nasal voice to begin with, plus she always had a cold: talking to that woman made me feel sorry for her at first; after a month it just gave me a headache.) She always asked about my boys and I never told her I was separated. That kept her calm, made her trust me.

I never minded the extra typing or paperwork or working through lunch. And Mr. Butler never badgered me about my short hours. I got a raise, like Ruth had promised, and the salary was okay. To stick to the three-thirty quitting time I had to be a part-time secretary. That meant $2.75 an hour and, still, no benefits. They put me through a real rigmarole, but I knew I'd get another raise; I knew the boys would get older; that the job had a future.

By the next spring, I was up to $5.50—which wasn't bad for 1975. I was on the move. Things were falling into place. Everything but Bobby. Between those two springs, I had Bobby to deal with—and Peg was right, he wasn't going down without a fight.

Bobby'd found out about the promotion and the raise when I got it—Tommy must have told him—and sure enough, the next day, he took a detour on his delivery route and came by for an inspection.

You could see him through the big bank window in his blue jeans, strutting across the shiny shopping mall floors, walking through the front door, a newspaper in his hand, minty Trident popping in his mouth.

The other secretaries and women tellers—we had two men tellers at the new branch—made a real fuss over Bobby; one of them even ran out afterward to see his truck (he'd parked his eighteen-wheeler in the mall parking lot) and watch him hop in, drive away. She took an early lunch just to do it. A young girl. "I wanna see if it's the same as my husband's," she said, but I'd seen her husband; he was a dumpy little thing, like her; it was Bobby she wanted to see.

I showed Bobby my desk and my nameplate, and he just smiled. But I noticed he stopped chewing.

That visit to the bank was a good thing—good for me, anyway. It let me gloat, got me some attention on the bank floor. But for Bobby, it was a wake-up call. He saw this was for real, that people respected me—decent people—and I was on my way . . . without him.

He started calling a few times a week. The same side-of-the-road call I used to get when we lived together, only now he had all the time in the world. He tried me the first few times at my office, but I'd put him on hold and leave him there.

So he started calling me at home—four-thirty, five o'clock, the same time he used to call with the excuses, the make-believe overtime that never showed up on his check.

"You just get in?"

"You checking up on me?"

"I'm just glad I caught you; you're so busy these days."

"That's right," I'd tell him. "I'm busy—busy at work, busy at home. So what do you keep calling me for?"

"I need to talk, Mary."

"You had twelve years to talk, Bobby."

He started sending me cards—schmaltzy Hallmark things with flowers on them: "Thinking of you," they'd say, or "Happy spring." I'm sure his mother picked out every last one of them.

He was careful what he sent; he didn't dare send one with the word *wife*.

On Mother's Day, I thought he might actually send real

flowers—for once—instead he dropped off another flowery Hallmark, this time with a poem about motherhood, and a crate of Tupperware. The poem talked about what a great thing it was to be a good mother like me—*so grand, with firm hand,* or some nonsense like that. The Tupperware was a complete set, forty pieces; it even had a hamburger mold and a funnel.

"Impressive," I said. "You pick this out yourself?"

"Of course."

"So you're hanging out at Tupperware parties?"

"Huh?"

"Tell your mother I said thanks."

The next day, Lucy grabbed me in the hall and started in about her son again, how he hadn't been over for two days.

"He missed Mother's Day?"

"Oh, no, he came over the day before. He's been so busy. And now I won't see him until the end of the week."

"And don't tell me . . . you're worried he won't eat?"

"A little, Mary. I know I shouldn't be, but—"

"Listen," I interrupted her, "you shouldn't have to worry about what he eats."

"I know. You're right. But I do."

"Why don't you make him some care packages?" I told her. "Pack a little extra for the wife. Have Joe drive them over."

She liked this idea. Her whole face lit up. She squeezed the banister, nodded her head.

"I could do that. . . . I could do that right now, even; I always have leftovers. . . ."

"Of course," I told her. "And I have just the thing to pack them in."

I ran inside and got my crate of Tupperware.

"Here," I said, "it's yours."

"Oh, I couldn't."

"I insist."

"This is too generous, Mary."

"You're the best tenant I ever had, Lucy—take it or I'll be insulted."

# Chapter 23

## BACK TO DOT

By late summer, Bobby knew he was getting nowhere with the calls, the cards, the Tupperware. But it was August: he knew that the boys were finished with Little League and still off from school. He knew they were bored, hot, on my nerves, and looking for a diversion. And he knew they missed their father; they'd missed him since the day I threw him out.

It was a Wednesday, about four o'clock, when he pulled up in his truck. I was inside, just home, marinating a London broil for dinner—the boys were buzzing around me; I'd made them help me with the tomato salad, set the plates—and there he was, out of the blue: Bobby and his eighteen wheels on a side street, horn blowing so you'd think your head would explode.

Everybody ran to their front porch when they heard the racket, including me.

"Hop in," he yelled the minute I got to the screen door.

"What's this?" I said.

"What's it look like, Mary?"

Twelve years and he'd never driven the truck home once. I'd

never even seen it, save for that one time at the bank. And now here it was . . . all that metal, a big MACK sign in raised letters across the front grating. A real show-off.

The boys shot past me, one on either side. I had the screen door halfway open by now, and they knocked it flying from my hand.

"Come on," he hollered, and they ran down the stairs, out to the truck, tried to climb up on their own. The truck was too high, though. Bobby had to jump down, walk around, show the boys how to climb in: left foot first, pull up with the right hand, stand, swing, drop into the seat.

They were in seventh heaven.

"You wanna get in, Mary?"

I wasn't about to hop in, not with all those people on their porches watching, not while I was separated—legally or not—and they all knew about it.

"It's not Saturday," I said.

"What?"

All of a sudden, he couldn't hear above the engine.

"You're supposed to come on Saturdays," I yelled at the top of my lungs. "Tuesdays and Saturdays. We agreed."

"Oh, don't be a hard-ass, Mary. I'll come back again then. Just hop in."

Stella was out on Helena's porch—as usual—and Judy was right behind her.

"I've got something in the broiler, Bobby."

"Call Lucy."

"She's at her son's."

"Stella," Bobby hollered, "you busy?"

She didn't answer.

"You busy?" he hollered again.

"We were just having coffee," she said.

"Stella won't mind coming over for a minute," he hollered—to me, to her—"will you, Stella?"

"Well . . . no."

"See, Mary. She's a good friend. She'll keep an eye on the broiler . . . and whatever else you've got going."

I didn't say a word.

"Just for a half hour," he said. "It's a new truck—see? It's thinner. I could never get the old one down the block."

I waved him away: "Just get them back for dinner," I said. "Half an hour, no more."

But he wouldn't budge.

"Come on, Mary, I wanna show you how she rides."

Stella and Judy didn't budge either; they were staring right at me—smiling, even—and Helena had her head poked out the door. Tommy got hold of Bobby's horn and started pulling it like crazy. "Come on, Ma," he yelled. *Honk, honk, honk.*

He really had me on the spot.

I put my hands over my ears—the girls did the same—and Stella ran straight down Helena's steps, came over to mine.

"You better go," she said, when she got to my stoop.

"You're a real pal," I said.

"That's what I always told you, Mary."

It's tough not to look like a villain when you throw out the father of your kids, even tougher not to feel like one. "It's a London broil." I rose to the occasion. "If I'm not back in a half hour, put it in the oven."

"I know how to cook."

"And if I'm not back in an hour," I continued—loud enough

so everybody could hear me—"call the police!" That got a good laugh from Helena. Then Tommy got going with the horn again— *honk, honk, honk*—and she yelled, "Mary, every window on the block is shaking. Get going or I *will* call the cops."

I switched places with Stella, hopped down my front steps, and went straight around to the passenger's side—by the time I got there, Bobby was right behind.

"I'm fine," I told him.

"I don't think so." He smiled.

"She can do it!" Tommy said.

"Yeah," Bobby Jr. chimed in.

"I'll stand back here just in case."

I had slippers on, and that made it tough, not to mention embarrassing—they were dress slippers, at least, with little heels— but I did what seemed logical: one step, pull, and swing. I landed on Bobby Jr., and God help me, I thought I'd crushed him, but he squirmed out from under me, and the girls started clapping.

"You okay?" I said.

"Fine, Mommy, fine." He rubbed his leg . . . and Tommy got hold of the horn again, started pulling.

"Bobby, close that door and get in here," I said. "Tommy, let go of that thing or I'll kill you." And we were off.

What a roll you feel inside when a truck starts moving. I had to hold my stomach. The boys were right between us, happy, sliding off the seats. I put my left hand over Bobby Jr. Bobby put his right hand over Tommy.

"Stay still," Bobby said, like there was a choice.

"There's no seat belts," I said.

"Mary, whatta you think I do for a living, chauffeur people

around? Hold the side bar with your other hand; we'll be fine once we get on the highway."

"The highway?" Tommy said. "We're going on the highway?" And he sat up on his knees.

"That's right," Bobby said. "Now sit right, both of you."

"Listen to your father," I said—I was getting nervous—and I reached across Bobby Jr., slapped Tommy on his knee.

"When I make a turn," Bobby said to Tommy, "hold on to my arm."

"I'll hold Bobby Jr."

"An even split," Bobby said.

The truck was up so high, the cars below looked miniature, and I told Bobby so. "Like Matchbox cars."

"You'll never cut off a truck again, Mary. Not after you see things from this angle. I should take everybody up here."

Bobby had to make a hard left, so he yelled, "Hold on," leaned in that direction, and pulled Tommy with him.

I got light-headed as we moved (I must have . . .) and I found myself looking across at him, watching his profile—he always cut a good profile—watching him yell orders at the kids, laugh . . . sweat running down his forehead. It's a lot of work to show off like that, keep your energy up, perform . . . and for the first time, I almost felt sorry for him: on the outs, living with his mother— in the doghouse, no matter the address—embarrassed as much as me (everybody knew about Dolores; people stopped by her restaurant just to see her).

Sweat was collecting in his eyebrows—they needed a trim— and I wanted to reach over, wipe his forehead. I didn't, but I wanted to.

We passed by the back of Lincoln Park, where he'd proposed to me—it's god-awful to look at from the highway side, that big metal fence surrounding it—and I craned my neck, stretched to see past the fence . . . to the Casino, the lake, but I couldn't. Then we passed by the Hudson Motor Lodge and I wondered if he'd ever taken Dolores there—or some other little bird.

The boys were happy, happier than they'd been in a long time . . . before or after I'd thrown him out, and I found myself thinking about Bobby, just Bobby—I was only seventeen when we married, true, but he was just twenty-three. A kid, really, like me—no matter what I thought at the time—shooting off to the beach with Paulie, spending his work money on drinks and rides . . . hanging out on the corner with his friends.

"The corner," they called it, and you were just supposed to know which one it was—even people outside Jersey City. Bobby had the kind of friends who all think they're famous. They all grew up together, and they all hung out in the same place. One of them, Tony Frogs, was on a TV game show once and he said it: "the corner," like everybody in America was supposed to know.

And I swear, sometimes they meant different corners—it would change—Duncan, Union, Lexington, but as long as it was one of their corners, where one of them lived, they knew what you meant, they knew where to meet.

Roosevelt was the big one. They had a dry cleaner, right on the corner of Roosevelt and West Side, and they hung out in front, so much that the owner used to let them have keys.

"You keep the trouble away," he'd tell them, and he'd let them open up in the morning so he could sleep late. Or he'd let them close up so he could go home early. He kept track of the money. He knew they wouldn't rip him off.

The clothes were another story. They'd have a double date, a dinner dance, or maybe a wedding, and a bunch of them would use their keys, sneak in on a Saturday night or a Sunday, go shopping through the suits—all cleaned and pressed . . . ready to be wrapped on Monday.

Bobby always looked good. So did his brothers. A different suit every weekend. A different coat, too. I told him flat out before our wedding: "No borrowed suits. There'll be pictures."

They'd get one of their little sisters—his friends, I mean—or maybe a girlfriend, to iron the suits, drape them back on the hangers. Even when they went out without them.

Saps. Bobby never even asked me to do it: I would have slapped his face.

He'd gone into the army, seen Japan, a bit of the world—true—but then he came right back to his friends, the corner . . . the borrowed clothes and the local dances . . . the shore. And I wondered what it was like to come home to me and my big belly right away—to my sick mother, my father stopping in and out, mad because his wife was dying, sorry because he couldn't do more. And my mother . . . mad and sorry, too: mad at my father, mad at the world . . . sorry for herself. Making trouble. Running out of time. The two boys before we knew it.

I wondered, that day while we were driving, how different it must have been from what he wanted, what he saw when he first looked at me on the Ferris wheel, in the diner that night, on those walks.

I wanted to fall in love again. I looked at this man across from me, my husband still, and I wanted to fall in love again.

But not with him.

I wanted to go back to that night on the boardwalk, thank

him for my shoe, keep walking. I wanted to go home the next morning, lie like always about where I'd been, who I'd been with, start from scratch.

I wanted to register for college in the fall, study, take care of my mother—not resentful like I was, but calm . . . calm because I knew I'd picked it, I'd made the best choice. The best for me, anyway. And I wanted to watch her die all over again. But this time with some sympathy. Some *more* sympathy. I wanted to get a job (a real job, part-time), say good-bye, tell her I loved her and mean it—not through gritted teeth, like I did at the end, because I was tired and she was a pain in my ass and I had two kids to take care of, one at home, another on the way—and then I wanted to graduate, get a job in New York, meet somebody, move . . . even stay local, teach . . . yes, maybe . . . teach at one of the private schools—just move . . . keep moving . . . move on.

But there was no scratch to start from. And who did those things back then?

My father thought college was a waste for girls—he told me so. Not my mother—but what did she know? She wanted me to marry a rich man. That was her big plan. Her, with her big talk, waiting in the car for Freddy the Jew for hours while he made a deal (my aunt Dot told me this—he sold swag on the side), waiting for my father while he played some club—that could never be me. I knew that now.

We all married early—even earlier than our mothers. Some of us. It was the early sixties: it was in style. I'm not making excuses, but it was in style.

And I wanted Bobby too. I couldn't help it. Bobby. He could have run, moved, just ignored me. He could have filed for divorce, same as me. But he didn't. Six months since I'd changed the locks, left his suitcase with Helena, and he was still there.

He was there. And so were my boys.

"Where we going now?" Tommy said. We were off 440, on Route 1&9.

"I wanna take you to my loading dock. I want you to see where Daddy works."

He was laying it on thick. My sons were loving it. Worse yet, so was I.

I needed to stop.

"Let's go home," I said. "Let's all just go home." And before I finished, I realized what I'd said.

"All?" Bobby said.

I paused, then answered him slowly: "I meant me and the boys, Bobby."

"That's not what you said."

Tommy and Bobby Jr. looked at me. Bobby stayed quiet, kept me on the spot.

"Just take *me* home," I told him. "If you want, you can keep riding—the three of you. I'll keep dinner waiting for the boys."

Bobby made a right turn at the jug handle and started to turn around. Tommy held his arm, and Bobby Jr. held mine.

"Have it your way," Bobby said. "Just remember, I won't wait forever, Mary—the ball's in your court."

We all leaned to the left as Bobby turned back onto the high-way. Bobby picked up speed and the roll came back. I squeezed Bobby Jr.'s arm and, like a reaction, he repeated the word *ball*.

*   *   *

"Where are the kids?" Aunt Dot asked when I called her that night.

"Here. Eating dinner. With me."

"And where's your husband?"

"Back on the road."

"Good," she said. "Drop them off with his mother. Come down."

I waited for the boys to finish eating, then shuffled them out the door, ran them over to Bobby's mother's. She invited me in for dessert when I got to the door. She probably had some Entenmanns coffee-ring cake on the table—she never baked either—but I said I had to run and drove straight downtown.

Aunt Dot answered the door in a house smock. She told me she was finished making loans for the day and she'd sent Aunt Beta to the store. I noticed she was a little slower, a bit surlier than usual, and I thought I smelled liquor on her breath—but Aunt Dot wasn't someone you questioned, at least not when you were only half sure.

You entered Dot's house through the kitchen, and that's as far as I got. "Sit down," she told me. "I'll make us some tea."

I sat in the chair she pointed to, while she walked over to her big black-and-white stove—a giant porcelain thing in the middle of the kitchen that she'd never changed since my grandmother died.

"You think he's changed?" she asked as she struck a match to light the burner.

"A little."

"And a little's good enough for you?"

I thought for a second, then said, "No."

"Well?" She blew out the match and turned to face me.

"It's a big move, Dot."

"You're a big girl, Mary."

"And it's not so simple . . ."

"Probably not."

I got quiet, and she sat down next to me. "Mary," she said, as soft as she could, "what's the holdup here?"

"I don't know."

"You still love him?"

"I might."

"That's fine," she said. "If you want . . . sleep with him after."

"Dot, I'm not like you."

"Oh, Mary." She laughed and slid her black Copacabana ashtray over so it was right in front of her, then reached for a cigarette. "You say that like it's the worst thing in the world."

I tried to apologize, but she beat me to it.

"Look." She lit up. "I've told you before—I'm sorry I didn't step in when you were younger. . . . I know how sick your mother got . . . and I know what she was like sometimes; I grew up with her. You got saddled, same as me—stuck with a house to run. But this . . . the no-good husband, the two kids right away . . ."

"Jesus Christ," I said, and I grabbed my car keys off the table. "For this I drove all the way down here?"

"I'm not finished," she said.

"Then finish fast," I told her.

"You got yourself in, and you'll get yourself out."

She pulled a business card from the pocket of her house smock and threw it on the table.

"You're still only part-time," she said, as I picked it up, fingered it. "Nothing in your name, no benefits unless they come from him."

I held the card up to the light so I could read it: the print was fancy and small.

"This man's a divorce lawyer—a good one. My friend Chippie used him when she finally left Jack."

The card said JEFF FRIEDMAN, ATTORNEY-AT-LAW—not Jeffrey, just Jeff.

"He cheated on you in your own house, Mary. Now you get that house in your name."

## Chapter 24

## QUID PRO QUO

I moved fast after that night with Aunt Dot. I didn't care what anybody thought—not Bobby, his mother, my father. I never even took time to explain it to the boys. Granted, I should have, but nobody's perfect, and I was surprised what a pleasure it was to fill out those divorce papers—so official! Mr. Butler helped me, a glint of hope in his eye: he'd found me wet-eyed over my coffee one morning. I had my weak moments . . . who wouldn't?

And I wasn't through with Bobby—my aunt was right about that. I should have been, sure, maybe—but I wasn't. I never thought he'd try so hard—even the way he cheated was lazy—but now that he was, I liked it. After all those years of waiting, hoping . . .

But that would stop if I took him back. It would stop, too, if I divorced him.

Or it might.

Either way, Bobby had an ego, just like me: he wasn't gonna

wait around forever—he'd said as much—and I saw the way other women looked at him. How long did I have before one of them moved in?

Jeff Friedman was a handsome Jew, my age, with dark wavy hair like Bobby's. A real shark—if he had his way, Bobby would still be begging for quarters.

He had an office on West Side Avenue, near Duncan—not far from Bobby's old corner—and it was small but he'd squeezed two leather couches into the waiting room. He wore bell-bottoms and jackets with wide lapels—rarely a suit—and he worked out at a gym in Bayonne during lunchtime, so he always smelled like soap.

Very punctual, too. I showed up five minutes early for our first appointment—4:55—and I'd no sooner sat down on his big brown sofa than he burst through the door at 5:00 on the dot, the sweet smell of Dial rushing in behind him.

"Mary?" he said, when he saw me. He had long legs, and those bell-bottoms flew when he made an entrance.

"That's me."

"You're younger than I expected."

"Well, thanks." I decided that was a compliment. "So are you."

"Open a file." He turned to the receptionist. "The last name's . . ."

"Nolan." I finished his sentence like I worked for him.

"Mary Nolan." He made sure she got it: "And hold all my calls."

Jeff had a leather couch in his office, too—though more of a loveseat—and when I sat down, I sank in deep. He swept past me, and for a second I thought he'd join me there, but instead he grabbed a yellow pad from the tall bookcase next to me, then slipped behind his desk.

"You've got big furniture for such a small office."

"Leftovers—we just redecorated in Livingston," he said.

Livingston was a nice town near the Short Hills Mall—very rich, mostly new. "What's in Livingston?" I asked.

"My other office."

"You've got two?"

"For now—we redecorate here in the spring."

He dropped his pad on the desk in front of him and sat down in his swivel chair—leather also—then he spun so he could face me head-on. "I'd like you to start from the beginning, okay?"

"Well." I slid to the edge of the loveseat and sat up straight. "I want a divorce."

"I know that much from your aunt, Mrs. Nolan."

"You talked to my aunt?"

"I thanked her for the referral; it's just good practice."

"And what else did she say about my marriage?"

"She said you could speak for yourself."

With that, he held up his pen in the writing position and crossed his long legs. "So . . ."

So, I started again. . . . I told him how we met and married in 1962.

He jotted a few notes; I went on.

I told him about the apartment on Winfield Avenue, what Bobby did for a living, our house. "You just want the big details, right?"

"Relax, take your time. This is all confidential."

I told him about my mother and what a strain that was, how she warned me not to marry him (it just flew out), about my two boys. He kept writing.

I told him about Dolores.

"This I can work with."

I went back to the apartment on Winfield Avenue; I told him how I'd given it my best shot. I told him about all those hours, days, weeks alone in our apartment: "Scrubbing and waiting" and that's just how I put it. I mentioned the flecks and specks on the linoleum: "You've seen them?"

"Oh, yes." He laughed. "I grew up in this city."

"Good," I said. "But it wasn't funny at the time."

I told him that I'd felt like I was disappearing (I left out the dreams about my mother—I didn't want him to think I was crazy), that I'd kept "hoping it would get better, change . . ."

"That's fine." He slid a box of Kleenex across his desk. I pushed it away.

"And it wasn't me who was disappearing," I continued. "It wasn't those flecks and specks either"—I wanted him to know I had a sense of humor—"it was Bobby, my marriage."

These things came to me as I said them (this was better than therapy—I didn't clam up like I did with Merna), and it felt good to say them, good to hear them out loud. Oh, yes, I was through crying: I told him my marriage was over. "Finished," I said. "It was over the day he moved Dolores upstairs—before that, even."

"He moved his girlfriend upstairs?"

"You can write that, too, Jeff—I've got nothing to hide."

"Your house is a two-family?"

"That new house was just a consolation prize," I told him,

"and the day he moved Dolores in was the day he moved out—those suitcases were just a courtesy."

I told him about my job at the bank, and he said, "Good for you."

I thanked him.

"But tell me about those suitcases."

I told him how I'd packed two bags for Bobby, changed the locks, left the bags at Helena's.

"Let me get this straight," he dropped his pen: "Your husband was sleeping with your upstairs tenant and you threw him out of the house?"

"Seven months ago today!"

"And you keep separate residences?"

"You could say that."

"So you're already separated."

"Not legally." I slipped back in the loveseat, proud and relieved. "Not yet."

"But that's what you want—a legal separation?"

"If it leads to a divorce." I'd already decided to be big about it, go for the "no-fault" divorce—that just meant an eighteen-month separation back then; they were all over the papers—and I told Jeff so.

"That's nice." He leaned back in his swivel chair. "But it's stupid. We can always settle—first let's threaten him with a trial."

"It's not like that," I said. "I'm not looking to squeeze him."

"I'm your lawyer; of course you are." Jeff smiled, and I saw he had nice teeth—not perfect, but white. He had a good, dark complexion, like mine, so they stood out. "How's he been acting lately?"

"All apologies, but . . ."

"So he wants to reconcile?"

"That might be the legal term; I'd say he wants more of the same."

"Let's get him in here; let's negotiate."

"I don't want a big fight, Jeff."

"Maybe you won't get one."

I told him I had two kids to think about, and he said, "All the more reason."

"I see how you got your two offices," I told him, "but this is overkill. . . ."

"Mrs. Nolan." He leaned forward on his desk. "You said it's been seven months since your husband moved out."

"Since I threw him out."

"I assume you've had mortgage payments, car insurance . . ."

"The usual."

"Has he offered to pay them?"

"We've got joint checking."

"Do you use it?"

"For some things. We've got joint savings too."

"Does he make deposits?"

I didn't answer. Bobby'd never made one deposit that I could remember—I needed a minute to think.

"And how much do you make an hour?"

It was still only $2.75. I didn't want to tell him.

"Fine, we can talk about that later. But in the meantime, Mrs. Nolan—in your own language—who's squeezing who?"

I sat all the way back in the loveseat and put my hand on my head. "My husband's not who you think he is."

"Good, then we've got nothing to lose."

Jeff was wrong. Bobby was a lousy husband, sure, but he was no rotten man—he'd shown me that in these past seven months. Still, I wasn't a lawyer, and I was better safe than sorry. I decided to scrap my idea, sue him for infidelity, or threaten to, because—besides my legal advice—it was true. I figured he couldn't argue with that one; even his mother couldn't take the witness stand and argue that point. She was a real bitch sometimes, but she was no liar.

"This usually goes with 'emotional cruelty.' "

"What?"

"The claims: they typically go together."

"Enough!" I told him. "Don't make me look pathetic." Jeff promised to leave that one off.

"Does your husband have a lawyer?"

"I doubt it."

"I'll send him a letter directly . . . he'll find one. Here"—Jeff handed me a buckslip with his name on it—"write down your husband's address."

"He's staying with his mother."

"Write down her address, then." He laughed, just like he did with the floors—only now I got irritated.

"Let's set some ground rules," I told him. "I never lived in some mansion in Livingston. And my husband's not a lawyer with two offices. But if you laugh once more at me or my family"—I thought for a second—"you're fired."

"I meant no offense, Mrs. Nolan. . . ."

"Then there'll be none taken."

"Toward you *or* your family."

"Just don't let it happen again."

Jeff looked frightened, not just taken aback—which surprised me. I wrote down Bobby's mother's address on the buckslip he'd handed me and gave it back to him.

"And one more thing," I said. "You'll see I was right about my husband—he won't fight the mother of his children in court."

"I hope you're right, Mrs. Nolan. Hey, just doing my job." He stood up, smiled, offered me his hand.

"So, how much is this costing me, anyway? You charge by the hour?"

"You can talk about that with your aunt."

"My aunt? Again with my aunt?"

"She said she'd take care of it."

"This is my divorce, Jeff—I'm the one paying."

"No offense," he said, and again he got nervous, "but I'm sure you can work that out with her."


"What's this?" I asked, when I called my aunt Dot that night.

"I told you I was stepping in."

"You should've called me first."

"You want him or not?"

"He's a little arrogant. . . . How much is he costing?"

"Of course he's arrogant—what do you care?"

"I want to pay you back."

"That's not necessary."

Aunt Dot was generous, but not like this. And I thought about Jeff, how rattled he got. "Does this man owe you money?"

"That's none of your business."

"What—he's a gambler?"

"Mary, you're right, I should've called you first. . . . Now, do you want him or not?"

"He's a good lawyer, right?"

"Oh, Jesus Christ," she said, and she hung up the phone.

The letter Jeff sent to Bobby said "I represent Mary Nolan; please have your lawyer contact me," and not much more.

Jeff read it to me over the phone, and I asked him what happened next. He said Bobby would get a lawyer. The lawyer would have to respond.

"So the lawyer's the one you threaten?"

"I'd rather have a sit-down, the four of us."

"Oh, no!"

"I recommend it."

"You can't handle this without me?"

"It's not as dramatic."

"You're unbelievable," I said. "Just send the letter; I'll be there if you need me."

"And don't worry," he said, "I've still got that box of Kleenex."

"Jeff, do me a favor: don't get on my nerves."

"These things get emotional, Mrs. Nolan. I just want you to know."

And they did get emotional. But for Bobby, not me. He showed up at my front door—his door, still—two days later, drunk, red-eyed, the letter in his hand. He rang the bell three times, and it was already after midnight. I sprang up from bed, put on my new terry-cloth robe—I'd bought it with my first paycheck to cheer myself up—and ran to the door.

"Open up." He pounded as I peeked through the little glass circle.

I unlocked the bottom lock, opened the door a crack—the top chain still hanging—and Bobby tried to push it all the way.

"You're gonna break the chain."

"Then open up."

"You stink of beer."

He kept pushing.

I watched as he pulled the door toward him—it was almost closed—then he put his shoulder behind it.

"You bought a good lock," I said, when the chain didn't break.

"Don't taunt me."

He pushed the door back and forth—fast—so the chain made a racket, and I heard Lucy's door open at the top of the stairs.

"You okay, Mary?" She poked out her head.

"I can handle this, Lucy. Go back to bed."

"Is that Bobby? Should I wake Joe?"

"He'll be gone in a minute," I told her. "Really, I'm fine." Then I turned to Bobby: "You're disturbing my tenant."

"She should mind her own business."

"I should call the police."

"Mary," Lucy called down again. "You want me to call for you?"

"You hear that?" I said to Bobby. "She wants to call for me."

"What . . . now I'm a criminal?" He stepped back, threw up his arms. "You send me this letter? You won't let me in?"

"Don't put on a show," I told him. "And lower your voice."

He stood still. Now that he'd moved back, I could see him clearly under the porch light. He'd been crying. His eyes were wet and bloodshot. Not just from drinking; I knew how they got then.

"A show?" He spoke softer. "You think this is a game?"

"That's not what I meant, Bobby."

It was only September, but it was cold out that night. He was wearing a windbreaker, very thin, and it wasn't even buttoned; I figured he must have been at Munzy's, a bar on the boulevard near Morton Place (a bad neighborhood by now, but his friends still hung out there). He must have been showing the letter to his friends—I was sure of it. They must have riled him up, sent him over.

I looked down at his teary eyelashes (you could see them from this angle) and, truth is, I felt bad for him—out there in the cold, practically crying on our stoop; for all I know he cried in front of his friends.

But like I said, he'd brought this on himself.

"This door's open enough," I said. "If you want, we can talk like this."

Bobby took a deep breath and exhaled. He was calming down—he had no choice, really. He stepped forward, leaned, almost fell, against the middle of the door, and brought his face up to the crack. Lucy flicked on the hall light and, standing there, the chain between us, we were practically in the same room. He pointed up and past me, toward Lucy, and raised his eyebrows to say, *Get rid of her.*

"You'll stay put if I do?"

"I'm not a dog, Mary—just send her away."

Even then—wobbly and wet-eyed—he stood his ground. All things considered, I was impressed.

I turned to Lucy and waved her away. "We'll only be a minute," I said. "I'm sorry for the noise."

She crept backward, pulled the door toward her. "Don't worry," she whispered, "I'll listen by the door."

"Thanks, Lucy," I whispered back to her. "I'm sure you will."

As Lucy's door clicked shut, I realized I should check on the kids. "Hold on a minute," I told Bobby.

"Where you going?"

"Just wait."

I left him there and ran to the boys' room. They were out like logs in their matching twin beds—or pretending to be—so I grabbed a jacket, quick, off the back of my kitchen chair and put it over my shoulders: it was one of my new suit jackets— short, blue, professional; in spite of the situation, it made me feel almost businesslike.

"Listen," I whispered, when I got back to the door—and I was glad I took a moment to collect myself. "I'm sorry you're upset—but what the hell did you expect?"

"Not some letter from a lawyer."

"I've got news, Bobby: that's how people get a divorce."

"But I don't want a divorce, Mary."

"Well, I'm sorry to hear that—because I do."

"So this is how you tell me . . . in a letter? On a stoop?"

"And just how was it that you told me about Dolores? Huh?"

He didn't answer.

"Be grateful it wasn't worse."

"I never said I was right, you know."

"You want a medal?"

"And what do you mean, 'worse'?"

"You better get a lawyer; that's all I can say."

Bobby told me that he didn't want a lawyer, that he wanted a second chance; and I told him he had it . . . about eight years ago. He told me he wanted another, and I said, "Sorry, you had that too."

"We've got two kids, Mary."

"That's right, and they're both sleeping."

"And you can't do this without me!"

"I never said I could."

Bobby was getting nowhere. He knew it. Plus, his mind wasn't working as fast as it usually did. "Look . . ." He didn't know what else to say. "I've got work in the morning. . . ."

"That's beautiful," I said. "You think I don't?"

"I've got real work, Mary."

"Oh, really?" I said—and now I lost all sympathy. I put my face against the crack—it was tough to keep my voice down. "Then get off my porch!"

"Whose porch, Mary?"

"My porch," I said.

"Is that what *he* told you?" He held up Jeff's letter.

"Never mind what he says," I told him. "When's the last time you wrote a check?"

"A check?"

"You never heard of one?"

"You packed a lot of things in those suitcases, Mary. I didn't see any checks."

"So . . . what? . . . You thought the mortgage disappeared?"

"The mortgage?"

"You thought those kids fed themselves?"

Bobby was good and confused now. He scratched his head, tried to come up with an answer. "You let the mortgage slip?"

"Of course not."

He squinted his eyes, thought for a second. "You want money, then ask for it, Mary. . . . I think it's you who's playing games."

I knew, then, that my husband wasn't squeezing me—I could tell by the way he said it. If anything, it was the same as always . . . he was just being lax. And I was no better off, really— but at least I knew where I stood.

"Tomorrow's your pickup day, no?" I decided to take matters into my own hands.

"You're damned right it is."

"Sober up," I told him. "We'll talk then."

"You'll let me in? We'll sit down? The two of us?"

"Go home, Bobby. The kids are sleeping. Let's quit while we're ahead."


The next day he stopped by at 6:00 P.M., right on time, for the boys. Tommy answered the door and brought him in. I stayed at my kitchen table reading the newspaper; I didn't want to seem eager.

"You look refreshed," I told him.

"Spare me the remarks."

Bobby Jr. came out from his room, and he had his Cleon Jones bat in his hand—the one Bobby bought for his birthday. It was still daylight savings, so they had a couple of hours before dark; I was wondering what Bobby had planned.

"Put that away," he said. "Today you're gonna visit with Grandma."

My two sons looked at each other, and I looked at them.

"We don't need all night," I told Bobby. "The boys can play around the block."

"You don't want them to see their grandmother?"

"I didn't say that."

"Good, because she's out on the porch."

Bobby Jr. put his bat in his room, just like he was told, and then he came back to the kitchen. Bobby signaled with his finger that he and Tommy should head toward the front door and they did that, too. I've got two good kids, but today they were like soldiers; they knew something was up. Bobby led them, from behind, through the living room, and I got up—a visit from my mother-in-law was a rarity—and followed close behind.

When we got to the front door, she was there waiting, sure enough . . . all dressed up in a pink pantsuit, her big black-vinyl pocketbook on her arm. I knew she didn't drive, so I asked where she was taking them.

"It's a nice day," she said. "We'll start with the park."

She grabbed them by the hands, which they were much too old for—and again, on this day, they went along with it.

As they headed up the block, I turned to face Bobby. It was seven months, now, since I'd let him near me alone. He'd come straight from work, save for picking up his mother, and the weather had warmed back up, so he was wearing short sleeves, a button-down—Bobby never walked around in a T-shirt like those truck drivers in the movies; neither did his friends. His arms still had a tan from the summer, though the left arm was darker than the right from Bobby's resting it on the truck window. The hair on that arm was completely blond. Bobby had work shirts in all different colors, almost like a uniform, and they were all formfitting, all cut the same. This one was blue, so it turned up the blue in his eyes. I'm sure he wore it on purpose.

"Come on," I said, and I led him straight back through the living room, to the kitchen. After seven months without him— or any man—I wasn't about to sit down on the couch.

"You want coffee?" I asked, when we got there.

"No, a beer."

"You didn't have enough last night?"

"I'm not living here," he said. "Don't nag me."

"I never nagged you when you did," I said, and I opened the refrigerator, grabbed a can of Miller Lite.

Bobby sat down and, under the bright light at my kitchen table, you could see that those bright blue eyes were still bloodshot.

"I've been thinking," he said, and he cut right to the chase. "You can't do this without me, and I don't want a divorce."

"We've been over this."

He opened the can, took a sip. I was still standing and he let his eyes run over me.

"That a new dress?"

I'd started wearing dresses to work, sometimes with a blazer. Nobody wore a suit every day. And this one had black and white horizontal stripes . . . flashy, but knee length. I could wear stripes back then.

"Don't worry," I told him. "I paid for it myself."

"I don't care who paid for it, Mary. You look nice."

"Then thanks," I said, and I sat down across from him.

"I've been thinking," he said again. "You rush into things."

I must say, he threw me with that one.

"Oh, really," I said, after I took a second to regroup. "Like what . . . marrying you?"

"I think so . . . yes."

Once more, he caught me off guard.

"Fine . . ." I told him. "Then that's all the more reason—"

"But you're in now," he interrupted me. "We both are." Bobby pushed his beer aside, leaned across the table. "You married me for life, Mary—and you weren't a kid." I opened my mouth to answer. "Young, yes. But not a kid." He sat back, pleased with himself. "I honor my commitments, I think you should too."

I thought about all the ways I could answer this man—my husband and soon-to-be ex—how I could bring up everything that led to this moment, how I could add up on my fingers all the nice things he'd ever said and done for me since we'd married, including the compliment he just gave, and I'd still have one hand empty. And how would that be different from Nicky or Paulie or the rest of his friends? How would that be different from my own father? Or his?

So he'd gone one big step further—he'd moved her in, got caught—and that was the one step he felt sorry for.

I was glad he put it that way—so hypocritical. I could always count on him for that.

"Get a lawyer," I said.

"Mary, I thought we could talk."

"We can talk about the divorce, Bobby—no more."

"I told you, I don't want a lawyer . . . I want another chance."

"And I told you you've had every chance you're ever gonna get."

"Mary." He reached over, put his hand over mine. "I'm your husband. . . ."

I wasn't expecting him to touch me. And now that he did, I wanted to have no reaction—like a statue, a stone. Instead, my heart jumped back to that diner when I was seventeen. It did for a second, anyway. (I could leave this out but I'd be lying.) I looked away from him, let my eyes travel down to the floor . . . the one we'd made love on. And you have to remember that this was the only man I'd ever slept with. . . . It was the 1970s, yes, and all over the world people were going to singles bars, picking up, doing God knows what—even Miss Warnock, Miss Hughes—but that wasn't me, that wasn't my life. . . .

"Keep your hands to yourself," I told him, and I pulled my own away.

"You made your point," he said. Again he reached for me. Again I pulled away. "Now, come on, Mary—let's just move on."

And *thank God* he put it that way. *Thank God* he made it seem so small. "A point," he called it—for all I know he was calling it "a tantrum" behind my back. He wanted to bring me to my senses, and that's just what he did.

"My lawyer thinks you'll fight me," I said. "I told him he was wrong."

"Did you hear me?"

"He wants to scare you with a trial."

"Do you hear me at all, Mary?"

"Do you?"

Bobby took a deep breath. This was half for drama, sure, but half because he suddenly found it difficult to breathe. He saw now—finally—that I wasn't kidding. He picked up his can of beer and finished it with one big gulp.

"You really wanna end this, Mary?"

"You ended it already," I told him. "I just want a divorce."

I'd never seen Bobby play football. Except for with the boys, I'd never seen him on any field at all. But I knew he was a good athlete. He said it when I met him, and he wasn't just bragging— I saw the way he caught that shoe, I heard his friends talk. He knew when he was losing, my husband—he knew when to throw in his best shot.

"I still love you," he said, and he looked straight at me. "And you can hire all the lawyers you want, Mary, but I know you still love me."

And maybe it was true that he still loved me—that he ever did. It wasn't the first time he'd said it, but close. Maybe I still loved him too. I felt *something* that day—we practically grew up together . . . it was hard to tell. But that plus seventy-five cents— as they say—would get me a ride on the Montgomery and West Side bus. And not much more.

Besides, I was tired of waiting. Tired of holding things together, hoping for the best. . . . If anybody needed to start from scratch, it was Bobby—it was my job to let him.

"We're married twelve years," I told him, and I answered in the most honest way I could: "That's very good to hear."

We reached an understanding that day, me and my husband— no Jeff, no Aunt Dot. There'd be no courtroom. No big fight. I told him that I wasn't out to screw him, but there were things that I needed to have. He told me he wanted us back together, and he didn't care about "the rest."

"You're not just pouting?" I asked him. "You won't change your mind?"

"I don't pout, Mary. Just don't get between me and my kids."

"I never thought you'd try so hard," I told him.

"You'll be sorry that you lost me," he said.

And I was glad this happened in the kitchen, my beautiful new kitchen with the orange flowers on the wall. I looked at the radio on the shelf above Bobby's head—a piece of furniture with a dial, not sleek and tiny, the way they are now—the one that played William B. Williams and his trivia, and I decided it was my mother who guided me past the couch (thank God I never sat down there) . . . my mother with her big, brown radio that arched on the top, and me. Alone.

*I'll be alone with my kids, too, now,* I thought as I walked him to the door. It was one of our finest days, really. *Lonely, yes*—but moving away from it. Not toward more of the same.

Chapter 25

## THE HOUSE

The one thing I had to push Jeff on was the house. At first, he said we could keep joint ownership. "People usually sell and split the profits," he said. "But you *can* still get right of occupancy." (Until the boys went to college.)

"I want it outright," I told him.

"Mary, that's not typical."

"Considering what happened," I said, "it's a matter of pride."

So he put it in the agreement—and Bobby balked a bit. At least his lawyer did. But in the end, this was the only real holdup—he signed.

## Chapter 26

## WOMAN'S CLUB

Peg and I were drifting apart. She had her own problems that year—a cancer scare. It was in the placenta, something Chinese women usually get . . . they found out after she'd had a miscarriage and my heart dropped—another rare disease. But they caught it early, thank God. She was in remission by the time I got my final decree. In between, though, she kept quiet, pulled away. That's how some people deal.

I tried to talk her through it—the surgery, the follow-up—but she'd turn it around, ask me about the divorce.

"Come on," I'd tell her, "this is nonsense compared to you."

"Just tell me," she'd say.

"Do you think they got all the cancer? Is your daughter okay?"

"I've got a team of doctors," she'd tell me, "what more can I say?"

So I forked over my stories, one at a time, took care of her as best I could. And I'd spice them up a bit, make it seem like more of a struggle.

"Bobby thinks I'm sleeping with Jeff." (Which he did.)

"He wants to take the kids away." (He mentioned it once, but didn't dare.)

I'd tell her what Bobby's mother was wearing. "The Pantsuit Queen," Peg called her.

And it was obvious, as I told her these things—I needed to get out more. I had nothing to talk about, not even with Peg. I'd spent years where the only visits were from my dead mother, my best friend on the telephone, Barbara Jean with the black eyes and sunglasses. And I wasn't about to head back to that Woman's Club—one more raffle and I'd shoot myself.

I started talking more with Helena when I got home from work, asking her about school, her first teaching job (she was student teaching). She was smart, she kept busy, she liked to compare notes: she'd ask me about the bank, the divorce—not just to be nosy, she seemed interested—and I'd answer. I didn't care if Stella and Judy *were* there (God knows why she tolerated them). I spent more time with Ruth, Miss Warnock, Miss Hughes. And the more I got out, the more I kept company, the more I liked it.


I never dated much that first year. For one thing, I never really wanted any man but Bobby. For another, he watched the house like a hawk.

I had one date with Jeff, just a dinner. He took me to the Casa Dante near Journal Square. Nicky and Barbara Jean were at the restaurant and Nicky must have dropped a dime from the pay phone—I know he disappeared, because Barbara Jean came over to our table and talked. When Jeff dropped me off, Bobby was waiting in front of the house.

"She's still my wife." He put his face up to Jeff's.

"And I'm still her lawyer!" Jeff snapped back—he stood right up to him. "You'd better watch your next move."

It was a wonderful scene, really—and I must say, I loved the attention. Jeff offered to get a restraining order afterward, but I figured, why bother? I didn't like Jeff that much anyway, and I knew Bobby was just blowing steam.

After that, I dated a cop named Bernie—another Irish guy, a hothead with red hair, but it kept Bobby in line. I'm sure he was writhing but he didn't dare make a move. Bernie rented rooms up the block from me—it was no love match, just companionship; we're still friends today. He was a recent divorcé himself, and he'd had some ride with his ex. I felt sorry for him. And he appreciated my company. He took me to a few movies, some dinners. Him, I let take me to Laico's; it's a real local hangout—we ran into everybody we knew.

Bernie made me feel special. He held the door when we walked into a restaurant and didn't start any trouble once we sat down (at least not with me). He asked me how my day went and told me all about his own. I was good for Bernie too—I listened, talked, flirted, let him kiss me. But no more. I made sure never to bring him into the house for more than a few minutes either. My boys became real tattletales to their father; I'll tell you that.

The real payoff with Bernie came for Miss Hughes. She married his brother, Dave. He was another cop, a detective no less, a bit older, with money to burn. He had his own two-family on Williams Avenue, where Bernie rented, and ever since his divorce a few years before, he'd been a big neighborhood "catch." He dated a regular line of beauties before Miss Hughes, but when he met her (I introduced them at the Williams Avenue block party), something just stuck. She never thought she'd end up with somebody local, but once she met him and got that engagement ring on her finger (I know they went to bed together before they married), she was a whole new person. She even developed a sense of humor.

"Call me Irene," she said right away. "We'll be neighbors, for God's sake."

"Oh, my," I said. "Is the neighborhood going up or are you coming down?"

"Let's say we're meeting in the middle."

I had to help her pick out the wedding dress; Miss Warnock was just too jealous.

"This is purely physical," Miss Warnock told her when she saw the engagement ring. I had them over for another spaghetti dinner to celebrate. "The man's been divorced, he carries a gun, what could you possibly have in common?"

"Your jealousy speaks louder than your words," Miss Hughes said (I never got used to calling her Irene), and she held her ring up to the light above my kitchen table—it was a full carat. She stuck up her chin and beamed.

Miss Hughes and I took the PATH train to New York one Saturday to look for a wedding dress while Bobby's mother watched the boys, and it was a happy day for me, in spite of my own marriage. We went up and down Fourteenth Street, where my mother used to take me, and then we took a taxicab to Division Street on the Lower East Side. We got nowhere—it was so long since I'd been to New York—so she decided to go to Kleinfeld's in Brooklyn the next day, and I drove with her. (Bobby's mother was glad for another day with the boys.)

Irene Hughes had slimmed into a fine figure of a woman since her days in the convent, and she was still only thirty-three. Her red hair, which she'd chopped into a bowl cut right after she'd left the sisterhood, was grown out now, all one length. It was beautiful and shiny and she kept it parted down the middle. She never tried to hide her freckles, which was to her credit, and I'd taught her to wear light pastel lipsticks and just enough mascara so she looked fresh, not overdone. True, she was four years older than me, but I looked at her like a younger sister. We picked a traditional white lace with a heart-shape neckline, and she still had those Irish soda-bottle legs, so we picked a hemline that was right to the ground.

"I'm proud of you," I told her. "You're moving on, just like me."

"I'll have the wedding at OLV," she said.

"It'll be a packed house. A real victory day."

"I hadn't looked at it that way."

"But Miss Warnock will."

"I wish she could feel better about this."

"She will," I said, "but not for a while."

And then it hit me: *How's she gonna have a church wedding when Dave is divorced?* So I asked.

"Oh, he's 'seeking an annulment,' " she said.

"An annulment!" I repeated. "On what grounds? He was married for four years."

"Incompatibility," she told me.

"You can do that?"

"Of course, they never should have been married in the first place—it's true, isn't it?"

From what I'd heard, I couldn't argue.

"So all he has to do is prove it—the incompatibility—and get her consent."

"Well, his ex-wife did remarry," I told her, after I thought for a minute. "So, you may have a chance."

"Oh, Mary, that wouldn't matter to the archdiocese," she said.

I said, "No, but it might matter to her!" (Miss Hughes had a lot to learn about life outside the convent.)

"And what about you?" She ignored me. "Have you ever thought of an annulment?"

I figured she was kidding, but she went on. "With children it would be more difficult, but not impossible. You should try, Mary—after the way he treated you. It would give you a clean slate."

*Amazing,* I thought. *Twelve years with a man, two kids, a whole marriage, and this woman—an ex-nun no less—thinks I can erase it.*

"I had my church wedding," I said.


"That line must have killed her," Peg said, when I told her.

"I don't know. These nuns are tougher than you think."

Peg's doctor gave her the good news about a week before my final court date with Bobby. It was still daytime in California.

"Hold on." I ran to the refrigerator, grabbed a bottle of white Corvo while she popped the champagne on her end. We toasted each other, coast to coast, over the phone.

Chapter 27

## BIG DAY

On the morning my divorce became final, I drove down to the Administration Building on Montgomery Street—the same one Miss Hughes just got married in—alone.

Since Bobby'd already signed the agreement, he didn't need to come.

I dropped the kids off with his mother—ironic, for sure—but I wanted to make certain they were out, busy, distracted all day. Tommy was eleven; you couldn't keep things from him. Especially if you were talking on the kitchen phone like I was the night before. Helena'd called—I had no private extension. And Tommy told his brother everything. They knew where I was headed. Mind you, I could have told them outright—I say this now—but that wasn't something you did back then. And I knew they'd be safe with my mother-in-law—she'd never mention a word; she might even drag them to church. . . . She greeted me with silence that morning—silence and a handshake, nothing more . . . save for a fake, tight-lipped smile.

It was August—a year since the truck ride—and it was hot. I

wore a light-green sleeveless dress with a matching short-sleeve jacket—I'd bought it for the occasion—and shoes (new, too) that were also green, but darker.

It's an ugly building, that nine-story green monstrosity, and as I pulled up, early, I remember wishing I'd worn a different dress—at least it was a lighter shade.

I parked right in front, walked in, and took the elevator straight to the seventh floor—Family Court, Chancery Division—where I met Jeff.

It wasn't an open court, so there were no spectators—mostly lawyers (they all knew each other, shook hands), a few couples (at least they looked like couples), and a few single women—or about to be, like me.

"How many do they take at once?" I asked Jeff.

"That depends on the day."

"What if they run past lunch?" I'd only taken the morning off.

"There's another batch at one-thirty," he said, "and this judge never misses a meal."

It was eight-forty-five, and there was no room left on the wood bench outside the courtroom, so I paced up and down the halls. Miss Hughes had had her civil ceremony in a judge's chamber—a friend of Bernie and Dave's—that June, and I wasn't invited (she kept it small, just family—I think she was embarrassed), but she'd told me the judge's name and I knew I'd remember if I saw the name on the door. They were painting, though, and all the signs were off.

I paced and paced for what seemed like two hours, and just before nine o'clock, a skinny blond woman joined the crowd.

She was crying from the minute she got off the elevator. We all looked up.

"What's with that one?" I whispered to Jeff.

"Well, she's not a lawyer . . . today must be her day."

The door to the court finally opened at 9:05, and as we trickled in, I watched to see where the blond woman sat, so I could sit far away. I found a seat in the back of the room, and Jeff sat down next to me. He was very proper and quiet in the courtroom but, like me, he kept checking his watch.

At 9:10 we all rose as Judge O'Leary glided in and took the bench like an emperor—he even flung out his arms before he sat. He was a fat man with food stains on his robe, but you didn't notice that right away. And I was glad for that, the way he carried himself—despite his appearance—because besides my marriage, which I rushed, and the birth of my children, which I never thought twice about, this was the biggest move of my life.

I watched as the stenographer set up her machine—she had a tripod like a photographer, and she set it up so her steno machine was right at the height of her lap. She was very self-sufficient, which is good, but still, she juggled, and nobody offered to help.

When she was finished, the judge cleared his throat into his microphone, very showy, and I knew he was about to begin.

Bobby was at work, driving, trying not to think about it, no doubt—he'd called the night before, right after Helena, to wish me "luck."

"You kidding?" I said.

"This was a tough call to make," he told me. "Just say thanks."

This divorce brought us closer—it can happen that way. I

never took time to get to know him before we married. It was the same for Barbara Jean, Judy, Helena—only Peg took her time. For the rest of us, it was like somebody blew a whistle at high school graduation: we all raced to the altar at once. And, yes, maybe I jumped Stella and Judy by a year or two . . . maybe I moved even faster because of my mother. . . . But now that I was getting to know my husband—now that he was far enough away to look at—he wasn't so bad. So long as I wasn't counting on him. So long as I wasn't waiting for him to show up, come home . . .

He'd look even better at the end of the day—I knew that—when this divorce was final, when those papers were signed.

I was beginning to relax when the judge called my name.

"What?" I yelled.

"Mrs. Robert Nolan," the judge said again.

Jeff stood up. "We're here, Your Honor."

"But . . . ?" I looked at Jeff.

The whole courtroom was staring. I got up and Jeff shuffled me toward the front of the room.

The judge pointed to the table marked PLAINTIFF. The sign was in Magic Marker on cardboard, very childish, like my boys would make at school, and behind the sign, in front of my face— once I sat—was a microphone.

"You never said there'd be a microphone, Jeff."

"I can't think of everything, Mary—just lean forward when you talk."

The blond woman kept crying, and I could hear her in the background as the bailiff swore me in. A man in a summer suit—her lawyer—came in, saying "excuse me," and hurried over to the seat next to her.

"I understand that this divorce is uncontested," the judge said, and before I could speak, Jeff answered him, "It is."

He picked up my certificate of marriage—"P1" he called it; I'd given it to Jeff beforehand—and the bailiff brought it over to me.

"Is this your certificate of marriage?" he asked, very dramatic.

I cleared my throat and the mike let out a boom.

"Yes, Your Honor." My voice echoed through the courtroom and it scared me. I waited for the echo to die down: "It. Is."

He asked if I'd been separated from my husband, if we'd "previously cohabitated," if I thought the property agreement was fair and equitable, if I thought there was "any prospect for a reconciliation" between me and my husband.

By the time I'd finished answering, the blond woman was a wreck. Her lawyer took her arm and had to help her out of the room.

The judge looked through the agreement ("P2," he called it)—we'd given it to him beforehand, like the marriage certificate—and he asked a few questions about the terms. "You're aware that the child support will decrease in five years?"

"That was my decision." I nodded.

The rest of his questions were minor, nothing I hadn't gone over with Jeff. I nodded, said, "Yes. Yes. Yes." I was waiting for him to get to the tough part—maybe some personal question (Jeff warned me that could happen)—but the judge never did.

"All right." He cleared his throat again. "I find that Robert and Mary Nolan have been separated for eighteen months. They have two children. A property settlement has been reached. There is no chance for reconciliation. And I hereby enter a judgment dissolving the marriage."

He looked at the papers on his desk and started writing.

"What's he doing?"

"Signing your divorce papers."

"That's it?"

"I'll get a copy in the mail."

"You mean this whole thing's over?"

"The divorce was uncontested." Jeff shrugged. "I'll bring the papers to your house."

At that point, the judge must have heard us. He leaned over and spoke into his microphone: "Would you like a copy today?"

"Um, yes." I leaned into my own microphone. "I'd like to see it, if I could."

"You can bring this around to my secretary," he said to Jeff. "She'll conform the rest of the copies today."

Jeff took the papers from the judge's hand, and held them up so I could see. He said, "Come on."

But I couldn't move.

"Come on," he repeated.

"Are you all right?" The judge looked down at me.

I leaned forward to answer into the microphone, but when I opened my mouth, I burst into tears.

"She's fine." Jeff walked over to me.

The blond woman walked back in with her lawyer. She'd calmed down by now—but she took one look at me and started in again.

Jeff touched my shoulder, but the tears kept pouring.

The judge put his hand over his microphone. "She can have a moment in my chambers," he said.

I tried to stand but my knees were wobbly; I fell back in my chair.

"Thank you," I sobbed into the microphone—I wasn't thinking—and I could feel fifty eyes on my back.

"You have to get up." Jeff put his hand on my back, rubbed it gently. . . . Who knew he could be so sympathetic?

"I'm sorry, I . . ."

"Just lean on my arm."

I stood up finally, and Jeff guided me out of the room. We walked into the judge's chambers, where a secretary was waiting. She was a friendly woman, older, with a floral print dress, and that made me feel better for a minute. But then I saw there were soup cartons on the judge's desk—empty, wet—and that made me cry more.

"It happened so fast," I told her, as she pulled out a chair.

"You're lucky," she said. "He used to go on all day."

The chair was green vinyl with metal arms. It had a tear on the seat, covered with silver duct tape, like my chairs on Winfield Avenue. The secretary took the papers from Jeff, picked up a file and some paper clips, and got busy behind her desk.

I looked over at Judge O'Leary's desk calendar with the coffee rings and stains from the soup cartons.

"I wanted today to be special."

"Here." Jeff handed me his handkerchief. "I carry this just in case."

"I would have been fine if it wasn't for that blond woman."

"Mary." He put his hand back on my shoulder: "You're fine, now."

I looked at the nameplate on Judge O'Leary's desk—engraved plastic in a metal frame: it was no better than my own at the bank.

"I've already got a job," I yelled over to the secretary. Who knows why I said this? It made sense at the time.

"That's nice," she yelled back to me. "Just don't mind the mess."

I wiped my face with Jeff's handkerchief and offered it back to him.

"It's yours," he said. "Take it out of my fee."

I wiped my face again, rolled the handkerchief into a ball.

"Listen," I said. I was feeling more in control of myself, and I wanted to say this. "No matter how I got you, Jeff, you did a good job."

"Shush." He put his finger over his mouth, shot his eyes across the room.

I put my hand over my own mouth to say, *I'm sorry.*

He shrugged and smiled to say, *That's fine.*

"You headed back to the bank?" he said loudly, so the secretary could hear him. "If you want, I can give you a ride."

"I'm parked out front," I told him.

"That's right," he said. "You got the car."

It took a minute for me to realize Jeff was joking—this was so unlike him—and by the time I did, he had the copies in his hand.

He folded them in three and, without his asking, the secretary gave him an envelope.

"I don't mean to be nosy," she said, "but you didn't take the day off? You're really headed back to your office?"

Jeff handed me the envelope with my divorce papers in it.

"My boss is lost without me," I said.

I put the envelope in my purse—the midsize leather purse with the zipper top that Ruth made me buy—and I thought about what Jeff just said about the car. It had been so long since

I'd packed my boys in, took them for a ride . . . some rice pudding. I'd come a long way since that night in the parking lot with Charlie—the night he said I looked like a grandma—and I wanted them to see me on this day. It was almost lunchtime. Al's was still open. I could drive straight to Bobby's mother's and pick them up in time.

"Maybe we got held up," I said to the two of them, and she laughed. Jeff laughed too. I stood up and peeled my dress off the duct tape. "Can I use your phone?"

She pointed to the black rotary-dial telephone on the judge's desk and I stepped over to it.

"He'll see me again tomorrow." They watched as I dialed Mr. Butler. "Let him stay lost for the rest of the day."

Chapter 28

## FOR LENA

It's been twenty-five years. They've all moved away—Judy, Stella, Ruth, even Helena.

I did well at the bank. And when real estate took off in Jersey City, I followed Mr. Butler downtown. I knew it like the back of my hand: he needed me. He got a broker's license, left the bank, hung his shingle out on Grove Street; I studied, got a broker's license myself—but mostly I helped him out with his deals. That job at the bank was just a start for me—a good job for a housewife. Just a start for him, too, it turned out. We made quite a name and a few bucks for ourselves downtown . . . him mostly, but I did fine. Good enough to retire early. Between that and the rents I get, I stopped working two years ago.

Helena did well for herself too—a teacher, then a principal. She took up politics, like everybody at the Jersey City Board of Education, and before we knew it she was freeholder. Then, in the early nineties, the mayor went to jail (I'd mention his name, but why bother? Half the mayors who ever did office in Jersey City went to prison) and Helena stepped into office. The first and only female mayor we ever had—she did a good job, too. She even gave me an "appointment" as her aide.

Aunt Dot never should have started drinking again. But she had a scare with the loan business (the FBI got busy in Jersey City), she lost her spirit, her contacts, her looks (these were her words—Dot always looked beautiful to me). She started hitting the Scotch in the daytime and locked herself in. At the end, Aunt Beta had to do the caretaking and, as usual, I had to step in. I didn't mind; I just wish they'd called me sooner—she was so proud, Aunt Dot, and you get busy when you're working, taking care of kids.

"It's your liver," I told her—she was already in the hospital. "You should have seen a liver doctor."

"I trust Dr. Rossi," she said.

"But he's a stomach doctor."

"I'm on my deathbed," she said. "Don't badger me."

And she was right. It was like she picked a checkout date. She died in my arms by the end of that week.

(I was glad I could give her that much.)

Dot left everything to Philly and Beta, but she left the house in my name, which was a bit of a shock to the whole family, me included. Beta moved in with Philly and Loretta—they take good care of her—so I rent all four floors.

Barbara Jean is dead, God rest her soul. She lost a son and never recovered; you never do.

\* \* \*

My father never remarried. With Bobby gone, he took on more of a role. Divorce was a big thing then, it jolted him—shamed him, really. He made special trips to the city just to see us. The band broke up in the sixties when the clubs in Newark burned or closed, but he and his friends played music at Bobby Jr.'s communion party, Tommy's confirmation, both their graduations from OLV. The kids were wary of him at first, but he was good with my boys—much better than he'd been with a girl— they got used to him, got to like having him around. (He stayed with Judy, even brought her around from time to time—but she was always nervous in front of me.)

Starting in 1976, I took a two-week vacation every August (Mr. Butler kept me part-time but paid me for all the days) and we would go to my father's farm. He even had a horse for a while, and the boys loved to ride—he taught them. The farm was in a little town called Dundee; it took us six hours in my old Buick to get there—they loved that ride, too, Tommy especially. Once we got upstate, the roads were empty; you could relax, speed up. I got more confident about my driving.

And my father was right at home up there. Our section of Jersey City was all little farms when he grew up—sustenance farms with a vegetable garden and a few chickens, maybe a whole coop, in the backyard. The house Bobby and I built stood where my father used to have a garden as a boy; we'd bought the lot from my uncle Birdie, who somehow managed to get hold of the deed.

My father took Judy up there with him to the farm, which I

knew, but when we visited she was always on her way out or already gone.

I'd always wished he had died first—I'm not ashamed to say that. Why wouldn't I? It's natural. She was my mother. But I never imagined he felt the same way. One night after dinner—we were at his last farmhouse; I'd already sent the boys to bed—I asked him straight out: "Why don't you marry Judy?"

He didn't answer me.

"It's been years," I said. "You're both single now." Her husband had died.

"I have a wife," he said.

I said, "She's not coming back, Daddy."

He said, "No, but she's not going anywhere, either."

When he got lung cancer in 1980, I took care of him too. It was the same year Lucy got sick—and it's no wonder, really: he smoked Camels, no filter, up to four packs a day. The doctors had to take out one lung, which humbled him, made him quiet, softer, more thoughtful. Not a bad thing, maybe—but I didn't like seeing him that way. We were sitting on my couch one day—this was after the operation, he was staying in my house—and I made him pull out his accordion.

He started to play "Heart of My Heart," a good sing-along, and he wanted me to sing, like at the boys' parties, only now I was alone. I got butterflies, even after all those years, but I wanted him to keep going, so I opened a bottle of Beaujolais (it was just after Thanksgiving) and we both had a glass. He leaned into the accordion as he played, put on his stage smile, flashed his white teeth (they were false now), and he started to sing: "We were rough and ready guys, but, oh, how we could harmonize." He tapped the notes like he tapped his foot. Right on time. Pitch-perfect. Never dragged them out. A lot of musicians sing like that—they give an indication, the right key, let the singer fill in the rest. So I tapped the notes with him, sang along.

"You sound good, Mary."

"Thank you," I said. I was thirty-five and still my face got warm.

"But then, you could always carry a tune."

I laughed. "That's not what you used to say."

"Oh, stop it," he said, and he kept playing. "You make things up."

He was sick and we were getting along, so I let it go—God knows how many things I said to my own kids when I was busy, mad, in the heat of the moment. He played and I sang for an hour, maybe longer. Then he got tired and took a nap.

He died the next year—by then we'd made peace—and, for once, Uncle Birdie gave me a proper discount. True, he could have picked up the tab—it was his own brother—but a leopard doesn't change his spots completely.


Bobby's mother died three years ago. She was a good little money manager, that woman—she left him a good chunk of change.

We got closer and closer, she and I, as time went by—my optional mother-in-law, the only kind to have. She always kept a place for me at her Thanksgiving table, and at first I just went over because I wanted the boys to see their family, have a grandmother, stay in touch. But people like her, they grow on you—very matter-of-fact, cold even—but straightforward, ethical.

She'd never say a thing behind your back that she wouldn't say to your face.

Toward the end, she even loosened up a bit. She liked my singing voice. And I got her singing too (the senility helped).

We'd sing while she cooked her big twenty-five-pound turkey. And this time it was my turn to tap—so I'd hit the kitchen floor with my shoe, keep time.

> *"Would you like to swing on a star . . .*
> *Carry moonbeams home in a jar . . .*
> *You'll be better off than you are . . ."*

And then her part:

> *"Or would you rather be a mule?"*

The other daughters-in-law, all four of them, would roll their eyes when we sang. I can't blame them; it's not like I helped with the cooking or cleaning. It was my day off, just like the men.

I got a Christmas card from Peg this year. First word in ten years.

"I found your address," she wrote.

California got to her. She became a real flake.

"Who you kidding," I said, when I called her. "I never moved for twenty-eight years." She didn't answer. I'd called on New Year's Day, 1999. I timed it that way—my gift—the voice of an old friend on the first day of a new year.

"To be honest, I thought you were dead." I was kidding.

"Well, I'm alive," she told me—though it turns out she came pretty close, had a terrible scare with breast cancer.

"Oh, my God; one or both?" I asked her.

"One," she said.

"Gone?"

"Just a lump," she said. Peg was never one for personal details— or for whining. "I had plenty to spare," she made a joke, "and you could never tell the difference. I'm fine."

She's moving back to New Jersey. John's retired, she's beat cancer twice, they're getting nostalgic; they want to come home.

"It's not like you left it," I told her.

"It wasn't so hot then," she said.

I couldn't argue.

"And don't think I'm coming back to Jersey City. Oh, no, Mary—we'll house hunt in Bergen County; that's close enough."

"La-di-da," I told her.

She'll be back this spring if she keeps to her word. We made a date for this summer—Seaside Heights!

The boardwalk's still there—scrappy but alive. And we'll walk, the two of us—no husbands, ex or otherwise, no kids— she promised. We'll walk from one end to the other. I bet we turn some heads.

Poor Lucy, she got sick the same year as my father, and that made Joe drink even more. The son came over four, five times a week. About half as often, we'd find Joe passed out on the front steps. One time, he even wet himself—that was the night Bobby saw him, showed his better side, carried the man up the stairs.

It was a shame to watch Joe; such a big man, and he'd always had dignity, even when he was half sloshed. I finally had to pull Lucy's son aside.

"I love your mother, Mark," I told him, which by that point was true, "and I'm sorry she's so sick. The boys love her too. But I can't have them seeing Joe this way."

Mark moved his mother in with him and his wife, and he sent Joe off to a clinic. In the end, Lucy died and Joe went three weeks after her.

I guess she protected him too.


I never remarried either. Never wanted to. The distance, slight as it was, kept Bobby in line, and so did the divorce papers. Plus he'd grown up . . . Nobody changes completely—Dot was right—but he mellowed . . . not right away, mind you.

And the boys were terrible. God forbid I brought somebody home. God forbid he smiled the wrong way, showed up five minutes late. Very few men came back for a second date. And the boys would tip off their father: he'd show up at 7:59 if my date was at 8:00. "Just thought I'd peek in, see what my sons were doing."

"Oh, Bobby," I'd say, "knock it off; you saw them three hours ago," and then I'd turn to one of my sons: "Did you plan this?"

My date would show up in the middle of this, my ex-husband at the front door, because this is the thing: your kids don't care about your happiness; they just want you around, they want you together. Finally I said, "Bobby, you're going about this the wrong way, you're gonna make me hate you, using my sons. . . .

You're a bad father if you continue, and shame on you—you selfish thing."

And he said, "I'm a damned good father."

"You used to be—that was the one thing I could say about you."

"One thing, huh?"

"One thing," I repeated myself. "And now I can't even say that."

"Mary, now you're getting cruel."

"Just back off," I told him. "Let me breathe or you'll lose me for good."

And I will say, he took my warning. But he never stayed too far away. And that impressed me—he certainly could have: there was no marriage binding him; he could see the kids either way.

I became his landlord, technically speaking. . . . Bobby could have lived anywhere; he pays his own way. He offered to move in when Lucy and Joe moved out, and I let him. Five years had passed, I had nothing to lose. I figured all the money went into the same pot, anyway, more or less, and the boys were about to head to college. It's not like we were millionaires. So I just charged him the mortgage payment—$350 a month. (My friend Muriel at the bank had the same arrangement with her ex-husband; so did a few other women I knew—there's a lot of two-families in my area.)

It wasn't so different from my grandma Angelina, really, when you think about it, because toward the end, my grandpa Louie slept most nights in his little bedroom downstairs behind the saloon. Only in my case, I held the deed; I was covered either way.

I wasn't dating and neither was Bobby . . . nobody special,

anyway. And it was nice to have him around—nice for the boys, especially—though it was a lot less nice when he brought a woman over.

But that didn't happen often, and he learned to keep his mouth shut when I had "visitors," and in time, it was him who took me out on dates. Slowly but surely.

He lived there until the boys finished college. We'd had two years living alone in the house by that point—the time the boys overlapped at school—and it was a good two years. A honeymoon in a manner of speaking. The one we never had. But then he asked me to marry him.

I thought about it, but not for too long.

"I can't do that," I told him.

"Why not?"

"Bobby, I think we're on to something—let's not ruin it."

"Mary, aren't you ever going to forgive me?"

"I forgave you already," I told him, "but I never forget."

He moved out after that—stayed away for a while too. He stopped calling, took out other women (I went out a few times myself). But then, slowly but surely, my phone started ringing . . . he'd find some excuse to stop over . . . the dates started again.


Both my boys have done well for themselves—no accident, really. I put in the time, made sure of it. So did Bobby. Tommy lives in Manhattan now, and he rewrites television scripts for a living. He makes good money, but I'm hoping one day he'll write his own. Bobby Jr. bought a house in Weehawken. It overlooks the Hudson River. He became a real banker, after

Rutgers—not like I was, or even Mr. Butler. He works for Chase Manhattan, and they even put him through graduate school. He got married last year to another banker (four degrees between the two of them), and they've got a kid on the way. His wife, Sharon, is expecting in June.

I like the idea of a new face in the family—a boy, I hope— but I told Sharon she's got no full-time baby-sitter in me.

"A drop-off here and there will do nicely," I said.

They see me at my best, my kids, and I plan to keep it that way.

People don't know where to go anymore when they miss the old neighborhood. Half the houses in Greenville are boarded up, and downtown's either degenerates or yuppies. I never said this when we brokered there, but the turnaround died off.

And Jersey City was once a lovely place—no matter what anybody says—all different ethnic types, races. But people had manners; they did for each other, stayed out of each other's way. And you never had a lock on your door. Even the bank was safe—when I started in 1974, the guard didn't need a gun.

And you can blame it on the welfare or on the blacks or on drug addicts, but who knows?

My uncle Birdie—he'll outlive us all—has a theory.

"You can laugh," he says, "but this was before air-conditioning. Air-conditioning and television. Before every house had an air conditioner, people sat outside on their stoops. So who was going to bother you, if I'm outside watching? And television movies . . . before that people were out walking to the theater, coming home—decent people—out on the streets until eleven-thirty, midnight. But then they started staying home. The air conditioner blasting, eyes glued to the TV set. The streets belonged to the criminals."

Me, I didn't need a scapegoat. I bought a condo on Willow Street in Hoboken last year. Hoboken's different—it went down faster and it came back faster. Hoboken was never so nice to begin with, really—it was a pit when I was growing up (it's just on the other side of the Observer Highway, but we stayed away), and the waterfront was hideous . . . so barren, so dirty, even worse than in the movies. But now you can walk here, it has energy, life. It's like a pop-up town from a children's book—connected old houses, spruced up and painted in all different colors; corner delis; restaurants and furniture shops. People move here, to this one square mile, from all over the world—they get their careers started, fall in love. The way they used to in Jersey City.

I paid top dollar for my condo, but it's worth it. I rent both floors in my house in Jersey City. Both floors in my father's house too. Aunt Dot's house has four units—like I said. I had it renovated in 1990 (used Mr. Butler's contractor), and I rent those too. If Jersey City comes back the way they say it will, I'll move into that house, right back to where it all started. Maybe I'll open a café of my own, a high-priced coffee shop like they have in Manhattan: I'll open it near Grove Street where the PATH train lets off; the neighborhood could use one.

My ex-husband will retire soon himself. And he's still a handsome man. He stops in here at Arthur's Steakhouse (I hostess on Tuesday, Thursday, and Saturday nights—it's three blocks up from my condo, right in the middle of Hoboken) and I give him a good table. Him and his friends. The same crew—Paulie, Limpy, even Nicky from time to time.

I've kept my figure—gained a few pounds, but that's to my advantage. In the winter and most of the fall I like to wear a coatdress (coatdresses—I've got five of them). Double-breasted, mostly, and sometimes with a plunging neckline. They look dig-nified; hug my waistline, my hips. I go light on the makeup—I still have good skin—and I keep my hair short, color it medium brown. I could never get away with my natural black; I have it done professionally. I don't wear red lipstick anymore—I did for years—just a full, rich pink.

Men still enjoy my company. Women also, but the men espe-cially. In the summer, I take off from hostessing. Bobby and I rent a place together at the shore near where we met, a sweet one-bedroom in Lavallette—most of the spring also . . . I tell people we "summer together." (Again, this took time.) But in the winter and fall, I'm right here.

On a good night we get three hundred to four hundred peo-ple in this restaurant, and I seat every one of them. Then I'm done. No paperwork, no mess to clean. I split tips with the wait-ers and bartenders. They're very generous, but I don't need the money. It's just nice to get out.

If an old friend or a new couple I like comes in, I take a break, sit down, have a glass of red wine. A lot of young girls move here, to Hoboken, straight from college, and they like to come in and see me, tell me how they're doing. I sit with them, too, if I'm not too busy. They go on about their careers, their stock options, their boy problems—they always pay their own tab, and I say, "Good for you." They tip less than the men; I'll say that too.

We serve a good steak dinner here at Arthur's—the chilly

months draw a better business for that type of food—but half these people come back for me.

I keep hearing that Jersey City is on the upswing. And then I hear another old friend moved away. I wish it took off fast like I said it would—maybe I wasn't lying when I sold those houses, just hoping. But when it does—and it will—I'll be ready. I'm one town over but just a few blocks from First Street—from where Grandpa Louie gambled, and Aunt Dot made loans, and Grandma Angelina cooked till she dropped.

Sometimes, on a Saturday after we close the restaurant, Bobby takes me to the Casino-in-the-Park for some dancing. They have a full bar downstairs, a live band, a proper dance floor. He likes to show me off. And vice versa. With a few drinks in him, he's not bad on his feet. We do the fox-trot, the Lindy—all the dances that were popular when we got married. (We never did them then.) People watch us as he dips me, we turn. We press together, spin out and away, then back again.

This is the part my mother missed out on—the middle. She had the early part, and the sickness brought her right to the end. She died at fifty-four, my mother, the same age I am now, already old. But the middle, that's what she missed, that's what I have now.

Let them all scurry to Short Hills and Harmon Cove—Staten Island even. It's taken me a long time to get here. I'm here for both of us—and I'm staying put.

## Acknowledgments

My family was extremely important in the writing of this book. For their help, support, and storytelling, I am extremely grateful. A special thanks to my parents, Tami and Willie, my aunt Betty Sbano, my late aunt Stella Sbano, and my late uncle John Sbano. Thanks also to my brother Michael and my sister Mary.

To David Kuba for his love and friendship; to Helene Stapinski for lending a hand when it mattered; to Joyce Johnson for her early and generous work on this manuscript; and to Melanie Burke for always being there.

To my other friends Katherine Taylor, Bobbie Kramer, David Porter, and Fern Flamberg for taking time from their own work to help me with mine; to Luc Sante, Lucy Rosenthal, Patty O'Toole, Mary Gordon, Michael Cunningham, and Sigrid Nunez—teachers who gave kind encouragement and useful advice.

Thanks to Jennifer Rudolph Walsh and Susan Kamil; and to Margo Lipschultz and everyone at The Dial Press.

To John Hughes and Bill Finnerty for sharing their knowledge of the 1970s Jersey City legal system and to Nancy Kist for bringing me to them; to Charlie Markey and Bruce Brandt in the New Jersey Room at the Jersey City Public Library; to Scott Balesteri and his parents, Frank and Marge; and to Roberta Jellinek for her ongoing support.

Thanks, finally, to Isabelle Alter and Thomas Maguire, now passed, who helped me immeasurably.

## ABOUT THE AUTHOR

Bill Gordon's work has appeared in *The New York Times Magazine, Mississippi Review, New York Press, Christopher Street,* and *Downtown.* He received an MFA from Columbia University. He grew up in Jersey City and now lives in New York.